THE
NEXT
TOGETHER

"A heartbreaking and unpredictable love story spanning time and space."

Melinda Salisbury, author of
The Sin Eater's Daughter

"Such an absorbing book. Lauren James spins together multiple timelines and plot threads to create a story that's complex and intriguing without ever being confusing. An accomplished debut."

Kendra Leighton, author of *Glimpse*

"An explosion of storytelling. It's everything that I love about books. Read it."

Alice Oseman, author of *Solitaire*

"Packed with humour, adventure, conspiracy and epic romance, *The Next Together* is a sensational debut that is sure to put you on the edge of your seat and keep you there."

Catherine Doyle, author of *Vendetta*

"A funny, gripping and incredibly imaginative story of true love and reincarnation."

Louise O'Neill, author of *Only Ever Yours*

THE
NEXT
TOGETHER

LAUREN JAMES

WALKER
BOOKS

In memory of Aisha Ahmad
1991–2011

You deserved so much more than life gave you.

This is a work of fiction. Names, characters, places and incidents
are either the product of the author's imagination or, if real, used
fictitiously. All statements, activities, stunts, descriptions, information
and material of any other kind contained herein are included for
entertainment purposes only and should not be relied on for
accuracy or replicated as they may result in injury.

First published 2015 by Walker Books Ltd
87 Vauxhall Walk, London SE11 5HJ

2 4 6 8 10 9 7 5 3 1

Text © 2015 Lauren James
Cover photograph of couple walking in meadow © 2015 Corbis Images

The right of Lauren James to be identified as author of this
work has been asserted by her in accordance with the
Copyright, Designs and Patents Act 1988

This book has been typeset in Fairfield LH, Avenir,
Adobe Caslon, DIN, GFY Sidney, GFY Michael

Printed and bound in Great Britain by Clays Ltd, St Ives plc

All rights reserved. No part of this book may be reproduced,
transmitted or stored in an information retrieval system in any
form or by any means, graphic, electronic or mechanical,
including photocopying, taping and recording, without prior
written permission from the publisher.

British Library Cataloguing in Publication Data:
a catalogue record for this book is
available from the British Library

ISBN 978-1-4063-5805-6

www.walker.co.uk

They will come back – come back again,
as long as the red Earth rolls.
He never wasted a leaf or a tree.
Do you think He would squander souls?

– Rudyard Kipling, "The Sack of the Gods"

PROLOGUE

The last time they were together, it was late evening and they were being followed.

"It's happening again," Katherine said, and immediately regretted it. Matthew didn't reply, only squeezed her hand a little tighter. She knew what it meant. They were going to die.

They ran. Katherine tried to be quiet, but her breathing was dangerously loud in the silence. Her heartbeat pounded in her ears. Matthew pressed a palm against the small of her back, urging her on.

She could hear footsteps behind them, growing faster and faster, gaining on them.

They turned a corner and ducked into a room. Matthew locked the door behind them with trembling fingers. They stared at each other, listening for the sound of their pursuers. For a moment there was silence. They had a few minutes, but that was all. They were going to be found. It was just a matter of whether they could finish their task first.

"Next time, we're moving somewhere hot and quiet before any of this happens," Katherine declared breathlessly.

"I like Spain," Matthew said and pulled her into one last, desperate kiss.

CHAPTER 1

K,

I'm going out to get some lunch. If you touch my bacteria cultures again you aren't getting any of my pancakes for at least a month and this time I'm serious. It wasn't funny the first time and it isn't getting any more hilarious, despite what you might think.

No more hiding my experiments.

Love you.

Matt

Folios/v7/Time-landscape-2019/MS-112

Kate poured glycerol into a beaker, measuring out what she would need for that afternoon's experiment. She wasn't really in the mood for labs today, but it was only her second session of biology practicals since university had started and she couldn't miss it. It didn't help that she was the only person without a lab partner, so she had to do double the work of the other first-years. Not that she minded the extra work particularly. She'd just enjoy having someone to gossip with, which – judging by the crowd gathered by the ice machine – was all the other students were doing.

She was opening up her lab book on her tablet when a harried-looking supervisor tapped her on the shoulder. She dropped her stylus and turned around. At the same time, she stuck her hand into her pocket, fingers catching on the locket she'd stuffed in there last week when it had annoyed her while she was working at a fume cupboard.

The supervisor gestured to the boy standing beside her. "Here's your new lab partner. He's just transferred from chemistry. You can get him settled, can't you?"

Then the supervisor disappeared in a flurry of stress and steamed-up goggles to deal with another fresher, who had just managed to drop a beaker of something foul on the floor and then stand in it.

Kate stared at the boy.

"Hi," she said dubiously. She fished out the locket and put it back on.

He stared back at her, his expression indecipherable.

Then he nodded hello. He was wearing a tweed waistcoat, of all things, over a ratty band T-shirt. His light-brown hair hung over his eyes in a retro fringe that seemed to be based on something from the late noughties. She was delighted to note that despite his doubtful fashion choices he was exactly her type.

"Welcome to my lair. Make yourself at home." Kate gestured to the lab, which was filling with the soft scent of rotting manure. Near by, a cluster of the Ice-Machine Gossipers, lab coat sleeves over their noses, were gathered around the spillage, offering advice to the flustered supervisor.

Kate turned back to the boy, who'd dropped his lab coat onto the bench like he'd been waiting for her permission. The coat was sparkling new, and he'd apparently been using it as a kind of satchel, as he pulled out an assortment of notebooks and what looked like his *lunch* (in a *biology* lab; did he have no survival instincts at all?) from its depths. As he rescued an apple from where it had bounced across the floor, she found her gaze lingering on the way his hair curled over the back of his collar.

He actually blushed when he noticed her watching him – a vivid pink staining cheekbones that she was frankly jealous of. Bone structure like that was wasted on a *chemist*. Kate pulled off her goggles to cover up the fact that she'd been caught watching him. She fought for a moment to free them from their determined grip in her tangled red hair.

He had *blushed*? She wasn't sure what to do with that, actually. Was it a good thing, a guy blushing when you looked at him? He might as well have a name tag saying, "Hi, I'm a shy, socially awkward scientist. Please don't look me directly in the eye or I might faint." Kate was just imagining him introducing himself as "a socially awkward scientist", his Scottish lilt skipping quickly over the words, when he cleared his throat and spoke.

"I didn't actually download a copy of the lab book. What experiment are we doing today?"

That was a bit odd. He sounded exactly as she had imagined he would: the same soft Scottish brogue. She frowned. Why had she assumed he would be Scottish?

"Cleaning up horse muck, by the look of it," she joked, glancing over at the students still gathered around the spillage.

He dimpled a smile at her, and relaxed a little as he pulled on his lab coat.

"What's your name?" he asked, looking her up and down. His eyes lingered on her lab-coat collar, which was decorated with badges and beads, but he didn't mention it. Which was good. He was hardly one to judge her for accessorizing her lab coat – there was half a ham sandwich poking out of *his* pocket. It should have been strange, but it wasn't.

"Kate Finchley," she said brightly, trying to convey a more normal aura.

His eyebrows rose in what looked like surprise at her answer. She wasn't sure why her name would be surprising.

"Matt," he replied. "Matt Galloway."

"Hi, Matt, nice to meet you. Welcome to biology, etc., etc. I know you from somewhere. Have we met before?" Or instead of being normal she could just act like his own personal stalker. That worked too.

"We haven't met before. I would have remembered." He blushed again and then stammered, "I mean, I haven't even been to this country before. I moved here for university."

She eyed him speculatively. He must be particularly intelligent to have got permission to study abroad. Since Scotland had gained independence from England after the last world war, almost twenty years ago, it had been practically impossible to get permits to study internationally.

Hmm. He didn't seem like he was lying. Where did she know him from?

She should probably get back to work and give him a week or so to settle in before she began to torment him more by *chatting* to him any further, or doing something equally terrifying like nodding to him in the corridor. It was obvious he was completely overwhelmed by her raw sexuality – or that was what she was telling herself, anyway, and no one could prove otherwise. But she couldn't look away. There was something … *familiar* about him.

He made no attempt to say anything else, just looked at her, nonplussed. Kate was afraid to continue any line of conversation in case he actually died from the blood rushing to his face, but the silence was awkward, so eventually she said, "Why are you transferring over to biology, anyway?"

"There weren't as many explosions as I was hoping for in chemistry." It sounded like a prepared response; he'd probably been asked that question a lot recently.

"Well, there aren't nearly as many giant octopuses as you'd want in biology either, sorry."

He grinned. "Shame. How's the physics department here?"

She could sense him eyeing her, and she tried not to feel uncomfortable. Her grandmother had once described her as a perfect Pre-Raphaelite beauty, which she took to mean that her figure was a little too soft around the edges to conform to twenty-first-century perceptions of beauty, and her hair was a vivid shock of red. Sometimes people at school had teased her for being ginger, but she'd always loved her hair too much for it to bother her. Either way, she was secure in her body image a lot of the time, but it didn't stop her feeling self-conscious when there was a cute boy looking at her like she was the most interesting thing he'd seen all day.

"I'd give the physics lot six out of ten. There aren't enough brunets," she said. There'd been a disappointing mixers event in freshers' week.

He grinned again, and Kate smiled back. Then she said, "But I hear their MRI research rivals Cambridge's."

"I'll look into that, then. If the octopi don't work out."

"I'm sure they will. No sea monsters today, though. We're testing fertilizer effects on the development rates of bacteria cultures."

"Sounds a lot easier than chemistry labs. I had to bring an acid to boil. On my *first day*."

"Ouch. Well, I'll look after you today." She handed him a pair of latex gloves. Their hands touched, just slightly.

> First contact established in time-landscape 2039

Kate shuddered, closing her eyes for a moment. She felt a little strange.

Carlisle, England, 1745

Katherine stared vacantly out of the carriage window, taking in the bustling streets of her new town. It was raining heavily, thick droplets momentarily cleaning the dirty cobblestones. They pulled to a stop with an abrupt clatter of horseshoes, and the coachman came around to hand her down. He smiled gently at her as she held tightly to his hand for balance.

> First contact established in time-landscape 1745

Katherine could feel herself relaxing in response to his touch and her expression softened, although she couldn't muster up a smile. She hadn't smiled properly in several weeks now.

"We must have the dressmaker sew you a new dress first," her aunt Elizabeth said, climbing out of the carriage behind her. "You simply can't wear that old thing when you're introduced into Carlisle society."

Katherine nodded vaguely. Elizabeth was so excited about taking her to parties and lunches, as if it hadn't been barely a week since Katherine's whole life had changed.

The coachman escorted them to the dressmaker's below a wide umbrella. Before leaving them, he confirmed that he would collect them later in the afternoon. He had a Scottish accent. In an attempt to cheer her up, the housekeeper at her grandmother's house had told Katherine stories of mysterious and dangerous Scottish savages while they were packing up her belongings. It hadn't worked. She'd been too distracted – her home was being disassembled around her and her grandmother was dead.

As they entered the dressmaker's, Katherine put her hand into her pocket to feel for the advertisement for the sale of her old home – the only home she'd ever known. It was to be sold, along with all the furniture.

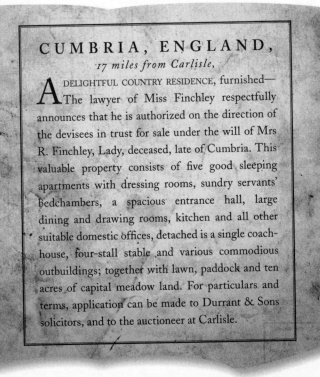

CUMBRIA, ENGLAND,

17 miles from Carlisle,

A DELIGHTFUL COUNTRY RESIDENCE, furnished— The lawyer of Miss Finchley respectfully announces that he is authorized on the direction of the devisees in trust for sale under the will of Mrs R. Finchley, Lady, deceased, late of Cumbria. This valuable property consists of five good sleeping apartments with dressing rooms, sundry servants' bedchambers, a spacious entrance hall, large dining and drawing rooms, kitchen and all other suitable domestic offices, detached is a single coach-house, four-stall stable and various commodious outbuildings; together with lawn, paddock and ten acres of capital meadow land. For particulars and terms, application can be made to Durrant & Sons solicitors, and to the auctioneer at Carlisle.

File note: Clipping from *The Times* classified advertisements

In the dressmaker's, Elizabeth settled on a light-green silk with pink braiding, and Katherine stood still while the dress was adjusted to her measurements. Katherine took care to express her gratitude to her aunt, but she felt awkward in the close-fitting, expensive clothing. She hadn't worn anything this fine when her grandmother was alive.

Katherine had a small circle of acquaintances, having spent the last few years looking after her grandmother. She didn't regret it, but now that she had to face the rest of the world she realized how introverted she had become. She was nearly eighteen and it was time to grow up. She shifted in the new clothing, suddenly feeling ready to start a new life with her aunt, uncle and cousin.

THE TIMES' OWN JOURNALIST seeks a young assistant to accompany him on a voyage to the Crimean front. Involves general MANSERVANT work as well as note-taking and transcribing. Persons influenced by idle and intrusive curiosity need not apply, nor any that cannot withstand the rigours of sea journeys. Letters, postage paid, addressed to M. Galloway, 104 Hatton Garden, London, will receive due attention.

Folios/v3/Time-landscape-1854/MS-2

File note: Clipping from *The Times* classified advertisements

Southampton Harbour, England, 1854

Katy glanced up from *The Times* advertisement that was clutched in her hand. She felt displaced and self-conscious amid the crowd of red-coated soldiers boarding the steamer. She was suddenly aware of the boys' clothing – the dull-brown breeches, shirt and jacket that she'd been wearing for years without worry. It had been a long time since she'd met new people. She'd grown complacent about her ability to pass as male. It was easy to keep up the act of being a pre-adolescent servant boy when people already believed it. It was entirely different to persuade new people. What if the journalist took one look at her and laughed her away, saying he'd wanted a man, not a skinny little girl?

Katy knew that her features were quite feminine, but with cropped hair and male clothing she hoped she would easily pass for an undernourished fourteen-year-old boy, instead of a girl of sixteen years. If she hadn't been so proud of herself for her achievement, she might have been a little offended by it.

She squared her shoulders and berated herself for being stupid. Then she went to find her new employer, weaving her way through the crowd of tearful families waving off the soldiers. Near by, a horse was being led reluctantly up the ramp to the ship. It paused every few feet to stare at the waves below as they crashed against the dock.

Katy climbed onto a crate of supplies waiting to be loaded onto the ship and looked out over the crowd. She spotted the journalist straight away. He was reading a newspaper with bags of luggage at his feet. He wasn't what she'd been expecting, but she knew instinctively that it was him. He looked completely out of place in his crumpled shirt and waistcoat amongst the crisply dressed soldiers.

He was young, only a few years older than her, and almost as thin. He was a mess of scruffy hair and spectacles and looked barely strong enough to withstand the sea breeze that swept through the harbour, let alone a war. She suddenly felt a lot more confident. There was hardly anything to him!

"Mr Galloway?" she asked. The man looked up from his newspaper and smiled at her. He had high cheekbones that defined his face and – oh! – dimples. Those were definitely dimples. *Oh.*

"You must be Christopher Russell! Matthew Galloway. Pleased to meet you."

"I— Hello." She mentally shook herself. She sounded like a fool. She was all flustered, just because he was quite striking, in a posh sort of way, if – if you liked that sort of thing. She swallowed.

She took his proffered hand a little distractedly.

> First contact established in time-landscape 1854

CHAPTER 2

M,

I'm shocked and horrified that you think I would consider doing such a terrible thing as mess with your experiments! I have more respect for my husband than that! I know you are in the middle of an important experiment at the minute. I wouldn't mess it up.

K x

P.S. You never said anything about me not messing with your lab book. Love you too!

Folios/v7/Time-landscape-2019/MS-113

UNIVERSITY OF NOTTINGHAM CAMPUS, ENGLAND, 2039

Kate sat at the desk in her room and stared blankly at the painted concrete wall. It was covered in pictures of her family that she'd stuck up the week before to try and make the university accommodation feel more like home. Her stomach was in knots. She felt like something hugely important had happened, but she wasn't sure what.

When her hand had touched Matt's earlier, she could have sworn something... There had been *something*. She blinked and tried to remember exactly what had happened. She had felt strange, like she'd suddenly relived the previous night's dream, one she'd completely forgotten.

Who was this guy? He seemed so familiar, but she couldn't quite place him. She didn't think she'd met him before.

Matt Galloway had come into her life and left her brain in uproar, and she didn't even know anything about him.

She touched her desk, waking up the computer screen in the table. She had to find out more about him, and the best way to do that was by "stalking" him on the Internet. Everyone did it, and she just wanted to find out what he was like – nothing weird. That was perfectly reasonable.

She found his university profile in seconds, but annoyingly it was set to private. The only thing she could access was the picture. It looked like it had been taken before a school prom – Matt, awkward in a suit and bow tie, seemed moments away from making an escape, the arm of someone who was perhaps an older brother slung over his shoulder, trying to stop him moving.

Kate looked at the picture and smiled. Matt really was cute. She hovered her finger over the SEND FRIEND REQUEST button, but didn't tap. Instead she did an Internet search for him. He must have some other social-networking accounts that were more accessible.

● ● ●   ■ search.co.uk   ×

← → C   search.co.uk   ★

Search

Matthew Galloway   🔍

<u>Web</u>   Images   Videos   News

Search results for "Matthew Galloway" (0.29 seconds)

<u>Central Science Laboratories (CSL)</u>
www.csl.org.uk

… biologists **Matthew** and Katherine **Galloway** (pictured below) have been working on the development of a bacterial fertilizer for use …

<u>Matthew Galloway | People | Central Science Laboratories (CSL)</u>
www.csl.org.uk/people

Matthew Galloway joined CSL after receiving his PhD in biology from the University of Nottingham in 2015. His main research area is …

<u>Breaking News: Terrorist attack in lab</u>
www.newsbreaking.com

In the early hours of this morning, **Matthew** and Katherine **Galloway**, two scientists employed by Central Science Laboratories (CSL) in the West Midlands, were fatally wounded …

<u>Lab quarantined after terrorist attack</u>
www.newsbreaking.com

Central Science Laboratories (CSL) has been quarantined following the accidental contamination of fatal bacteria …

<u>Science and Sass</u>
www.science-and-sass.com

Welcome to the blog of Katherine **Galloway**, a biologist with too much free time and a slightly nauseating obsession with her (gorgeous, wonderful) husband, **Matthew** …

<u>Matthew Galloway – United Kingdom profiles</u>
www.linkedup.net

Connect with professionals named **Matthew Galloway** in the United Kingdom now!

Other search results:

<u>Matthew Galloway – free online encyclopedia</u>

Matthew Galloway was a Scottish reporter with *The Times*, and is …

<u>**Career**</u> – <u>**Personal Life**</u> – <u>**Legacy**</u>

<u>See more results</u>

All of the websites were over twenty years old, from before World War III had even begun. They clearly weren't about her lab partner, although coincidentally this other Matthew Galloway guy was married to someone called Katherine. Kate grinned. She and Matt were clearly meant to be.

Kate clicked on the first link. It was the website for an old science laboratory and the article outlined its research into crop fertilizers. She skimmed it, looking for the first mention of Matthew Galloway.

> Recently two of our biologists Matthew and Katherine Galloway (pictured below) have been working on the development of a bacterial fertilizer for use in agriculture. They have found that they can make the fertilizer safer and reduce the hazard to local wildlife by varying the bacteria used.
>
> This work could lead to commercial applications for the fertilizer, as the environmental side effects had previously limited its viability for a large range of crops.

It definitely wasn't an article about her lab partner. Kate was about to click out of the link when the photo finished downloading, and she paused in shock. She enlarged it and peered closer at the scientists, trying very hard not to overreact.

The photo was of a man and a woman wearing lab coats dotted with stains, goggles around their necks. They were holding up beakers of fluorescent liquids and smiling cheerily at the camera.

They were standing close together, shoulders pressed against each other.

They looked *exactly* like her and Matt.

That was a picture of her, and her new lab partner. *From more than twenty years ago.*

There wasn't just a passing similarity – they were identical. Katherine Galloway even had the same freckle on her cheek as Kate. How could that be possible? How could she be in a photo taken over twenty years ago? Her parents had both been only children, and Kate didn't look much like either of them. As far as she knew, the woman in the photo wasn't anyone in her family at all. Kate would have known if she had a relative who looked identical to her. Or at least, she thought she would.

Wouldn't she?

Carlisle, England, 1745

Katherine shivered, rubbing her arms to try and warm them. Aunt Elizabeth had wasted no time in taking control of her niece's love life, pushing her straight into conversation at a dinner party with the first in what was sure to be a long line of eligible bachelors. Katherine had made her escape as soon as possible with the excuse that she wanted to explore the host's garden while it was still light. There was an icy nip to the air, but it was infinitely preferable to what was inside.

The party was at a house on the outskirts of Carlisle, and the city wall was just visible behind the guests' carriages. The ancient stone blocked the view of the countryside beyond. She walked down a grove of lime trees alongside the drive and came to a pond, green with algae. There, she leant against one of the trees and watched a pair of ducks, tails wiggling, as they dived into the muddy water. She could hear the quiet conversation of the coachmen at the carriages where they waited for their employers, and she felt herself slowly calming. It had been a long day – talking to strangers took so much energy. The ducks startled suddenly and swam into a clump of reeds; Katherine heard the sound of footsteps on the gravel, and she turned to watch the approaching figure.

It was her aunt's coachman. He came to a stop a foot away and looked at her hesitantly, holding something out.

"It's a blanket, Miss," he explained. "You look cold."

She was caught off guard. "Th–thank you." She took it, unfolding the material. It smelt musty, but she wrapped it around her shoulders regardless. She hadn't realized how cold she was.

"Would you like me to take you home, Miss Finchley?"

"This isn't my home," she found herself saying, too severely.

His eyes widened momentarily.

"I should apologize. That was…" She faltered. "I miss my grandmother. I miss my home, my *real* home. My aunt and uncle are pleasant enough, but I never even knew I had an aunt, until after my grandmother had passed away. They never spoke to one another. I have no idea why."

The coachman shifted, seeming uncertain, and ran a hand through his hair. Eventually he replied, looking like he knew he shouldn't. "Your aunt and uncle are good people. I think you will like it here."

"I hope I do." She shouldn't be speaking to him like

this – he was just a servant. It was inappropriate. She met his gaze then, already aware that her expression was showing too much of her desperation. She was scared. She wanted to feel happy again, just a little, but it felt like she never would. The excitement she'd felt at the dressmaker's on the day she arrived hadn't lasted long.

She hadn't paid much attention to a mere coachman before, but now she saw he was quite handsome. He was a little older than her – about nineteen or twenty – tall, but not intimidatingly so, and more gangly than well built. She swept her eyes up and down his body. When she looked back at his face, she found him watching her.

"I'll be by the carriage if there's anything else you require, Miss," he said, blushing and turning away quickly with a bow.

"What is your name?" she asked, desperate for him not to leave.

He paused, and turned back to face her. "Galloway. Matthew Galloway."

She held out a hand to him. He hesitated and then took it, shaking it formally, lip quirking upward as she said teasingly, "Good evening, Mr Galloway." She knew it was wrong to interact like this with a servant, but she felt strangely relaxed around him.

"Please call me Matthew," he said, then blushed again, which she couldn't help finding endearing. "You should probably avoid doing so if anyone else is present, however."

"Very well. Then you may call me Katherine, but again only in private."

He smiled at her, and she found herself smiling back. She remembered the stories her grandmother's housekeeper had told her about the Scottish savages. Even if he was Scottish, Matthew didn't seem like a savage. The Highlanders were supposed to eat human flesh and drink blood from wounds. They were ferocious, murderous barbarians. Matthew Galloway didn't look like that at all.

> Time-landscape 1745 progressing as planned

104 Hatton Garden,
London

Dear Christopher Russell,

I was pleased to receive your application for the position of manservant this morning, especially as it came with such excellent references from Lord Somerset. Ensuring that I am fed and watered and have not misplaced my glasses will be a step down from working in the house of a lord, I suspect, but I'm happy to take you on if you are willing. I understand from my editor that the voyage to the Crimea is long and extremely hazardous. This job is therefore a big commitment, so your response was appreciated, especially at such short notice. In fact, it was the only reply I have so far received.

To be quite honest, it had not occurred to me to hire a manservant until this week end, when a woman I encountered on the omnibus suggested it, quite out of the blue. So I'm not entirely sure of the proper process of things, but I'm sure we'll find our way.

The regiment is departing from Southampton docks tomorrow morning at nine. I look forward to meeting you there. You should prepare for a stay of several months, with a possible extension if the war continues beyond that point.

Regards &c.,

Matthew Galloway

War correspondent for <u>The Times</u>

Folios/v3/Time-landscape-1854/MS-3

Off the coast of France, Atlantic Ocean, 1854

"So, Christopher, I'm glad you could make it in time!" the journalist Matthew Galloway said to Katy, as they joined the queue for dinner. The ship had left the harbour hours before and was steadily making its way out into the Atlantic Ocean on its journey to the Mediterranean, where the

British Army was gathering for war. The sun was setting, streaks of orange and red reflecting off the quiet waves. "I wasn't sure if it would be possible to get an assistant at such short notice. But you applied very promptly."

"Please, call me Kit," Katy insisted, stepping forward to avoid being trodden on by a boisterous soldier who was keen to jump the queue in front of her. The soldiers had calmed somewhat since the departure, which had involved a lot of cheering and singing, but the deck was still filled with noise and laughter. "And it sounded like a wonderful opportunity. My previous employer was only too happy to let me join you."

In fact, the whole adventure had been Lord Somerset's idea.

Three days ago, she had been in the library of Lord Somerset's house. She had wanted to finish the book she was reading before she went to collect a delivery from the greengrocer's. Strictly speaking, she wasn't allowed to read the library's books, but she had found herself alone in there when waxing the floorboards the previous summer and had started reading one of the novels. Ever since then she'd been obsessed with them. The day passed so much more quickly when she could occupy herself during dull chores by trying to guess what would happen next in the story she was currently reading. Usually the lord and lady were in town and the country house operated with only a small staff, so there was plenty of time to read without being caught.

She was on the last chapter of her book when the door

opened. She jumped and then froze, too scared even to turn and see who it was. If it was her employer, Lord Somerset, then she would be in trouble – she may even be let go.

The floorboards creaked as whomever it was walked towards her. She held her breath, hoping it was the maid come to light the fire, or even one of the children. She could make an excuse for herself more easily then.

"Oh, I'm sorry. I didn't know anyone was in here," a surprised voice said. She let out a relieved breath. It was not Lord Somerset or his wife, but their guest, a general in the British Army. "Should you not be working?" he added, looking her over.

She gave a short bow. "I'm sorry, Sir. I'll get back to my duties."

"Very good," he said, inspecting the bookcase.

She tried not to run out of the library, although she was keen to escape as fast as she could.

Later that afternoon, she was summoned to meet Lord Somerset. She'd knocked self-consciously on the half-open door to his office. She was going to get dismissed for avoiding her work. She shouldn't have risked reading books while the lord and lady were in residence – however good she was at sneaking around, it was only ever destined to end in disaster.

Somerset was writing a letter. To her surprise, instead of firing her on the spot, he indicated that she should sit down, which she reluctantly did. It was a few minutes before he looked up from his letter. He stared at her for a long moment and then nodded.

"Now, then – Kit, is it?" he said.

"Yes, Sir."

Katy had been living as a boy, Kit, since she'd been kicked out of the orphanage at the age of twelve. For a while she'd had to live on the streets, looking after herself, until a girl she was friends with had managed to secure her a position as a kitchen boy in the house of a lord. He was an army general, which meant he was almost never at home and so the work was lighter than it otherwise might have been. Katy had been lucky, especially as the girl could have dressed as a boy herself and taken the job, instead of kindly giving Katy the idea.

"You can read, can't you, Kit?" Lord Somerset enquired.

She swallowed nervously, and decided her best tactic was to lie outright. "I asked Lady Somerset's permission, Sir."

He blinked, looking taken aback. "For what?"

"To read the library books."

They eyed each other. Katy crossed her arms and then uncrossed them, flustered.

Somerset waved his hand, and ink from his pen splashed onto the table. "Oh, that. I'm not concerned about the books. I'm grateful to George for bringing it to my attention, though. I'll need to talk to the butler about assigning the staff more duties if you have so much free time during the day." He gave her a knowing glance, and she looked down, embarrassed. "I called you here for a different reason, however. I've been looking for someone like you. I assume you can read well?"

"Yes, Sir."

"Good. And how old are you?"

"Sixteen, Sir." She was confused and nervous.

"Perfect," he said. "I have a special task for you, Kit. Something that might put your abilities to good use. You are a loyal servant. You've been here for several years now. Well, it is time to prove your loyalty. *The Times* newspaper is sending a journalist to the front in this damn war with the Russians. The decision's causing an awful fuss, as you can imagine. What a ridiculous idea! A *civilian*! At the front, poking into the army's business!" he scoffed, looking scandalized. Katy was impressed by the sheer number of exclamation marks she could hear in his voice. She had never heard him so angry.

"We can't stop it," he went on. "The government has got involved, and so we've got to let this journalist report on what's happening. Freedom of information and all that. We've even got to provide the man with rations! Like he's fighting for our country, instead of spying on us!"

Katy frowned in disapproval, which seemed to be what he was expecting from her.

"Anyway, the man has placed a classified advertisement, requesting an assistant – a young manservant who can read and write. I want you to apply. Then you can make sure he doesn't get into any bother, or send home any military secrets to be printed in the goddamn national newspaper."

Katy considered the proposal carefully. He wanted her to go to the front in the Crimea and spy on a journalist? Was this some kind of creative punishment for reading his library books? It seemed a little bit of an overreaction.

"I don't understand, Sir," she said.

"I spoke to Cook. She told me that you are trustworthy. You clearly have intelligence. I think you would be very well suited to the position. I think I can trust you to report back to me frequently with information."

Katy had always wanted to travel, but she wasn't sure she felt comfortable spying on someone – even a journalist.

"It would mean a great deal to me, Kit," Lord Somerset said. "Otherwise … well, I could certainly find another kitchen boy. One who didn't steal my books." He raised an eyebrow.

She repressed a sigh. "Very well, Sir."

Lord Somerset had given her a reference then, which she'd taken silently. Her head had been full of questions, but she decided her best option was to ask none. Considering that the meeting had changed her life, it had been surprisingly short. She hadn't felt she'd been adequately briefed for such a covert mission. Nevertheless, she'd applied for the job in *The Times* that evening and received a reply the next afternoon, which had quelled all her hopes that her application would be too late and she could get out of it.

> Time-landscape 1854 progressing as planned

Katy had done some research on the war against Russia and had read some of the journalist's articles, and she felt ready for the job. Hopefully she'd have a nice little trip and be back in a few weeks. Hopefully the journalist would be easy to manipulate and wouldn't be interested in sending back too much information about the war.

It had struck Katy that having a reference from Lord Somerset probably hadn't been a good idea. It was hardly subtle for her to have been employed by an *army general* before serving the journalist. She couldn't believe Somerset hadn't thought of that himself. Luckily, Matthew didn't seem to know that her employer was part of the British Army – yet.

They sat down to eat with a cluster of soldiers and a few of their wives, who were accompanying the regiment. The group was debating the origins of the meat. One man, who claimed to be a butcher, was adamant that it was horsemeat.

"So, why are we going to Bulgaria?" Katy asked Matthew, to distract herself from thoughts of what they were eating.

"It's where the army are based, while they prepare to march on the Russian forces in the Crimea. We'll be sailing around France and Spain to the Mediterranean Sea and then landing in Varna in Bulgaria. See." He pulled a map of their route from his pocket. "It's going to take several weeks to gather the British and French troops in Varna, and then we will journey to the front."

Weeks, she mentally repeated in disappointment. They were going to be gone far longer than she'd anticipated. "Are we just going to follow the army around, then? Making notes on what they do?" she asked.

"Yes. I'm the first journalist ever to go to the front," he said proudly.

"But how did news get home from wars before?"

"Well, we usually just … take the news from foreign newspapers." He coughed. "We tried to hire soldiers to report for us, but they weren't very particular about when they wrote. So I agreed to go out and report back properly – to get an accurate report, for once."

"What do you mean by an 'accurate report'?"

He took a bite of food, thinking, and then said, "When the soldiers reported to us from other wars, we later found out that they had been quite selective about what information they chose to share. They made everything seem as if it was going perfectly, out of loyalty to their regiment. Which is fair enough, but it meant that by the time the news got home of what the situation at the front really was, it was far too late for anything to be done about it."

Katy frowned. It didn't sound like Matthew was intent on spilling secrets to the enemy, but rather that he wanted to protect the British troops. "What kind of thing could be done about it?" she asked.

"Well, donations of warm clothing can be sent to soldiers in cold conditions, for example. A little thing like that can make a big difference, but if the public doesn't know it's needed, it won't happen."

Katy nodded. This wasn't what Lord Somerset had told her at all. What Matthew was doing sounded like a good thing.

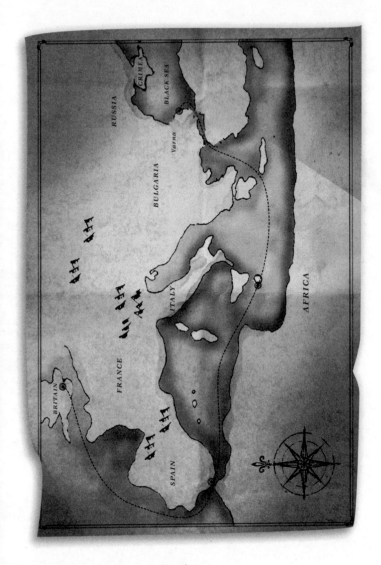

Folios/v3/Time-landscape-1854/MS-4

File note: Initial voyage of the British Army to Varna,
          Bulgaria, during the 1854 Crimean War, when Britain
          allied with France against Russia, to try to control
          the expansion of the Russian Empire into the south
          around the Black Sea, and to stop Russia getting
          control of British trade routes to India

CHAPTER 3

Katherine, darling,

I was deeply flattered by the highly personal remarks you kindly left for me on my lab book. So considerate of you to leave them somewhere you knew I'd see them straight away, along with the rest of the lab.

To show my appreciation, here's a coffee. They had run out of sugar so I used salt instead, but it should taste all right.

(You still aren't getting any pancakes. People who insult their husbands don't deserve breakfast in bed.)

M x

Folios/v7/Time-landscape-2019/MS-114

Carlisle, England, 1745

Katherine was growing tired of her new place in Carlisle society. The parties were interesting enough, but Elizabeth kept introducing her to prospective marital matches, which she found tedious. Most were pleasant, but she couldn't bring herself to talk to any of them for longer than ten minutes before wanting to escape. Her usual tactic was to sneak out into the gardens, where Matthew would be waiting with the carriage to take them home. It was peaceful outside, with the light and noise from the house filtering out across the driveway. He would hand her a shawl that he'd started leaving under the seats instead of the musty old horse blanket, and she would give him a glass of whisky punch. Then they would explore the gardens together, breathing in the refreshing cold night air.

She knew she shouldn't be spending so much time with a servant, but he was so engaging. He understood her. He let her talk about her grandmother, or just be silent as she recovered from the close scrutiny of society. He spoke to her as if she were a person instead of an object at an auction. They were only talking, anyway. There couldn't possibly be anything wrong in that.

"Matthew," Katherine said one evening as they wandered down the long slope of the rectory's lawn, admiring the stars which blinked occasionally before disappearing behind dark clouds. "You are Scottish—"

"Well observed," he interrupted, raising an eyebrow at her.

"No, I meant, what brought you to Carlisle?"

"I came to work," he said, as they stopped by a well. "My family live on the Scottish border, about ten miles north of here. They own a farm in the hills. In the morning you can't see anything but mist for miles around."

"It sounds magical. Why would you ever leave?" Katherine tried to picture the mountains of Scotland. An image of Matthew running around chasing cattle entered her mind.

"I wish I'd been able to stay," he said. "All I ever wanted was to be a farmer, like my father. But there were – there are – struggles for money. I send as much of my wages home as I can."

"Do you miss them?" Katherine leant over the wall of the well to peer down it. The black water below reflected the starlight, and she took a deep breath of the clean smell. She missed her grandmother.

"Yes. But I know that because of me they have enough money to survive now."

"I hope you will be able to pay them a visit soon."

"As do I. Maybe I should join the Rebels – that would give me a chance to travel!" He smiled.

Katherine was silent for a moment, unsure what the Rebels were, but not wanting to sound ignorant. Matthew's smile faltered as he waited for her laughter, so she asked, "The … the Rebels?"

He stared at her for a moment. "You haven't heard about the Jacobites?"

"No," she said. The word Jacobites did sound familiar,

but she couldn't place it. "Who are they?"

"Charles Stuart is making a claim for the throne again. You know about the uprising during his father's time?"

Sudden clarity struck Katherine, bringing her brief history lessons to the forefront of her mind (she'd always preferred the natural sciences to history). A revolution at the end of the last century had ousted King James II. His son, James Stuart, had made a claim to the throne of England and Scotland some years ago. He had managed to become recognized as the true monarch by several countries and had attempted an unsuccessful invasion of England in 1715. But that was thirty years ago, and there hadn't been a real threat since then. Was James Stuart's *son* now going to try to claim the throne of England?

"Of course I know about the uprising. It didn't succeed. Why would his son repeat something destined to failure?" Katherine asked.

"Charles Stuart – or Bonnie Prince Charlie, as they call him – has sought out the Highland tribes. He thinks that with their support he'll be able to win."

Katherine stopped walking, the shawl sliding down to her waist. "The Scots? Will they help him, do you think?"

"They already are. He landed in Scotland several weeks ago."

Katherine shivered and absently pulled the shawl back around her shoulders. "He is *raising an army*? In Scotland? Why is no one talking about this?"

She tried to picture the Highlanders forming an army.

In all her imaginings about the Scots, she had never thought of such a terrifying – but exciting – possibility. A part of her wanted the uprising to happen – the prospect was so thrilling. It was such a world away from tedious parties full of long conversations about beaus and silks.

Matthew shrugged. "There isn't much of a threat. Most people are aware of the situation, but as you said it has almost no hope of success. The biggest piece of news – Charlie's landing in Scotland – happened when your grandm—" His eyes flicked to hers. He knew that she found it hard to think about her grandmother's death. "I mean, before your arrival. You missed it. The latest news is that the Rebels are going to bypass Edinburgh and march straight on to England."

"England!" Katherine said in horror. "They may attack Carlisle."

He looked at her gravely. "Yes. But we've got some defences and a garrison. Well, you can hardly call it a garrison. No conflict was ever expected, so our defence consists entirely of a few old men with gout who have been here since the last uprising."

"You think that will be enough?"

"Perhaps not," Matthew admitted. "It is likely that the Rebels will be stopped before they get to England and Carlisle, but if they reach us, then we will have to prepare our defences. In Edinburgh they are setting up cannons."

"How terrible." Katherine tried to imagine the occupants of Carlisle having to decide whether to fight or surrender to the Rebels. She shivered again. How could this be happening? If the Rebels reached Carlisle, the citizens could be in real danger. Suddenly the uprising didn't seem so thrilling any more.

> Warning: Danger in time-landscape 1745 imminent

> Intervention recommended

  >> Intervention denied

Terrorist attack in lab

162 Comments

In the early hours of this morning, Matthew and Katherine Galloway, two scientists employed by Central Science Laboratories (CSL) in the West Midlands, were fatally wounded during a confrontation with security guards after an attempt to steal important research from the facility.

The scene of the attack, West Midlands

Evidence indicates that the scientists were planning to release the weaponized bacteria in central London, in the first of a series of terror attacks. Their motives are currently unknown, but may be linked to the growing unrest in Europe.

During the attempted theft, three security guards were attacked. Shots were fired in defence, and in the struggle to detain them, both Galloways were shot.

CSL, a research group funded by the Department for Environment, Food and Rural Affairs (DEFRA), employed the Galloways as scientists, to research a fertilizer that uses bacteria to distribute nutrients to crops. This fertilizer would increase crop yields indefinitely, as it has the capability of reproducing naturally in the ground. In particular, their research focused on the potential environmental impact of the bacteria.

In the course of their research, the pair apparently became aware of the potential applications of the bacteria as a weapon, as the spores of the bacteria can be fatal upon inhalation.

A scientist told this paper, "Bacteria spores are resistant to many types of radiation, disinfectant and temperature changes, so any outbreak would be hard to control once in the ecosystem, particularly if it entered the water supply."

Folios/v7/Time-landscape-2019/MS-172

Home > News > Terrorist Attack

Lab quarantined after terrorist attack

98 Comments

Central Science Laboratories (CSL) has been quarantined following the accidental contamination of fatal bacteria at the site.

A statement has been issued by the director of CSL saying that the bacteria was still in the early stages of development, and any potential outbreak wouldn't spread far enough to lead to loss of human life.

The lethal bacteria was released during a confrontation between security guards and former CSL scientists Katherine and Matthew Galloway last week. The pair were killed as they tried to steal samples of a fertilizing bacteria, which has the potential to be used as a weapon. Evidence indicates that the Galloways were planning to release the bacteria in central London, in the first of a series of planned terror attacks.

MI5 has found evidence that the Galloways were altering the bacteria to make it more dangerous to humans. Its effect would be similar to the spores of the weapon anthrax.

An expert said, "The scientists' research had been focused on allowing the bacteria to spread easily over large distances for distribution over farmland. This makes it a particularly virulent weapon."

The CSL buildings, located in the West Midlands, have been put into long-term quarantine. The press release says this is "unlikely to end in the foreseeable future".

Kate stared at the newspaper articles, which had appeared in the search results for "Matthew Galloway". Matthew and Katherine Galloway – the ones who had worked at CSL – had been terrorists. They had tried to steal from their lab. They had attacked security guards. She was amazed.

Who were these people? Could she possibly be related to this Katherine Galloway? She'd never heard of her. If there had been a terrorist in her family, who looked just like her, surely she would have been aware of it?

She went back to the search results, scrolling through other news articles for answers. After war began in 2019, the investigation seemed to have been completely abandoned in favour of reporting on the stand-off between England and Europe. World War III had been short, lasting only three years before both sides began threatening the use of nuclear weapons. This had led to a reluctant and uneasy peace, which had lasted ever since.

The next link Kate found was for Katherine Galloway's blog. Kate then flicked back to the news article. Someone who spent their free time analysing TV programmes and going on dates with her husband couldn't spend the rest of her time making a biological weapon. Could she?

SCIENCE AND SASS

Welcome to the blog of Katherine Galloway, a biologist with too much free time and a slightly nauseating obsession with her (gorgeous, wonderful) husband, Matthew.

Sorry (not sorry) about all the reblogged pictures of shirtless men.

About me

Pictures

Proposal

Ask

I might not be online for a while
21 June 2019 (40 notes)

Matthew and I have some stuff to do. I can't tell you what. I know, I know: that's cryptic and infuriating. But I really can't. I just wanted to tell you, in case I can't post again. I love you all. And I'm sorry.

Tags: this is probably overdramatic and unnecessary, apologies for all the drama

Oops I haven't been posting much
12 June 2019 (7 notes)

Things have been happening recently that I just can't find it in myself to joke about. I guess we all have to grow up eventually, right?

Tags: I'm scared, and I don't know what to do

The new series of OITNB just went up …
4 June 2019 (5 notes)

… but I can't watch it yet because Matthew is INSISTING on taking me out for a romantic dinner. RIDICULOUS.

Tags: I should never have married him, he has no respect for the sanctity of Netflix

Rolls around on floor whining
2 June 2019 (3 notes)

I spent *all* day doing an experiment that failed because I forgot to put one thing in the mixture, my life suuuuuucks.

Tags: I'm going out with Matthew to drink away my sorrows, I apologize in advance for any drunk blogging which may henceforth occur

< Previous posts

Carlisle, England, 1745

Katherine woke up after another bad night's sleep. Everyone in Carlisle had been seized by terror as the Rebels marched closer and closer to England, and rumours of the monstrous Highlanders changed daily. They were described varyingly as murderous giants who ate babies, or weak farmers who wouldn't be a threat to a country cottage. Her aunt and uncle talked constantly of their fear that the Rebels would take over the city and kill their son. Katherine's dreams had been filled with attacks on the city by giants, and she felt exhausted that morning. She sat up, rubbing her eyes to try to dispel the headache lingering behind her temples.

Katherine stared at the painting that dominated the wall opposite her bed. It was of her grandmother – a younger, brighter version of the woman she had known – with her husband. Since her arrival, Katherine had often wondered why Elizabeth would have a picture in her home of the mother whom she had not spoken to for so many years. Katherine had always felt too embarrassed to ask. Her aunt had kindly taken her in after her grandmother's death and she hadn't wanted to cause a fuss.

She got out of bed, suddenly awake and invigorated with curiosity. What had happened in her family? What secret was being kept from her?

She would need to go back to her grandmother's house soon, to start organizing her possessions now that the house was to be sold. She had been avoiding it for weeks. She wasn't ready to face ripping apart her home and throwing away all her grandmother's things. It would make it all too real. Although perhaps she might find the answers to the rift between her aunt and grandmother there.

After dressing, Katherine leant out of her window, watching the hens meander around the herb garden. She wished her life was that simple. She couldn't even bear the thought of going down to breakfast, where she would have to endure her aunt and uncle's endless discussions about the Jacobites.

She spotted Matthew leading a horse back to the stables, and quickly slipped outside to follow him, eager for a distraction.

He was talking to a maid when she reached the stables. The servants' heads were close together, their conversation serious and intense, while the horse idly plucked at a patch of cow parsley.

Something turned over in the pit of Katherine's stomach, but she shook the feeling away, annoyed with herself. Matthew could talk to whomever he wanted.

A cherry tree cast a dappled shadow over them, and the sunbeams shone brightly off the girl's dark hair. Katherine thought it was horrible. She crept closer to hear what they were saying.

"There is still a long way to go until victory," Matthew said.

"Yes, but the attack is the first step," murmured the maid. "After that everything that happens is important."

Katherine edged a little closer, being careful to keep out of sight. What were they talking about?

"What do we do?" Matthew asked the maid.

"Nothing, yet. You only need to act when the siege happens. That's when you can change things."

"So we wait?"

"Yes," the girl said, suddenly walking around the building, towards where Katherine was hiding. Matthew followed. Katherine tried to back away, but she had nowhere to go. They caught sight of her and stopped in their tracks.

"Sorry," she said apologetically. "Did I interrupt?"

Matthew exchanged looks with the servant girl. She curtsied, clearly embarrassed, and then walked towards the house.

"No. It's quite all right," Matthew replied. "That was my cousin."

"Oh," Katherine said, casting a fresh eye over the maid. She recognized her, now that she looked more closely. Katherine tried to remember her name, but she hadn't really paid the girl much attention before now.

Katherine swallowed, trying to act normally. "I can see the resemblance." Matthew and the maid had a similar bone structure, all sharp edges and angles. *Anise* – that was her name.

"You do? Where?" Matthew asked.

"The delicate eyelashes," she said, trying to sound teasing.

Matthew mock-sighed at her, so she added cheekily, "She carries them better, though. She's more elegant, somehow. And there's something about her posture that is just more dignified."

"Excuse me, Ma'am, but I have better things to do with my time than be insulted," Matthew said stiffly, but his

eyes twinkled. He bowed before turning to w
into the stable.

"Don't stumble!" Katherine called after h
formal posture broke as he laughed. She caug
him just inside the door. The stable was cold, and musty
with hay dust. A pigeon perched in the rafters, cooing
softly. It was so much more welcoming than the house,
where Katherine was always a little scared she would mess
up the brightly polished furniture.

"So, did you hear about Edinburgh?" Matthew
commented, rubbing the nose of the mare absently.

"No. What has happened?" It was hard to concentrate
on what Matthew was saying. The conversation between
him and Anise was going round and round in her mind.
What had they meant?

He grinned. "The city of Edinburgh surrendered, and
the Rebels have taken it. The mayor gave Prince Charlie
fifteen thousand pounds!"

Katherine drew in a gasp. "Good heavens!" That meant
the Rebels were barely a hundred miles from Carlisle.

"Before they reached Edinburgh, they passed through
Dunblane," Matthew continued. "I heard a story about one
of the Rebels. It is not as interesting as many, but I thought
it was good."

"So, what did he do?" Katherine was feeling
uncomfortable. Matthew was a little too excited that
Edinburgh had surrendered. Anise's words came back to
her: *You only need to act when the siege happens. That's when
you can change things.*

"The Rebel read a *Bible* passage as they rode through the town."

"A *Bible* passage? Which one?"

Matthew cleared his throat. Then he closed his eyes, preparing himself as if he was about to perform a Shakespearean monologue. Despite her concerns about his loyalties, she couldn't help but beam in delight at his pose. Without opening his eyes, he said, "Stop smirking."

Katherine controlled her expression. "Sorry," she murmured.

He shushed her, and after a moment he began speaking, voice strained to sound intentionally mysterious: *"Remove the diadem, and take off the crown… I will overturn, overturn, overturn it: and it shall be no more, until he come whose right it is; and I will give it him."*

The quote sent a shiver down her spine. Matthew looked at her wide-eyed expression with satisfaction.

"That's … scarily apt," she said after too long a pause.

"It does make you wonder, though, doesn't it?" Matthew said. "Perhaps Charlie should get the crown."

Katherine watched him carefully. "You support the Rebels?"

Is that what Anise had meant by "you can change things"? Were Matthew and his cousin plotting to help the Jacobites with their invasion?

For a moment he looked almost panicked. His shoulders had set into the same nervous posture that he'd had when she'd discovered him talking to his cousin, but quickly his expression settled. He shrugged then, gaze fixed on the far distance. "I don't really know enough to have an opinion."

Katherine tried to keep her expression blank, but she was concerned. Was he lying? He always seemed to know more about the Rebels than anyone else, even if they claimed to have the latest news. He certainly knew enough to form an opinion about something so important.

"I am rather naive about politics too," she said eventually, trying not to show her suspicions.

She ignored the way he watched her as she returned to the house.

> Delay predicted in time-landscape 1745 due to mistrust

CHAPTER 4

M,

You're not supposed to tell me you put salt in the drink!!!!! That's the WHOLE POINT! You're so bad at this, wow.

By the way, Clare was asking to see a picture of us, since she couldn't make it to the wedding. I uploaded some from the big day as well as that fantastic one that your mum showed me from school, where you are wearing entirely denim. It really suits you, brings out the colour of your eyes. Hope that's ok! Clare thought it was incredible.

So did Mick and Olivia. And I thought denim was underappreciated in the modern age!

See you later. We need milk.

K x

Folios/v7/Time-landscape-2019/MS-115

Near Portugal,
Atlantic Ocean, 1854

Matthew handed Katy his pen and a notebook. She stared at him questioningly. They were on deck, and after two days of travelling, she was starting to get her sea legs.

"I thought we could start taking notes," Matthew explained. "I could teach you a bit of shorthand to speed the process up."

She let out a heavy sigh. "I'm not going to get to relax until we arrive at the front?" After dipping the nib into the ink, she waited for him to begin talking.

"After several days, the journey progresses smoothly, with good weather and few delays." He paused for a moment to think.

Katy found herself distracted by the lines of his shoulders and the surprisingly well-defined muscles that were visible under his shirt. She let her eyes drift over the hair falling across his forehead. His spectacles were just about clinging to the brink of his nose. One sharp movement and they'd fall off. He pushed them up absently, and she shook herself. What was she *doing*? She was here to spy on him, not admire him.

There was something familiar about Matthew. She wasn't sure what it was, or if it was anything more than her own urge to spend more time with him, but he seemed like an old friend. His mannerisms were recognizable, comforting. The feeling was both strange and welcome at the same time.

She shook herself and tightened her grip on the pen, trying to ignore the tone of his voice, lilting and low in her ear, and concentrate instead on his words.

"Good," he said, when she'd written almost a page of notes for him. "You'll have to practise shorthand before we get to the front. We don't want to miss out on any important information because you struggle to keep up."

Her smile faded. For a moment she had felt contentment, but the reminder of their purpose made her remember herself. She couldn't be friendly with Matthew. She was here to manipulate him. She swallowed.

"You should write a letter to your aunt and uncle," Matthew said suddenly. "I'm sure they'll want to know you are safe. We can post it when we land."

She stared at him, confused. "My aunt and uncle? I don't have an aunt and uncle. I grew up in an orphanage."

He frowned. "Oh. I don't know why I thought that. My apologies."

There was a pause. Katy didn't know what she'd said that had led him to believe she lived with her aunt and uncle. Oddly, the mistake didn't feel completely wrong. She brushed the thought away – she'd never had an aunt and uncle. Had she?

Matthew stood up then, clearing his throat. "I think we should go inside. You've caught the sun."

Katy felt her face in surprise. The weather had been windy all day, but her arms and face were reddening, so he was probably right about going indoors.

No.: 411

Date of admission: 11 December 1838

Child's surname: Unknown

Child's forename: Katherine

Date of birth: Unknown   Place of birth: Unknown

Parents' names: Unknown   Gender: Female

Reason for admission: Destitution

Attended school: Yes

Leaving age: 12

Folios/v3/Time-landscape-1854/MS-1

File note: A 19th century admissions book for Freeman's Orphanage

NOTTINGHAM, ENGLAND, 2039

The next morning, Kate was dressed by six. She hadn't slept at all. She had just lain in her tiny, uncomfortable uni bed, listening to her neighbours party noisily, with everything she'd discovered about Matthew and Katherine Galloway running through her head. She'd been invited to the party, but had felt too confused by everything she'd read online to go.

She grabbed a cup of coffee and a slice of cold toast from the dining hall, waving to her friends when they called at her to sit with them. Instead she ate as she walked to catch the bus to her grandparents' house. She was going to get answers. One of them must know something about this Katherine Galloway.

"ID?" asked the soldier by the door of the bus, and she scanned her thumbprint on the machine. It flashed green, confirming she was an English citizen.

"Where are you headed?" he asked. "Do you have a permit to travel off-campus?"

"I'm going to visit my grandparents. They live in Beeston."

She showed him her permit, which he read carefully and then scanned into the machine. "Don't travel into the city centre today, Miss Finchley," he warned. "There's another protest in Market Square about the rationing. They're arresting demonstrators."

"I won't. I'm just going to get some of my gran's cake. I miss home cooking," Kate joked.

He nodded, letting her onto the bus. "Safe travels."

She stuck a toothpaste tablet in her mouth, enjoying the fizz as it cleaned her teeth.

*   *   *

When she arrived, her gran opened the door with flour-covered hands. "Kate! What are you doing here? I thought you'd be too busy partying to visit until at least the third week of term." She kissed Kate on the cheek, before pulling her inside.

"I'm homesick," Kate replied, breathing in the smell of her grandparents' house. She'd spent half her childhood there, after school when her parents were still at work. "But don't tell Mum and Dad I came round. I haven't been to visit them yet."

"Making the most of your freedom, are you? Come in. I'm just making bread. Your nana is still in bed."

Her gran turned to the stairs and shouted for her wife. "*NANCY! KATE'S HERE!*"

There was a long silence, and then a reluctant reply came. "I'm up. I'm *up*. This had better not be another lie to get me out of bed!"

Her gran shook her head, before walking into the kitchen. Kate followed, grinning to herself. She hadn't realized how stressful she had been finding university life until she came home, and suddenly she felt completely relaxed. Growing up and leaving home was great, but sometimes you just wanted a good hug from your grandmother.

"Tea?" her gran asked.

"Sure," Kate said. She sat down at the table, pressing her fingerprint to the on-screen scanner to log in. She pulled up the article she'd found the night before, enlarging the picture of the Galloways. Her gran was telling her an anecdote about their latest poker night. "... and Anthony said he'd let Nancy win back her money if—"

"Gran?" Kate interrupted her.

"Yes, sweet pea?"

"Do you know who this is?" Kate asked.

Her gran turned to look at the screen. All of the colour drained from her face. Her nana wandered into the kitchen in a dressing gown. She headed straight for the coffee pot.

"Morning, Kate," she said and then stopped as she took in their pale faces, the abandoned teacups. "Flo…?" When she saw the screen, she let out a short sob. *"Kate!"*

Kate looked between her grandmothers. For the first time they looked old to her — old and tired.

"Who *are* they?" Kate asked, suddenly scared.

"That's our daughter." Nancy took Flo's hand.

"Daughter? But … I thought Dad was your only child."

"We had a daughter too. Katherine."

"She died," Flo said, voice almost inaudible. "A long time ago."

"I … I read an article about them. Her and her husband, Matthew." Kate was suddenly, violently, regretting coming here and asking questions about this. She hadn't meant to hurt her grandparents. "It said they were scientists and terrorists."

Nancy closed her eyes.

"*Why?* Why would they do that?" Kate asked.

Neither replied.

Then Flo sighed. "Sit down. I suppose you're old enough to hear about it now."

"I'll make tea," Nancy said, squeezing Flo's hand.

Flo quietly went upstairs, and Kate sat at the kitchen table, feeling very young. She minimized the photo. She should never have done this.

Nancy put a plate of cake and a cup of tea in front of her.

"I'm sorry, Nana," Kate said, voice small.

"Oh, darling. It's all right. We've had a long time to come to terms with what happened."

Kate picked at the cake, nudging a slice of apple until it pulled away from the crumb.

"Why don't you tell me how you found that picture?" her nana asked.

Kate hesitated. What could she say? *It was all for a boy, Nana. Sorry to bring up your dead terrorist daughter.*

"I was investigating. There's a boy in my class who has the same name as Katherine's husband. He looks similar too."

"Oh." There was a long silence. When Kate looked up next, Flo was back, holding a folder.

"I haven't looked at any of this since it happened," she said. "Nancy has, but I – I couldn't."

"Do you want to now?" Kate asked, looking down at the yellowing papers apprehensively.

"Yes. You should know the truth."

Kate opened the folder and then spread the sheets out. There were letters, photographs and some other more official-looking documents, including a marriage certificate. It announced that Katherine Finchley and Matthew Galloway were legally bound in the eyes of the law, giving a date of only a few months before the war had begun in 2019. There were several postcards too – the bright pictures showing vivid scenes of exotic locations. On the back, their foreign stamps curled away from the dried paper.

K — I'm having lots of fun without you, as you can imagine. (I'm only joking a little bit.) This conference is everything I want in life sun, sand, and four talks a day about health and safety. Nearly everyone here is French and I can understand just enough of their conversations to know that they are a lot cleverer than I am, which is always reassuring. My presentation is tomorrow, so I will probably have eloped with the ENS Directeur de Biologie before then just to avoid it. (He has the most impressive beard I have ever seen. I took a photo for you, but let's ignore the fact that I got caught doing it and had to pretend I was entranced by the lapels of his jacket. If you ever fancy a trip to Paris, I now know a very good tailor.)

Love, Matthew x

Katherine Galloway
Office 110
Central Science Laboratories
West Midlands
UNITED KINGDOM

Kate turned to the photographs. The printed pictures were a treat for her, as even before the war they had been going out of fashion, and now they were a rare, unnecessary luxury. Most of them were of Katherine and Matthew's wedding, but there were a few holiday snaps mixed in. Kate ran her fingers over the smooth, glossy paper, taking in the old-fashioned clothing.

Katherine Galloway was radiant in a lace wedding dress, eyes caught on her husband. The man looked so much like Matt that Kate could hardly take her eyes off him either.

"I hadn't realized how much you look like her," Flo said. "You've grown up so fast. I was really pleased when your parents named you Katherine, although I was surprised too."

"What was she like? Katherine, I mean."

"She had gorgeous, shining red hair, just like you," Nancy said. Kate automatically brought up a hand to her hair, flattening the wayward curls. "She was really vain about it. She was very funny too, like you. She was always so kind and patient with everyone, which is why it was such a shock to the family when she was accused of being a terrorist.

"The wedding was only a few months before the war started. Everyone was ecstatic at Katherine's choice of partner. Matthew was very charming and intelligent – a research scientist, like her. It was like a fairy tale. They looked so beautiful together."

Nancy paused, looking down into her tea. Flo rested a hand on hers, and took up the story. "They must have been very good at concealment, because no one had a clue that anything was going on. We were so proud to have a scientist in the family, someone working at the cutting-edge of genetic modification."

"I don't know about you, but I never really understood what she was saying when she explained it," Nancy added.

"Me neither. I liked looking at the pictures of bacteria, though. They were always so colourful."

"I think they add in the colours with a computer afterwards, love," Nancy said.

"Do they? Well. Anyway. We were both very proud of her. But then, just before the war began, everything changed. She hadn't rung us for weeks, and she wasn't answering any calls. Not from us, or from your dad. At first we just assumed they were caught up with work. But then when they missed Nancy's birthday, we began to get concerned. We went to their house and found it ransacked, papers everywhere. It was a complete mess. Katherine and Matthew were nowhere to be found."

"We were frantic," Nancy added.

"We had no idea what had happened or how to get hold of them – whether there'd been a break-in or if they'd been kidnapped or what. I tried calling their lab," Flo said, "but I was told that there was an emergency situation and the place had been quarantined. We told the police they were missing." Flo's hand trembled as she lifted her mug and sipped distractedly at her drink.

"That evening two soldiers came round," Flo continued. "They were *enormous* – huge, serious, dangerous men. It was frightening. They told us that Katherine – our little girl – had been caught making a biological weapon that she and Matthew were going to release in London."

"Obviously we didn't believe them," Nancy interjected. "They didn't even tell us what terrorist organization they were supposed to have been working for. We asked to see her, and they said she'd been killed, along with her husband, at CSL. Katherine and Matthew had been stealing research. They had attacked the security guards who were trying to stop them. One of the guards fired – in defence, they said – and … and…" Nancy stopped to clear her throat.

Her voice was rough when she spoke again. "It was such a shock and so confusing. We didn't know what to do. We just … we let them go." She drew in a shaky breath. "I should have tried harder, to fight for my Katherine, but I knew it was beyond me. I could scarcely handle her death, let alone try and fight to find out what exactly had happened."

"We did the best we could," Flo reassured her. "We couldn't have done any more for them."

"Could you not have tried to tell someone?" Kate asked, quietly horrified that they had never found out what had happened. "Was there no one who could help?"

Flo shook her head. "It would have been too dangerous for us to mention to anyone that our daughter had been accused of being a terrorist, not with the war looming."

"We had to trust that we knew our daughter, and that she wouldn't have been involved in something bad. She was a good person. I've never stopped believing that ever since."

Kate let out a choked-off sob, and launched herself at her grandmothers, pulling them tightly into a hug. "I'm so sorry, Nana, Gran. I'm sorry. I didn't mean to make you relive such painful memories."

Flo patted her back and then stroked her hair. "It's OK, dear. You had to find out sometime."

"Most of the time I think that they couldn't possibly have done it," Nancy said, when Kate sat back down. "They were both so lovely. But it was all such confusion at the time, with the war and then the stalemate. We spent every day terrified that someone would drop a nuclear bomb and destroy the world. I don't know how we could have found out the truth, in the middle of all of that."

"I – I saw her blog," Kate said. "She seemed so... She didn't sound like a terrorist. She was complaining about missing a TV show."

Her grandparents shared a wry glance. "Katherine was a good person," Nancy said.

"Did... Do you think that her husband made her do it?"

"Matthew?" Flo said in surprise. "Oh, no. He was a darling. He wouldn't have hurt a fly."

"Katherine was always the one forcing him into stuff," Nancy agreed. "Do you remember when she made him go abseiling, Flo?" Nancy let out a laugh. "He hated it. In all the pictures he had this absolutely pained expression on his face, like he would rather have been anywhere else in the world."

"And Katherine was there, grinning away, completely oblivious."

"But he did it, for her. They were such a sweet couple."

Kate drank her tea, gulping down the cooling liquid. She felt exhausted. "I'm so sorry."

"We know, sweet pea. We know."

FOR THE INFORMATION OF THE GENTLEMEN & COMMONERS INSIDE THE WALLS OF CARLISLE

If the rebel forces gain entrance to the city of Carlisle, they will raid your houses of any valuable goods and destroy the rest, and take your wives and children for their own. They do not act with restraint, reason or intelligence. The Highland savages will destroy our noble city.

You may be assured that within the walls of Carlisle, at the castle garrison, there are those who will stop this treasonous attack. These men have so much gallantry and honour that they will, to the last piece of bread or drop of blood, keep Carlisle as English land.

ALL VOLUNTEERS ARE WELCOME AT THE CASTLE TO DONATE ANY TIME AND MONEY THAT CAN BE SPARED TO THE CAUSE.

Folios/v1/Time-landscape-1745/MS-2

File note: Part of a notice posted in Carlisle town square as the city prepared for the siege by the Jacobite forces during the 1745 uprising

Carlisle, England, 1745

Katherine had spent hours thinking about the conversation she'd overheard between Matthew and Anise, and she could only come to one conclusion: they were spies for the Rebels, and were planning to help the invasion if the Rebels reached Carlisle. Katherine couldn't just sit by and watch that happen, not when there was a risk that her family and her home could be attacked. She needed to stop Matthew and Anise. She would have to find a way to prove what they were doing and have them arrested.

She was supposed to be socializing with the other guests at a dinner party. They were all discussing the uprising too and panicking over the siege at Edinburgh. She let the conversation go on around her as she plotted how to reveal Matthew and Anise as traitors. She was drawing a blank, apart from pretending she was a Rebel too.

Then she realized how ridiculous she was being. She decided to just talk to Matthew. Now was the perfect opportunity: he was waiting for them outside by the carriage. He wouldn't be able to leave or avoid her questions. She stood up from the card table.

"Excuse me," she said to the other guests. "I need some air."

She left the party, ignoring her aunt's disapproving look from the fireside. Then she walked outside and scanned the driveway for Matthew.

He was lying on the roof of the carriage, staring at the stars and singing quietly to himself. Katherine stood with her arms crossed, listening to him in a futile attempt to decipher the words of the song, but his accent was so thickly Scottish that they sounded like nonsense. He seemed so harmless, sprawled out like that. It was hard to imagine that sweet, gentle Matthew could betray Carlisle – but she was convinced that his conversation with Anise hadn't been entirely innocent.

She loudly cleared her throat. Matthew quickly sat up and looked down at her. He was slightly dishevelled and sheepish with embarrassment at having been caught singing.

"Katherine!" He dropped to the ground, avoiding her gaze. He began fiddling with the mare's bridle, while his embarrassment faded.

She set a hand on her hip and said, in as coy a voice as she could manage, "Does my aunt know you use her carriage as your own personal theatre?" She raised an eyebrow.

"You're very witty, Katherine. In fact, I would say that your humour has no match. To what do I owe the *unequalled* pleasure of your company?"

She couldn't help but grin. He might be a traitor, but he was a very charismatic one. His lips spread into an answering smile.

"Sarcasm is the lowest form of wit, Mr Galloway. Can you take me home, please?" she asked.

He looked towards the house in surprise. "Is the party over already? Where's your aunt?"

"She's still inside. You can return for her later, but I want to leave now."

"What's the matter?"

"Nothing." Was she that obvious? She couldn't bear to think of him as a Rebel. A traitor.

He came towards her, frowning.

"I'm perfectly well, just feeling a little out of sorts. Could you take me home, please?"

He stared at her for a moment before nodding resignedly. "If you're sure."

Katherine realized how close they were standing. If anyone had been watching they would have thought he was about to kiss her. She twisted away, feeling her stomach flip over with something like fear at the thought.

He opened the door to the carriage, but she shook her head. She had to use the journey home as an opportunity to talk to him. "I think I'll sit with you tonight. I need some fresh air."

She couldn't read his expression, but she suspected that he was annoyed with her.

He silently closed the door and gestured to the driver's seat. Katherine began to climb up, thinking he was too angry to lend a hand, but after a moment she felt his arms around her waist as he guided her into the high seat. She smiled to herself as she watched him arrange the horses' reins around her.

Once he was seated beside her, she understood his annoyance for what it was: embarrassment. The seat was uncomfortably small for two adults and she was pressed closely against him. Through her thick skirts, she could feel the muscles in his leg move against her as he shifted position. She flushed. Perhaps she should have waited until their arrival at her aunt's to speak to him.

The carriage made its way down the narrow streets and through the square, with its towering cross, then past the quiet cathedral. The only sound was the clip-clop of horseshoes on the cobblestones. After several minutes, Matthew cleared his throat, his breath clouding the cold air. "What happened this evening?"

She didn't reply immediately. She was wondering how she could introduce the subject of the rebellion. Eventually she realized she had been silent for too long and said shortly, "I can't stop thinking about the uprising." She was getting a headache from all of this intrigue. She wasn't suited to being devious.

He turned to look at her questioningly. It took her a moment to focus her attention away from the fall of his hair, the startling hazel of his eyes.

"I think that we should do something to protect Carlisle, in case the uprising reaches the city," she said finally. "We can't just sit here and wait for them to attack us."

"Ah," Matthew said after a long pause. "Well, the town leaders are trying. They've raised a militia and tomorrow they are recruiting volunteers from the city to help improve the castle's defences – repairing broken walls, reinforcing the gates, deepening the moat, fixing broken cannons, that sort of thing. They need all the help they can get. I'm – I'm actually going to offer my services. I'm not working."

She tried to hide her surprise. He was going to help *protect* the city? Was he lying, to try to reassure her that he had no Jacobite leanings? "That's very charitable of you," she murmured.

He looked pleased, although he tried to hide it. She realized suddenly that he had been trying to impress her. It was flattering. If she hadn't overheard his conversation with Anise, she would have liked him all the more for his loyalty to the city. Then another thought occurred to her. Perhaps he was planning to destroy the cannons, to completely ruin all the weapons without anyone even realizing. Could she charm him into letting her join him at the castle, and then stay close enough to stop him doing anything treacherous?

"I wish I could help too," she said. There was a short silence. Katherine took a deep breath. "Matthew...?" she ventured.

"Yes?" He sounded resigned, like he knew what she was going to say.

"Do you think I would be able to help?"

Matthew didn't laugh like she had been expecting. "Katherine, I understand why you would want to. But you are a woman. Not only a woman, but a member of the gentry! It would be a scandal."

"I don't care! I can – I can *dress as a boy*! People do it all the time! At the very least I could *try* to help."

"What people? Besides, your aunt would never allow it."

"I don't care what my aunt thinks," Katherine said resolutely. "She isn't in control of my life. I can hide it from her. I can tell her I'm preparing my grandmother's house to be sold."

That part at least was true, and it did afford the perfect

excuse. Katherine could work at the castle without anyone knowing about it.

Matthew seemed to be deciding whether he wanted to argue further, or just accept his fate now and save the yelling. She leant more heavily against the seat where their shoulders were pressed together and lowered her voice. "*Please*, Matthew. I think it's so brave of you, volunteering to help. I want to join you."

His eyes flickered across her face in indecision. She licked her bottom lip in genuine anxiety, but when his gaze dropped she knew she had him.

"This is a senseless idea," he eventually muttered, mouth pinched. "This is going to end so badly."

She exhaled in relief. "But you'll help?"

He let out a long-suffering sigh and nodded. "I will. We are going to have to be really careful."

"It'll be fine," she said eagerly, ignoring his pessimism. He stared at her, silently conveying all his doubts at her breezy conviction. She rolled her eyes. "I promise I shall be careful and do everything you say, or else you can do something bad to me as punishment."

"A threat isn't at all menacing when it's as vague as that, but, yes, I will do something *really scary* if you behave like a fool."

"Well, look on the bright side. If it ends badly, you can tell everyone much you hated the whole experience."

He snorted. "Yes," he said dryly. "It will go down in history as the gospel truth on 'Why Not to Trust Katherine Finchley Ever, Under Any Circumstances'."

She laughed giddily, falling into a boneless sprawl against his arm, already wondering how she could convince Matthew to lend her some of his clothes. He nudged her shoulder with his own and smiled down at her. She held his gaze, feeling the buzz of it under her skin until he had to look back to the road.

"So," she asked after a contented silence, "may I borrow a shirt? Maybe a pair of trousers?"

"Hmm," he said. "I think my clothes would overwhelm you."

She sat upright and stretched out her arms alongside his to measure the difference. Her fingertips reached the base of his thumb. As the carriage hit a bump in the road, she fell against him again. He was warm in the cold night air. A shiver ran down her spine.

"I think your clothes will fit me just fine," she murmured. Her voice sounded huskier than she'd ever heard it.

They stayed pressed together without acknowledging the touch until the carriage pulled into the drive. When he helped her down, she balanced a hand on his shoulder, gripping tightly enough to feel his muscles flex under his cotton shirt as he supported her. He brushed a curl of hair away from her eyes, the tips of his fingers rubbing against her cheek, and she shivered.

"I'll give some clothes to Anise," he said in a low tone. "Meet me by the stables tomorrow morning around nine."

She cleared her throat, nodded. After a pause, he stepped back. She walked to the front door and then turned back towards him.

"Matthew… Thank you." She said it wholeheartedly.

He gave her a lopsided smile. "It's my pleasure."

He said it so sincerely that it brought a faint blush to her cheeks and she suddenly couldn't meet his eye.

> Progress in time-landscape 1745 following desired schedule

> Previously reported mistrust between subjects may work to the advantage of the program

It wasn't until Katherine was safely in her room and drinking warm tea that the giddy head rush wore off, and she started to panic. What was she doing? She was, well, flirting was the only way to describe it. She was *flirting* with a servant, getting close to him to test his loyalties to the Crown. She was planning to lie to her aunt and spend the day with him, dressed in his clothing. What was she *doing*? If anyone found out she would be ruined. Her grandmother would be appalled.

Katherine shuddered as she pressed her hands against her temples. Then she thought of the conversation between Matthew and Anise. They were planning something, something that could help the Rebels invade the city. She couldn't let that happen. She was going to do this for her city, for her family. She was going to do this for England. And if there was a part of her that remembered the warmth of Matthew's skin against hers, she ignored it.

CHAPTER 5

KitKat 12:47:04   Hey Matthew

KitKat 12:49:39   Matthew

KitKat 13:05:52   Matthew?

Gallows Humour 13:07:43   Katherine, I can't talk rn.

KitKat 13:08:01   :(

Gallows Humour 13:09:10   All right, what's up?

KitKat 13:09:36   !! What's your favourite hobby: dancing in the woods, singing, collecting things, talking to small animals, or baking?

Gallows Humour 13:10:33   .... what

KitKat 13:10:55   I was just, you know, wondering. What would you say the answer was?

Gallows Humour 13:11:30   I don't understand what's happening right now

KitKat 13:12:08   Just a wife who wants to know more about the man she loves, babycakes. Is that such a bad thing? I'm sure there are things you don't know about me.

KitKat 13:12:53   Like did you know that until today I'd never tried Pimms?

Gallows Humour 13:13:37   Are you drunk?

KitKat 13:14:10   Um. No? Well, they were giving out free samples at the supermarket when I went to get lunch and I got a little over eager.

Gallows Humour 13:14:59   Please say you're at home, and not scandalizing the doctorates in the lunchroom.

KitKat 13:15:48   ......

Gallows Humour 13:17:12   Katherine?

KitKat 13:18:22   I'm, er, not in the lunchroom. Any more.

KitKat 13:18:45   Who would your ideal prince be? Your childhood friend, Prince Charming or a strong warrior?

Gallows Humour 13:19:10   I don't want to know which Disney Princess I am. I've told you before, stop doing online quizzes. Leave it.

Gallows Humour 13:22:19   He would love me for myself.

KitKat 13:22:57   Tell me about your dress.

Kate felt almost sick with nerves as she waited for Matt to arrive for their next lab session. She couldn't believe that it had only been a few days since they'd met. She felt like her whole world had changed since then. It felt like a lifetime ago.

She hadn't slept well since her grandparents had told her about her aunt, and even when talking to her friends she hadn't been able to concentrate on any of their first-year gossip. She kept having odd dreams about the Galloways, but they were never in the right place. They were always too far back in history, dressed in old-fashioned clothing.

Matt arrived while Kate was arranging their incubated Petri dishes. He struggled out of a black waistcoat and into his crumpled lab coat. Kate took the opportunity to admire the tight fit of his jeans. When he spun round to face her, she jerked her gaze up guiltily.

"Morning!" he said cheerfully. He ran a hand through his hair. It stuck up straight for a moment and then collapsed in on itself, pointing in all directions.

"Hi," she mumbled. How was she going to bring the subject up? Could she just ask whether he happened to have any terrorists in his family? She settled on, "I need to talk to you later."

"Sure," he said, surprised. "We can go and get coffee, if you want?" He grinned at her, and then his smile faded. "Hey, are you OK?"

"Uh. Not really."

"What's wrong?"

She sighed, looking around the lab. She really didn't want to do this here. Everyone else was working quietly. By the looks of things, most of her lab group were hungover.

"Kate?"

She swallowed. "Is there anyone else in your family called Matthew?" The words came out uncertain, a little hesitant.

He stared down at his lab book. "Oh."

"You know, then?"

"Yeah. I know."

"Why didn't you say anything?"

"I recognized you. Obviously. You look just like her. But you didn't seem to recognize me. I didn't want to mention it in case you didn't know." Matt leant in close, voice pitched low. His eyes were clear, earnest. "Do you believe they did it?"

Kate lowered her voice too. "No." She fished in her bag for a few sheets of paper among the bundle of photographs and documents that her grandparents had let her borrow. It was a jokey PowerPoint presentation that her aunt had written for her uncle. "Look at this. I found it in some papers my grandparents gave me. Do you really think a terrorist could have written it?"

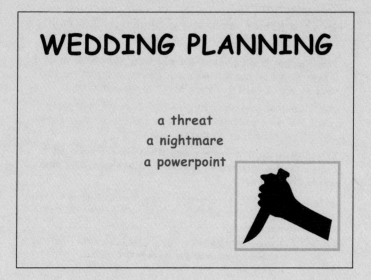

WEDDING PLANNING

a threat
a nightmare
a powerpoint

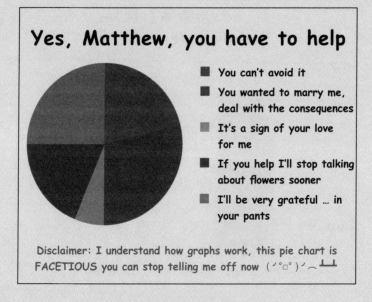

Yes, Matthew, you have to help

- You can't avoid it
- You wanted to marry me, deal with the consequences
- It's a sign of your love for me
- If you help I'll stop talking about flowers sooner
- I'll be very grateful ... in your pants

Disclaimer: I understand how graphs work, this pie chart is FACETIOUS you can stop telling me off now (´°□°)´ ～ ┴┴

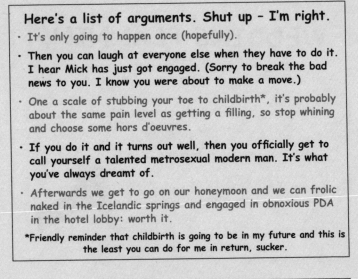

Here's a list of arguments. Shut up – I'm right.

- It's only going to happen once (hopefully).

- Then you can laugh at everyone else when they have to do it. I hear Mick has just got engaged. (Sorry to break the bad news to you. I know you were about to make a move.)

- One a scale of stubbing your toe to childbirth*, it's probably about the same pain level as getting a filling, so stop whining and choose some hors d'oeuvres.

- If you do it and it turns out well, then you officially get to call yourself a talented metrosexual modern man. It's what you've always dreamt of.

- Afterwards we get to go on our honeymoon and we can frolic naked in the Icelandic springs and engaged in obnoxious PDA in the hotel lobby: worth it.

*Friendly reminder that childbirth is going to be in my future and this is the least you can do for me in return, sucker.

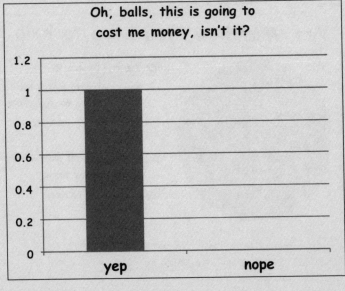

Oh, balls, this is going to cost me money, isn't it?

1.2	
1	
0.8	
0.6	
0.4	
0.2	
0	
yep	**nope**

CONGRATULATIONS ON OUR
ENGAGEMENT, HONEY!!1!

Folios/v7/Time-landscape-2018/MS-32

"Don't you think she's funny?" Kate asked, grinning, as Matt finished reading it.

"I guess," Matt admitted. He tilted his head, staring at the pie chart with a look of bemusement. There was a nick on his neck where he'd cut himself shaving. "She's got a very … *distinctive* sense of humour."

Kate felt a little offended on Katherine's behalf. "I think she's hilarious."

Matt was still staring at the paper. "Kate," he said, slow and thoughtful. "Do your grandparents have any more of this kind of stuff?"

"I dunno. Why?"

"Because it might have the answer."

Kate was surprised by the excitement in his voice. "What? How?"

"If they have any of Katherine and Matthew's research, like their lab books or something, it might help to prove that they weren't making a weapon – that they were just doing their jobs."

"That's true! We can go and visit them after labs if you want. You really think Katherine and Matthew might be innocent?"

He nodded. "Ever since I found out about my uncle and your aunt, I've thought it wasn't right. My parents don't want me to get involved. They think I should just leave it alone, but I can't." He folded his arms and then unfolded them. "Actually ... that's why I'm here."

"What?"

"I applied to Nottingham Uni so I could get into England. I wanted an opportunity to visit the lab they worked at, to see if I could find any evidence to prove that they didn't do it. It's the whole reason I'm here."

"Wow," Kate said. "I only came here because a girl at a careers fair told me they did good field trips. But I do want to prove that Katherine and Matthew are innocent. Will it be dangerous?"

Matt didn't reply, but Kate knew the answer. This wasn't going to end well. They stared at each other, like rabbits caught in the same headlights.

Strait of Gibraltar, 1854

They were a week into their journey and Matthew had already started interviewing soldiers for his first article. He was planning to post it to *The Times* as soon as they landed at Varna, Bulgaria, in a fortnight. He flashed a charming smile at one of the officers supervising the cooking of dinner in the kitchens, dimples appearing in his cheeks.

"Sergeant Woodward, may I introduce myself?"

Katy's heart sank. Matthew was in journalist-mode and he was annoyingly efficient. He sounded experienced and responsible. He would definitely be able to pick up on anything Katy did to try and influence him to change his articles.

The sergeant looked at the two of them with mild interest. He pulled a fat cigar from his mouth and nodded.

"I'm Matthew Galloway, war correspondent for *The Times*. Lord Raglan may have mentioned that I was accompanying this regiment?"

Katy was suddenly alert. Lord Raglan was her employer, Lord Somerset. Raglan was what he was called by the general public. That must be why Matthew hadn't been suspicious of Katy's reference. He only knew the famous army general as Lord *Raglan*. If he found out who Lord Somerset really was, he might guess that Katy was spying on him. She winced.

The officer chewed on the end of his cigar thoughtfully, before replying, "I do recall my superior mentioning something to that effect. Frightfully odd business. What if the Russians got hold of your dispatches and discovered our tactics?"

Matthew gave a nervous laugh that failed to convince either Katy, or the sergeant, judging by his expression.

"Anything I send will be long out of date when it reaches the Russians," Matthew said. "I will make sure there are no breaches in security. That would do more harm than good, and I intend to do good here."

"What do you mean 'good'? How can a journalist help the war effort?" the sergeant asked.

"I'm dedicated to providing Britain with the most accurate account of the war that I can, Sir," Matthew responded. "I believe that a regular supply of news straight from our loyal and valiant army will encourage people at home to support the war effort."

The sergeant, cheeks red from the clouds of steam in the kitchen, looked pleased at this compliment to his regiment. "So how might I be of service, Sir?" he asked.

Matthew pulled out his notebook. "I understand that you have already visited the army encampment at Varna, when you accompanied another regiment there. May I ask you a few questions about your experiences at the front so far?"

The sergeant nodded, and Matthew asked him some basic questions about the army's conditions. He interrupted a monologue on the officers' misuse of their revolvers to ask, "Were there any problems with the administration of the army?"

"Last time I was there, there weren't enough interpreters," the sergeant said. "You could never understand a goddamn thing the locals were saying. Of course, there was the usual lack of mechanics, wheelwrights, and the like – but that's only to be expected during a war when the demand for repairs is so much higher."

"Of course. Anything else?"

"Well..." He looked unsure, but said, "There wasn't enough forage for the horses. Some of them became very colicky – it was terrible. I dread to think what condition they're in now."

Katy wondered, not for the first time, whether what Matthew was doing – reporting on the everyday lives of the men at the front – wasn't such a bad thing. People at home should know what was happening, especially if a lack of supplies had an impact on the war.

"You're awfully quiet," Matthew asked as they made their way back onto deck. "Is anything the matter?"

A familiar feeling of guilt rose in her throat. She watched a seagull spiral overhead before asking carefully, "Are you going to put everything he said into your article?"

"Of course," he replied easily. "Why wouldn't I?"

"I don't think it would help anything. I mean, his complaints weren't really important. No one is going to care about bad tobacco, are they?"

"Maybe not – but they will care that the horses are being kept in bad conditions."

"I just think it's a bad idea to report on something which you haven't seen for yourself," she replied. "He could have it all wrong. Why don't you wait until we arrive in Varna and are able to see if he was right?"

Matthew agreed with her idea, and Katy tried,

unsuccessfully, not to feel guilty. Her loyalty to Lord Somerset, her employer, had to be her first priority.

Carlisle, England, 1745

It was the morning after her conversation with Matthew about volunteering at the castle. Katherine was brushing her hair when Anise knocked quietly on her door and entered her bedroom. She was carrying a wrapped package, tied with twine.

"You asked for this, Miss," the maid said.

"Oh! Yes, thank you." It was the clothes from Matthew. She took the package, noticing that he'd tucked a pheasant feather into the knot of the binding. She clutched it tightly.

"Will there be anything else?" Anise asked. She spoke quietly, almost under her breath. Katherine would never have guessed that she was a Rebel if she hadn't overheard her conversation with Matthew the other day. She seemed so shy and restrained now. She had been completely different when talking to Matthew.

"Have you had any news of the Jacobites?" Katherine asked. She had to see if she could find out anything from this girl. She might be able to get an idea of their plans.

Anise didn't answer for several seconds, and then finally said quietly, "I haven't, no."

Katherine cast about for something else to say. "What – what do you think of the rebellion? Do you think it has any chance of success?"

Anise shot her an odd look. "I don't really know much about it, Miss."

"Oh, really? I thought I heard you discussing it with the coachman." The minute she'd finished speaking she realized it had been the wrong thing to say.

Anise blinked at her. "Excuse me, Miss." She turned and left the room without a backward glance, or even a curtsy.

Well, that hadn't worked out at all.

After unwrapping the package, Katherine quickly pulled Matthew's shirt on. It was freshly laundered, but it still smelt of him. It was slightly too large around the shoulders, but the trousers fitted almost too well – they were very snug. Next she pulled on the waistcoat. The simple act of dressing in men's clothing felt *naughtier* than she'd expected. It felt almost delightfully illicit.

When she was dressed, she looked at herself in the mirror. The result was better than she had hoped. She was a little too pale to really pass as a working boy, but it would do. She pinned her hair under a cap.

Matthew was grooming a horse in the stables when she went to meet him. "It fits well," he said, a blush rising to his cheeks as he took in the sight of her wearing his clothes.

"Yes, it does. Shall we go?" Katherine found herself fidgeting nervously. She was suddenly very aware of how revealing the trousers were.

They walked to the town square, where a meeting about the uprising was to take place. Matthew collapsed onto the steps that led up to the large cross in the centre of the square. He yawned into his palm. Katherine sat beside him. She reached down to arrange her skirts without thinking. She smiled and stroked her hands down the trouser legs instead. She could get used to this. Her initial self-consciousness was gone.

People were starting to stream into the square – a few elderly men who formed the castle's garrison and the volunteer militia, which was made up of younger local men. The latter was more of a social club than a military force, and they strolled up in a dense gang, talking loudly to each other and catcalling at a passing maid.

Then the colonel arrived. He was in the middle of an intense monologue and surrounded by members of the city council, who were listening raptly to his words. He was old – over sixty. Katherine couldn't remember seeing anyone of his age in the army before, but it might not be a bad thing, especially if it meant that he had a lot of experience. In his smart uniform and shiny boots, he was in stark contrast to the rumpled, hungover men of the militia.

The soldiers, young and old, fell silent, watching his approach. Katherine climbed onto the higher steps so she could see him over the crowds. Matthew scrambled up beside her to get a better view of the spectacle.

The colonel regarded the group of men dispassionately. Eventually he cleared his throat. "My name is Colonel Durand. I've come from London to help prepare the defences of Carlisle. I've looked at the current situation, and there's a lot to be done, but I'm confident that Carlisle will soon be able to withstand any attacks.

"However, I will need people to restore the cannons, dig ditches, and clear the farmland so there's a clear line of sight. The most important job is to improve the strength of the castle walls, which are in poor condition. The mortar is at least two centuries old.

"We're also going to be collecting provisions of food to store in the castle in case we have to face a siege. I hope the citizens and militia of Carlisle will help their city in its hour of need, and by the time we next meet I believe we will have more confidence in the state of the preparations." He gave a short bow and there was a smattering of applause from the militia. Katherine was almost certain it was ironic.

Katherine, however, was immensely satisfied with the meeting. Colonel Durand seemed so confident and experienced. She felt sure his strategies were sound. It was a little concerning that he had outlined in such detail how bad the defences were, though. He had made Carlisle seem like an easy target. They would have to work hard to make sure the city could stand up to any attack. She looked over at Matthew to see how he had reacted to the news of the weak defences, but he was staring out across the square, his expression impossible to read.

CHAPTER 6

New post on **Matthew Galloway**'s profile page:

10 hrs • West Midlands
Saw you and Kate left labs early today with a bottle of Pimms…!
Don't worry, I sent the experiment off for analysis.
… have fun! ;)

Like • Comment • Share

Folios/v7/Time-landscape-2019/MS-147

Near Greece, Mediterranean Sea, 1854

Katy was celebrating a poker victory against a sulking Matthew when a bugle sounded. A sailor then explained briskly that there was an opportunity to bathe if they wished. Katy was delighted. After a fortnight of hot weather and confined conditions, she felt really grimy.

It was only when the soldiers' wives went below deck to wash in private that she realized what it meant. The men started undressing on the deck without a care in the world.

Katy tried to look away, but she was surrounded by naked men of all shapes and sizes, cleaning themselves with warm water and soap. Then Matthew stood up, unbuttoning his waistcoat.

"What are you doing?" she asked, panicked.

He shot her a strange look. "I'm going to wash, Kit. I suggest you do the same. We might not get another chance for a while. We are not due to disembark for another week."

Katy felt like she was going to explode from embarrassment. She watched in open-mouthed horror as Matthew pulled his shirt over his head.

"Can't I go somewhere private?" she asked.

Matthew tipped a bucket of water over his head as she desperately tried to keep her eyes above waist level. Everywhere she looked there were … men's parts.

"Why would you want to do that? There are no women here, Kit. Everyone's the same. Just get on with it."

She began by slowly washing her hair – something she could do fully dressed while only risking looking a bit strange. Most of the men had finished washing by now, and were standing around talking. They were still naked. She reached under her shirt and quickly cleaned her armpits, neck and shoulders as best she could, which wasn't very well at all.

"Kit! What are you doing?" Matthew asked. "Don't be ridiculous – just take off your clothes. Does it look like anybody cares?"

She didn't know what to do. She grasped for a plausible explanation. "I can't," she whispered.

"What? Why?"

"I – I can't… Matthew, please. Don't make me!" She gasped. She couldn't breathe. What was he going to do when he found out?

Up until then he had been baffled, but now he stepped towards her, looking worried. "Kit, what's wrong?"

She couldn't get out of this. She was going to have to tell

him. He was going to work it out for himself at this rate. She stepped closer and made sure no one was within hearing distance.

"Matthew…" She exhaled, took a breath.

And then she turned and ran.

> Progress in time-landscape 1854 may be affected by the actions of subject allocation "KATY"

UNIVERSITY OF NOTTINGHAM CAMPUS, ENGLAND, 2039

"How did you find out about Katherine and Matthew Galloway?" Kate asked Matt as they walked to her grandparents' house.

"My brother. A while back he found an article online about our uncle, saying he was a terrorist. He confronted our dad about it and Dad admitted it was true. He'd always told us that his brother had died in a lab accident. After that we just started investigating. My brother's good online. He's … um" – Matt lowered his voice – "kind of a hacker."

Kate spun round to face him. "That is so *cool*. You mean he's, like, an actual political activist?"

"It's kind of stressful, actually. He's pretty famous, in all the wrong ways. On forums and stuff. I'm always worried he's going to get caught."

"Wait, is he famous-famous? Would I have heard of him? What's his name?"

"Well, he's called Tom, but online he's known as Spartacus."

"What?" Kate stopped in her tracks, and Matt turned back in surprise. "Your brother is *Spartacus*?"

It was her guilty secret, but she was obsessed with conspiracy theories. Any hint of a hidden agenda made her instantly suspicious. She always felt that there was something shady going on. Spartacus was one of the best-known hackers. He was dedicated to trying to reveal the conspiracies of the government. Kate followed all of his posts almost fanatically.

"… Yes?" Matt said, hesitantly.

"No *way*." She bounced a little on her toes. "I don't *believe* it!"

"Urgh." Matt sighed. "You know who he is. I should have known you were into this stuff too. The hair – it's a dead giveaway."

"He's only been my idol for the last three years or so! He's amazing!" Kate gushed, choosing to ignore the hair comment. Suddenly this drama seemed a lot more fun. "Can I meet him? Please? *Please*?"

"I'm not sure. Kate, do you have a crush on my brother?"

She blushed pink, and avoided his gaze. "What? Of course not."

Matt raised his eyebrows at her.

"OK, maybe a little," she admitted, going even redder. "I used to, anyway." She started babbling, embarrassed. "He's really famous on the Internet! His blog is *amazing*. He's made people start really thinking about what the government tells us. He's a huge part of history. Plus, he's really funny."

Kate looked at Matt, hopefully, but he just shook his head

like he was ashamed to know her, and carried on walking.
She had to jog to catch up.

Carlisle, England, 1745

Katherine was balancing on her tiptoes so she could peer
out of the mottled glass window of the castle's supply room
and watch the militia dig out the moat far below. The
soldiers were thigh deep in muddy water as they steepened
the sides of the river banks. It had started raining and
they resembled miserable drowned rats. Considering how
arrogant they had been at the meeting that morning,
Katherine couldn't say she felt sorry for them.

The garrison had been stationed in the castle for years,
and working there was not easy. The castle was on the
northernmost side of the city, facing Scotland. It was set
into the high stone wall that surrounded Carlisle. As the
colonel had observed, the ancient buildings were in bad
repair, and they were cold; the roughly hewn stone walls
were stained with dripping water. Cannons had stood on
the battlements for decades, ready to fire at any attacking
enemies through the narrow slits in the parapet. Now they
were rusting and broken, and Katherine and Matthew had
been assigned the task of renovating them.

They had been given a better job than the men below,
though, Katherine decided, contented. She knelt down
on the stone floor beside Matthew, who was diligently
rubbing off the endless layers of rust on the first in a long

series of ancient cannons. She poked the metal. A bolt fell off in a gust of orange dust.

"I presume this is not as glamorous as you were expecting, My Lady?" he teased.

"I preferred you when you were half asleep. You were much nicer." After a pause, she added more seriously, "It is exactly what I was expecting. I didn't think the Rebels would be firing at us immediately. The most vital things are often the dullest."

She meant what she said. She didn't mind the work. She had known that it was going to take a while to find out if Matthew was planning anything and this was a good opportunity. He probably wouldn't do anything while she was around, but if she kept a close eye on him, he might give something away anyway. Matthew continued rubbing rhythmically at the metal. She tried not to watch the movement of his shoulder, the tight play of muscles under his shirt.

"At least this is something you can help with," Matthew added, "which is fortunate. If we had been given duties digging out that moat, you would have struggled."

"I'll have you know I am an expert at trench digging," she said. "It's an important skill for a young lady. I would struggle to find a husband without it."

He grinned. "I should hope so. I would be wary of a wife who was unable to dig a perfect tunnel."

"My point exactly, Matthew, thank you. If even *you* require such a talent, imagine the demands of a man who actually has standards." It was so nice, talking to him while dressed as a boy, without having to worry about what anyone would think if they saw them.

"You think you are a lot funnier than you are, you know," he replied, not looking away from the cannon.

"I am extremely amusing! I don't think you are listening properly." Matthew was struggling with a stubborn patch of rust, and she leant closer. "You have to rub it harder, or nothing will happen," she offered.

He snorted, and mumbled something under his breath. She frowned, trying to work out what he'd found funny. "What?" she asked.

He looked up with a naughty grin. *"Said the actress to the bishop."*

What actress? What was he talking about? "Oh," she said in confusion.

He seemed to realize his mistake, because he looked ashamed. "It's supposed to be funny. I expect you wouldn't have heard it before. It's something the servants say a lot."

She nodded, memorizing the joke so she could try to work out why it was funny later. Then she stuck her head inside the barrel of the cannon to pull away some of the looser layers of decay. The barrel immediately began to fill with dust, and she pulled out again quickly, trying not to sneeze. Matthew quickly moved his eyes back to the cannon, focusing too carefully on the metal, and she knew that he had been laughing at her.

Servants were strange.

Inventory of Provisions &c.
in Carlisle Castle

Approximately 130 bushels of meal & 210 bushels of wheat

270 bushels of potatoes

800 pounds of cheese

500 pounds of butter

400 tons of coal

A large quantity of candles and all the straw we could get

2 chests of medicines

About 27 bullocks

Between 30 and 40 sheep

Necessary utensils for dressing of victuals

Wine and other provisions sent in by the gentlemen, or brought in by the militia

CHAPTER 7

Matthew Galloway commented on the post *"Does anyone remember a time when* Katherine *and* Matthew **weren't* having sex?"* along with twelve others:

Like • Comment • Share

Matthew Galloway Why is this happening? I hate you all. (I don't think there is anything crazy about our sex life, thank you very much!)

7 hrs • Like

Folios/v7/Time-landscape-2019/MS-148

Near Greece, Mediterranean Sea, 1854

Matthew found Katy hiding in the stairwell, crying into her handkerchief. He ducked down beside her, shirt still clasped in his fist as he'd run after her while he was dressing.

"Kit," he said softly. "What's going on?"

She looked up at him, trying to hold back a sob. His hair was still wet and water dripped down his collarbone.

"I'm so sorry."

He patted her shoulder. "Please tell me what's wrong."

She brushed away her tears. "I can't. You'll hate me."

"Surely it can't be that bad."

She took a deep breath. "I can't undress because … I'm not a boy." His face was blank so she added, "I'm a girl."

She felt a moment of release, which disappeared as

she watched the confused expression on his face give way to something like surprise, then horror, finally settling on anger. His face hardened and her gut twisted to see him shut her out. His hand slowly moved off her shoulder, before tightening into a fist. She grabbed his arm in desperation as he pulled away and stood up.

"Wait, Matthew—"

He shrugged her off, turning his back to her and beginning to slowly, carefully, dress. There was a flush of angry pink spreading down between his shoulder blades. She watched him, not knowing what to say. When he had finished buttoning his shirt, he walked away without turning back to look at her.

For a long moment, she stared after him. There was a lump in her throat that wouldn't go away however much she swallowed.

> Subject allocation "KATY" in time-landscape 1854 is a potential problem

> Subject allocation "MATTHEW"'s response to "KATY"'s lies indicates that any future revelations of her dishonesty may severely hamper desired progress

> Too late for intervention – monitor situation carefully

Carlisle, England, 1745

The next morning, Katherine went to meet Matthew at the stables, excited at the prospect of another day at the castle. She hadn't managed to catch him doing anything treacherous yet. He hadn't shown any sign of being anything other than the kind, slightly awkward coachman he appeared to be. She had tried to bring up the topic of politics several times, but he had only ever had perfectly uncontroversial things to say, and the conversation would often drift to gentle, flirtatious exchanges despite her most dedicated efforts to remain on topic.

Secretly she knew that her desire to expose him as a Rebel wasn't the real reason she was eager to get to the castle. The truth was she enjoyed spending time with Matthew. Katherine had never spent so much time giggling.

Matthew was filling a water trough when Katherine arrived. His movements were quiet and steady in the peace of the silent stables.

She bounced up to him, delighting in disturbing his solitude. "Good morning!"

He didn't smile back. "Katherine."

"Shall we go to…?" She trailed off, taking in his expression. "Matthew, what's wrong?"

"Anise told me that you asked her about the rebellion. She thought you sounded suspicious."

"I … er—" She flushed, unsure what to say.

"What are you doing, Katherine? I don't know what you think you heard, but we aren't Rebels," Matthew said, not giving her a chance to explain. "You don't need to question my – my *cousin*."

She swallowed. "You said that if the seige happens you were going to 'change things'. You're planning something with her."

"No! We aren't. We're—"

"Matthew, just admit it!" Katherine exploded in a fit of frustration. "You are a Rebel! You were talking about doing something, during the siege."

"We only want to help."

"So … you do admit it? You are spying for the Rebels? I *knew* it!"

"No! What?" He looked appalled. "I'm not spying on anyone."

"I don't understand," she said, confused. She wanted to believe him. She wanted to be able to trust him and know that he was really the person she thought he was.

"We want to help the *English*," he explained. "I don't want the Rebels to win. I want to defend Carlisle. I thought you knew that! I want everyone here to be safe. I would never want anyone to invade the place where people I … care about live."

"But you're Scottish."

"The Scots aren't some sort of barbarian race, Katherine. We have common sense. Having Charles Stuart on the throne wouldn't necessarily be a good thing for the country. Anise thinks we can be useful. She believes that with the right knowledge, we can help."

"But you're servants. What do you know that could possibly help?"

"Oh," he said, dully. "Right."

"I didn't mean it in that—"

He took a step away from her. "I thought you were different. I didn't think you cared about social classes."

"I don't, I…" She didn't know what to say. She couldn't pin her flying thoughts down into any kind of order.

"You were spying on me. You thought I was a Rebel. That's why you've been talking to me, all this time."

She froze.

"You were spying on me," he repeated quietly, like he was only just believing it. "All this time I thought we were…" He sighed. "I thought we were friends." He said it softly, regretfully, and the sound of it hurt somewhere deep in her chest.

"We *are* friends," she managed to choke out, the reassurance ringing false even to her ears. "I had to make sure, that's all. You were acting a little suspiciously, and I needed to ensure that you—"

"All this time," he interrupted, "you were watching me and waiting to see if I made a mistake. Was every conversation a lie?"

"No! Spending time with you, it's… You healed me, Matthew. I was so miserable here, after my grandmother died. I was alone in Carlisle, and you made me happy again. None of that was false. I just had to be sure that you weren't lying to me."

As soon as she said it she realized how terribly she'd

been acting. Of course Matthew hadn't been lying to her: everything about him screamed honesty. She was the one who had lied and deceived and hurt him.

"I can't talk to you now," he said and turned away.

> Previously scheduled progress in time-landscape 1745 has been affected by the actions of subject allocation "KATHERINE"

> Project may not proceed at projected rate

CHAPTER 8

<u>House rules for a certain Matthew Galloway if he wants to</u>
<u>taste my DELECTABLE chocolate cake again any time in</u>
<u>the foreseeable future</u>

1) No discussing our sex life in any kind of disgustingly explicit detail on the internet ever again. Seriously, I am scarred for life.

2) Clare asked me why I kept twitching earlier and whether you were being too rough with me. I hate you I hate you I hate you, get out of my life.

3) Yes, that includes vaguely dirty innuendos, Matthew! Mum congratulated me on the obvious strength of our physical relationship!!

4) Do you have any idea how soul destroying that is?! Kill me now, right now. I'm not even joking.

Folios/v7/Time-landscape-2019/MS-149

Near Greece,
Mediterranean Sea, 1854

Katy breathed in the musty scent of the stables below deck as she ran her hand along the flank of a docile mare whose stall Matthew was sitting in. He hadn't looked at all surprised when she'd appeared in his hiding place. After a nod of hello, she held out a tot of rum as a peace offering. He took it, and knocked it back with barely a wince.

"Sit down." He gestured to the straw-covered floor. She considered objecting – *he* was sitting on a barrel of water – but decided not to push her luck. She sat, pulling her legs up to her chest and staring determinedly at her knees.

"I'm sorry I didn't tell you," she said. "But you'd never have employed me if you'd known. And I have been living as a boy for so long that it's not something I talk about with anyone."

He was silent. She grimaced at her knees, trying to think what else to say. It felt so wrong to be openly discussing something she'd hidden carefully every day for years, something her livelihood depended upon.

"How long?" he eventually enquired. He was fiddling with a curry comb, and his head was bent, so his fringe hid his face. Although it was obvious what he meant, he added, "How long have you been living like this? As a boy?"

"Four years. When I left the orphanage, I would have had to go to the workhouse. This was a better choice."

"Four!" His surprise broke his carefully blank tone, putting a touch of the Matthew she knew back into the formal voice he'd been using. "How old are you?"

"Seventeen at Christmas." She paused, and then asked something she'd been wondering for a while. "How – how old are you?"

"One and twenty." She was a little surprised. She'd expected him to be older. He'd achieved so much at such a young age. "And has no one known that you're really *female* all this time?" He said the word "female" in a lowered tone, as if it was a swear word.

"No. That might change when I get older and never grow a beard, though."

"What is your real name?"

"At the orphanage they called me Katy. Katherine."

"Katherine," he repeated quietly, and her reaction to the sound of it was stronger than she'd expected. She turned away, hoping he wouldn't notice.

He dropped the comb then and sat up straighter. He still wouldn't meet her gaze, but his shoulders had dropped and he seemed more relaxed. He carefully looked her over from head to toe.

She had a sudden bout of dizziness, and when it stopped she wasn't sure where they were. *For a moment it had seemed as if they were in an actual stable on land, the morning sun lighting up the straw in a golden glow and Matthew gazing at her clothing with dark eyes, his lips parting…* She blinked the image away, and they were back in the dingy bowels of the ship, and instead Matthew was staring at her like he was finally letting himself compare the Kit he knew with the girl underneath the clothes. When their eyes met, it felt like he was seeing right through her.

She said gently, "You can ask anything you want."

"Does it hurt?" he said in a rush, and immediately his blush deepened.

"Does *what* hurt?"

"Being, ah, bound? You must have been bandaged for weeks, *years*, without a break."

Surprised, she unconsciously wrapped her arms around her chest. He watched her carefully. It was a perfectly innocent look, but it still made the hairs on the back of her neck stand up. "Oh. Not much. It hurts a little now as I haven't had a chance to take the bindings off for a while. There isn't anywhere you can be alone here."

"But not being able to move freely, in all that time?"

"Haven't you heard of corsets?" Katy asked with a wry laugh.

"I suppose."

"Having my hair cut short is the hardest part," she confided. "I wish I could wear it long."

"It must be very hard for you," he replied, eyes twinkling. His tone was almost teasing, if still slightly formal.

"It is. This hairstyle makes me look like a twelve-year-old boy."

"Well, maybe a bit…"

"Matthew!" she said, mock-offended.

He shrugged helplessly. Looking at him made her chest ache.

"You're not keeping any other secrets from me, are you?" he asked, shakily. "I'm not sure I could take this again."

She choked out a laugh as her stomach twisted. "None," she lied.

For the rest of the day she found herself walking more delicately, like a girl. Why was it harder to pretend now that Matthew knew? She just felt more feminine all of a sudden. She reminded herself she was a boy, at least for now, and tried to walk with long, confident steps.

Carlisle, England, 1745

After their argument in the stables, Katherine and Matthew avoided each other for almost four days with awkward and sometimes even aggressive determination. She would see him grooming the horses and turn the other way, or he'd be talking to a servant when she went to ask for hot water and would conveniently disappear before she reached them.

On the fifth day, Katherine decided that she had to find him and apologize. After lunch, she hovered uncertainly at the stable door, but he didn't even look up. Instead he bent closer over the bridle he was cleaning, rubbing the saddle soap into the leather forcefully. She stood in the doorway, trying to come up with the perfect way to describe how sorry she was.

Before she had sufficiently collected her courage he spoke. "I didn't think I would see you again now that you have found out everything you wanted about me, Miss Finchley."

"I can assure you that I wasn't only here for that, Matthew."

"Oh? Did you want to gather enough evidence to have me arrested or perhaps sent away for disrespecting your rank?" He seemed resigned and disappointed.

"No! That's not how it was." Did he really think everything between them had been a trick, to get him into trouble? She opened her mouth and then closed it again.

"I should have realized at the beginning," Matthew said. "During our carriage journey together ... that night." He swallowed hard. "You were just trying to get close to me to find out if I was a traitor. It was stupid of me to have thought, even for a moment, that it was anything else. You're practically nobility."

"I wanted to be friends with you before I ever suspected you of any involvement with the Rebels," Katherine said. "But once I had overheard you and your cousin speaking, I... Well, I had to investigate further. When you said you were volunteering, I saw an opportunity, and I took it." Even as she said it, she knew it was the wrong thing to say.

"An *opportunity*," he repeated dully. "Is that all I am?"

Suddenly she was furious. "Oh, please. Did you not think of me in the same way? Why else would a servant want to *get close* to an unmarried girl with a dowry, *Matthew*? I'm sure it wasn't for my *tantalising conversation*."

He actually took a step back, as if her words had physically hurt him.

"I..." He stopped. "I suppose it only makes it worse if I say I wanted to speak to you because I thought you were beautiful."

She gaped at him. Did he really think that was a

compliment? He had wanted to be friends with her because of how she *looked*? That was how every man she'd ever met saw women – as objects, possessions. She'd thought he was different.

He hadn't noticed her silent fury, and continued, "I thought you were beautiful, and funny, and knowledgeable. You were so sad, but you still took the time to speak to me as if I was a person, not just a servant. I have never met anyone like you. You're one of the bravest people I've ever known. You thought you'd found a Jacobite spy, and so you decided to spy on *them*. I don't understand you at all. If you'd been a serving maid, I still wouldn't have been able to stay away from you."

"You … you really saw all of that? In me?"

"Yes. But then I found out that you've just been playing with me all along, and now I feel as though everything was a lie."

"I wanted to be friends with you too," she admitted in a rush. "I was a fool. I am ashamed of the way I have treated you. I do things without thinking sometimes. I didn't even know anything about the Rebels before you told me about them. I got caught up in something I didn't understand and I hurt you. That's the last thing I ever wanted to do. I wish I could go back in time and stop myself ever being so thoughtless."

"You were *thoughtless*." The way he said the word made her realize how terribly she had hurt him. She stepped hesitantly towards him, but he turned away from her.

"I should get back to work," he said, to his saddle soap.

She bit her lip, trying not to let her disappointment show. "I am really, truly sorry. It was all my fault, and I wish you'd forgive me."

"I forgive you for being a fool," he said with a heavy sigh. "But I'm not sure we can be friends the way we were before."

Katherine's vision blurred with tears. "You are right, of course," she said, tight and quiet.

She had wanted him to fight for her or to give her some confirmation that the connection between them hadn't just been in her imagination. But she shouldn't have expected that of Matthew. He was too noble, too moral and too loyal to do the wrong thing, even if it was what he wanted. His ideals were clear-cut. Risking Katherine's honour wasn't something he would do in any situation – she could see that now. He was better than Katherine. She always took what she wanted without considering the consequences.

She couldn't force Matthew to change his decision, though, however much she wanted to. It was the right one, after all. They needed to stop this … this *dalliance*. It was ridiculous, a danger to both of them, and it needed to end before it went too far. She walked slowly back to the house without another word. She felt as though she were splitting in two.

> Relationship advances in time-landscape 1745 rejected by both subjects

> The social dynamics of this time-landscape may make any relationship between the subjects impossible

> Consider situation further

NOTTINGHAM, ENGLAND, 2039

After a shocked pause when Kate's grandparents had stared at Matt in surprised recognition – apparently they hadn't believed her when she said he looked *just* like her aunt's Matthew Galloway – they had been ridiculously, effusively thrilled to meet him. Flo had pulled Matt into a long, hard hug. Nancy had begun to quietly cry.

"You look so like him," Flo said. "It is just … it's crazy. Such a coincidence that the two of you should end up at the same university. How is that possible?" She shook her head. "I can scarcely believe it."

Once they had recovered sufficiently from the shock, they had both begun embarrassing Kate as much as possible by talking rapidly about how she never brought anyone home and how nice it was to meet him. Kate suffered it all quietly, while slowly turning redder and redder, but when Nancy wanted to show him Kate's baby photos she interrupted. There was a line that she wouldn't let them cross, and it involved a particular picture with a dropped ice cream and a seagull and many, many tears. She definitely didn't want Matt to see that – ever.

It had taken a bit of persuasion, but finally Kate's grandparents had agreed to let them look in the loft for any of their aunt and uncle's old stuff. Kate had explained that they just wanted to find out more about their namesakes.

They headed upstairs, where Flo directed Matt to lift up the polystyrene ceiling panel of the loft, with all the precision of a military general. A shower of dust fell onto his head when he worked it free, standing on the toilet so he could reach.

"Nice look," Kate teased as he wiped the dust away, grimacing.

"Kate, you go up," Flo ordered. "The ceiling is a little delicate up there. You are lighter. Matt might fall through."

Torch in hand, Kate climbed up. She lay on the dusty floor of the loft for a moment while she caught her breath. The loft was full of old crates and boxes, and a Christmas tree wrapped in a sheet. All Kate's old toys were up there too. She had rescued them from a clear-out the year before. Her mum had been about to throw them away, but Kate, who had always known she wanted children one day, had wanted to keep them for the future. Her grandparents had come to the rescue by offering to store the boxes in their loft.

Kate closed her eyes. If she was going to hide something here, somewhere a search wouldn't find it… She turned to look at the chimney breast, where it disappeared into the roof. After picking her way through the crates to the brickwork, she moved aside boxes and squeezed past an old filing cabinet, so she could get at the wall.

She prodded at the bricks cautiously. To her surprise, one of them moved. Kate grasped the edges of the loose brick and tugged it until it slid out with a dry grinding sound. The hole was filled with cobwebs, so she blew into the opening. When the dust and dry mortar had cleared, she shone her torch inside. The light lit up a plastic bag. Her heart jumped into her throat.

She tugged the bag free, brushing away a brown layer of grime. The bag was surprisingly heavy, and inside were several notebooks, some papers and an ancient laptop that was bulky and old-fashioned. Kate whooped delightedly.

"You've found something *already*?" Matt called up, amazed.

"It was in the first place I checked!" It was like she'd already known where it was.

"What a coincidence," he said as she carefully passed the package down to him. He handled it just as reverently as she had. "Where was it?"

She paused. She couldn't tell him that she'd decided to ignore all the boxes in favour of following a weird hunch and checking inside the wall. It sounded crazy. "It was … er … it was in one of the boxes."

"That's brilliant! It's like you knew it was there all along."

She didn't comment.

Matt helped her down. They grinned triumphantly at each other, their faces so close together as she dropped to the floor that their noses were almost touching.

His eyes were shining. *His lips parted slightly as he helped her down from the rigging. The rain was just starting up again. He gazed at her with wide eyes and she could feel the gentle rock of the boat. The crisp smell of the sea filled her lungs, and—*

No, that wasn't right.

She blinked.

They were in the bathroom of her old house? Yes: she remembered dyeing her hair black at this sink during her goth phase. She'd stained the tile grout and made her mums crazy.

She blinked.

No, that wasn't right either. She'd never lived here. It was Nana and Gran's house.

She focused on Matt, whose gaze had always steadied her, and felt herself re-centring and finally she remembered where she was. She swallowed.

"Did you … did you feel that?" she asked.

He looked at her, expression blank. "Feel what?"

"Nothing," she said weakly.

CHAPTER 9

Katherine, you do know I can add rules to this too, right?

5) Katherine is no longer allowed to steal my 85% cocoa dark chocolate just because she's run out of the disgusting, sugary, tasteless crap that masquerades as chocolate in her wildly distorted world view. That stuff is expensive and you just don't appreciate it enough, sorry.

6) Stop borrowing my fountain pen. It genuinely does ruin the nib despite how impossible you think that is. I can tell the difference!

7) I do have more things to complain about and I'll be back when I can actually think of them.

Folios/v7/Time-landscape-2019/MS-149

Near Turkey, Aegean Sea, 1854

"Matthew, is that a bird?" Katy asked. They were walking around an almost deserted deck, admiring the Turkish coast. It was their third week at sea and they were due to land any day now. Katy had been warily eyeing the black clouds collecting ominously overhead when she'd caught sight of a brown blur, high up in the rigging.

Matthew peered up, following her pointing finger. "Yes! It's an owl, trapped in the rigging. It's tiny!"

The deck was treacherously wet, and they gingerly made their way over to the rigging, holding onto each other as they walked, to avoid slipping.

"We need to help it." Katy rolled up her sleeves and tentatively put her foot on the rope, testing it. It held her weight, and she began climbing up the thick ropes to the bird.

"Katy, what are you doing? You can't do that!" Matthew hissed.

Grinning, she looked down from her perch above his head. "Are you *scared*?" She giggled, before turning back to the rope to climb further.

"Some people are just too reckless for their own good," he muttered.

She held in her laughter this time. She needed to focus on climbing.

The bird was tangled in the ropes and completely motionless. It was obviously exhausted from trying to escape. She manoeuvred beside it, moving slowly so she didn't scare it.

"Be careful!" Matthew called up. Preoccupied with the tiny creature, she acknowledged him with a small flick of her hand. She brushed her fingers over the bird's soft feathers. It startled but let her gently unwrap the tangled rope. Once free, the bird flapped its wings madly, wriggling until it slipped out of her grasp. Leaning back against the rigging, she watched it fly off until it was barely a speck on the horizon.

When she looked down again, Matthew had a small smile on his face. "Well done. But please come down before you fall into the sea!"

She laughed out loud, the excitement of having rescued a living creature making her dizzy – or maybe that was the height.

It was harder climbing down, but as she reached the bottom, Matthew was there to help her the last few feet, his gentle hands around her waist. He was closer to her than she had realized, and she could see the small kiss-curls in his hair where it had dried from the rain. He didn't pull away and she stared into his eyes, her smile dropping and her breath catching.

A sailor let out a wolf-whistle and Matthew stepped back quickly, releasing her waist.

"Steady there, lads," the sailor called.

The tips of Matthew's ears went pink.

"It's starting to rain again," he said quickly. "Shall we go back inside?"

> Time-landscape 1854 on schedule

Carlisle, England, 1745

After the conversation with Matthew, Katherine had run all the way back from the stables to her bedroom. Now, she dropped onto her bed, worming her head under the pillow and pressing her face into the eiderdown. The sound of the world dropped away to a muffled dullness and she breathed in the warm, trapped air caught under the blankets. She hated herself and was angry that Matthew had made her feel this way. She pressed her knuckles into her eyelids, pushing away the bright colours of the world, until she saw white stars, wishing she could do the same with her emotions.

She was such an idiot. Aunt Elizabeth was forcing respectable men on her almost daily and she had to choose a servant to fall in love with? She gasped and sat up. *Fall in love*. Was that what had happened?

She was in love with Matthew.

In love. With a servant.

There was a tentative knock at the door. She flattened her hair and rubbed the tears off her cheeks.

"Yes?"

Elizabeth entered, looking at her with concern. "Katherine, what's wrong? Are you ill?"

"No. I'm fine, really." Katherine didn't know what else to say, but she didn't want her aunt to leave. It was nice to have the company. It might stop her from thinking about Matthew for a few moments.

Then Katherine's eyes fell on the painting of her

grandmother. Now seemed as good a chance as any to ask about the argument, and it would provide a further distraction from her thoughts.

"Why didn't you ever talk to Grandmother?" she asked.

Elizabeth looked momentarily disconcerted and then set her jaw. "You don't know?"

Katherine shook her head. "Grandmother didn't talk about it. I didn't even know I had an aunt until after she had passed away."

"Oh," Elizabeth said, quietly.

"I'm sorry. We don't have to talk about it if—"

"No, I can tell you. It's a story that you should know. It does concern you, after all." Elizabeth brushed her skirt, picking at a loose thread of the embroidery. Katherine waited, trying not to lean forward too eagerly.

"Do you – do you know anything about your parents?" Elizabeth asked at last.

"I know that my mother died giving birth to me," Katherine said slowly, unsure where this was going. "My father died before I was even born."

"Well, that isn't quite true. Your mother did die in childbirth, but your father, as far as I know, is still alive."

"What?" Katherine cried.

"He was a servant in our house, when we were growing up. Your mother, my sister, was seventeen when they tried to elope. They were caught and brought home. Your father was dismissed. Your mother, as it turned out, was with child, and, as you know, she passed away giving birth to you. I doubt very much your father knows of your existence."

Katherine was shocked. Her father had been a servant.

Her aunt continued gently, "I had already married your uncle by then, and when I found out what had happened... Well, I was very angry with my mother, your grandmother. I felt that it was wrong not to tell your father about you, especially after your mother died. Mother disagreed. She said it was better to be an orphan than the daughter of a servant – and an illegitimate daughter at that.

"We argued about it for months, until one day when she said that she never wanted to talk to me again. She denied me access to you too. I wanted to raise you myself, but she said that she would not allow it. She couldn't trust me not to find your father." Elizabeth bit her lip. "She did love you. Very much. I still think she was wrong not to tell your father, but you had a happy childhood, didn't you? That's what matters." The words came out small, like she was reassuring herself.

Katherine took her aunt's hand and squeezed it. "I had a very happy childhood. And I'm very happy now, to be here."

Her aunt looked up at her, smiling weakly. "I tried to make the right choice."

"I think you did. It sounds like it was a difficult situation, for everyone."

Katherine wasn't sure what to make of it all. Her grandmother, her lovely grandmother, had done that? She still couldn't believe her father had been a *servant*. Just like Matthew.

Elizabeth was watching her carefully, and she forced

herself to speak. "Thank – thank you for telling me."

"I'll leave you to your thoughts. It's a lot to take in." Elizabeth paused by the door. "Mother wasn't a bad person. She just loved you too much. Her daughter had just passed away. I think she was afraid your father would take you away from her."

Katherine nodded thoughtfully, and then Elizabeth was gone and she was alone once more. She collapsed onto the bed with a sigh. Her father had been a *servant*, and he might still be alive. It wasn't the idea of meeting her father which kept going round and round in her head, though, but the notion that she should have been raised a servant, just like Matthew. They were not so different, after all.

CHAPTER 10

8) NO UNAUTHORIZED ADDITIONS TO THE LIST, MATTHEW.

9) ESPECIALLY NO RULES THAT ARE ACTUALLY JUST LONG, EXTENDED RANTS ABOUT CHOCOLATE, OF ALL THINGS. WHAT THE HELL! GO CALL YOUR MOTHER IF YOU WANT TO BITCH ABOUT ME. KEEP IT OFF THE FRIDGE!

10) Also, stop finishing things off and not adding them to the shopping list.

11) Or at least stop putting the empty packets back in the cupboard! I only went shopping yesterday and now I have to survive a whole week without porridge oats. You are a terrible person.

Folios/v7/Time-landscape-2019/MS-149

UNIVERSITY OF NOTTINGHAM CAMPUS, ENGLAND, 2039

"Katherine is kind of a sassy chick, isn't she?" Kate commented. They were in Matt's dorm room, looking through the documents that Kate had found hidden in the loft, which had included Katherine's diaries, from when she was a teenager up until university. Kate was reading through a long diary entry about the first time Katherine and Matthew had met. Katherine had apparently fallen deeply in lust on the very spot. The entry used the words "delectable", "buttocks" and "I want to bite them".

Matt and Kate hadn't told Kate's grandparents about the laptop or the notebooks. Nancy and Flo just thought they had found an old overlooked box of Katherine's diaries and other letters.

Matt "hmm"ed. "Sassy? If I didn't know any better, I'd think she was a teenage girl. She speaks like every Internet meme combined."

"She *is* pretty awesome, I agree. Matthew must have been in constant awe of her startlingly witty repartee." Kate grinned. There was no doubt in her mind that Matthew had been head over heels for her. Katherine, that was. *Obviously*.

"I guess," Matt said, slowly, like he was trying to work out how to explain himself properly. "But I think she just sounds … innocent, you know? In a way that no one really has been since the war. It's refreshing, but sad. She has no idea what is waiting just around the corner."

"Yeah," Kate said softly. "But we don't know what she was messing with yet."

Matt picked up the laptop. "This might be able to help with that."

"Do you think it still works?" Kate asked.

He frowned, brows wrinkling in a way she had to admit she found adorable. "Well, there's only one way to find out."

After some research, they discovered an article online about old computer systems and worked out that the lithium-ion battery would be dead after so long. Matt said he would be able to make a rudimentary charger by removing the battery completely and connecting copper wires from a cable directly into the power supply. He started work on it while Kate read through some more of Katherine's diary entries.

There was some dreamy poetry about a uni romance, which made Kate feel an achingly strong second-hand embarrassment. The poetry referenced chemistry for some reason and was framed with groupings of meticulously arranged heart-shaped sequins.

deep resonance

like electrons pulled inexorably
towards the nucleus

the strength of the attraction between
carbon and hydrogen

my heart to yours

It wasn't long before Matt interrupted her by calling out, "Flick the switch, Kate!" He proudly arranged his newly connected cable on the table in front of her. They both held their breath in expectation of an explosion of sparks, but the cable only gave a small flash. A blue light on the front of the laptop flickered and then stayed on.

Kate threw an arm over Matt's shoulder, hugging him. "Well done, clever clogs."

Matt looked pleased. They took a deep breath as he opened the lid of the laptop. There was some dust on the keys, but otherwise it was surprisingly clean. They weren't actually expecting the laptop to turn on, despite their luck so far, so when the startup screen flashed on, Matt nearly knocked the laptop off the table in surprise. Kate held her breath until the login screen appeared.

"Wow," she said. "What are the chances?"

"I know." He sounded awed, slightly breathless.

"I feel like I just ran a marathon. My heart's racing," Kate said.

Their excitement was short-lived, though, because they needed a password before they could login.

"How are we possibly going to work out what the password is?" Kate asked.

Matt ran a hand through his hair. "We're just going to have to speak to Tom." He sounded annoyed, as if having to introduce Kate to his brother was the worst scenario he could possibly imagine.

"Your brother? The hacker?" She sat up, a little too quickly, obviously showing a bit too much enthusiasm, because Matt frowned at her. "Isn't he in Scotland?" she added, trying to sound disinterested.

"No. He studies here too."

"Spartacus lives here? Like, just across campus?"

"Yeah." Matt didn't look like he was going to make an attempt to move any time soon.

"Shall we go and see him, then?" she prompted, still trying not to sound too eager.

"Sure."

As Matt put on his shoes and found his keys, Kate waited for him by the door, metaphorical tail wagging, like a dog hoping to go for a walk. Finally he was ready to leave.

20 July 2010

I had another dream yesterday. It was one of those achingly real ones, where you wake up and feel like half of your heart has been ripped out, because the perfect dream boyfriend your subconscious made up doesn't really exist.

This time it was another regency dream – I've probably been watching too much _Pride and Prejudice_. It was the same guy, because apparently I have a Type and it's a guy who I made up in my head. Cute hair, a bit shy. Cheekbones. He was riding a horse. (I am a walking stereotype.) He was called Matthew.

Folios/v7/Time-landscape-2010/MS-6

File note: Diary of subject allocation "KATHERINE", aged 16

Carlisle, England, 1745

Katherine and Matthew were eating their lunch on the battlements in silence, while looking out over fields which might soon be filled with approaching Rebels. Earlier that day a messenger had arrived at the castle, bringing the news that there had been a battle at Prestonpans and the English had lost. Everyone had started panicking, especially as the English army wasn't prepared for an attack yet. It needed more time to gather enough soldiers. Most people were now convinced that the Rebels were unstoppable and that the city of Carlisle should be evacuated.

It was all anyone could talk about, but Katherine and Matthew sat in silence. Ever since their argument a few days ago, any conversation between them was almost painfully awkward. They were both unable to relax around each other and felt almost like strangers. Despite this, Katherine still insisted on volunteering at the castle and Matthew always accompanied her, although he made it clear that he didn't want to be there – at least, not with her.

Katherine broke the silence. "I was speaking to my aunt the other day. She told me that my mother eloped with a servant."

Matthew turned to her in shock. "You … your father was a servant?"

She nodded. "They wanted to marry, but they were caught and separated. My mother died in childbirth and my grandmother raised me. My father doesn't know I exist. I think … if they had succeeded in their elopement, I would have been *raised* as a servant."

Matthew made no answer.

"My aunt wanted to tell my father that he had a daughter, but my grandmother disagreed. It split the family apart. I believe that my aunt still loved my mother and would have forgiven her, had she lived. Our family is more important to my aunt than respectability. I hadn't fully understood that about her before. However, I feel sure that if I wanted to make a" – she swallowed – "less than ideal match, shall we say, she wouldn't entirely disown me. I also think that if my mother was prepared to live the life of a servant for love, then I could too." All the time she was speaking, she carefully avoided looking Matthew's way.

"I'll bear that in mind," Matthew said, coolly.

"Matthew," she said, turning towards him, "I cannot apologize enough for my mistrust of you. Please, please forgive me. I cannot bear it."

He shifted and his shoulder brushed against hers. Still he continued to stare across the fields. She admired the shape of his nose, the curl of hair against his forehead. His Adam's apple moved as he swallowed. Finally he turned his head, and caught her eye. She didn't drop her gaze.

"Katherine," he said thickly, voice low, with the slight hint of a warning. Her eyes flicked to his lips, which were so close to her own.

"Matthew…" The sound was barely more than a breath in the air, but it seemed to physically touch him. He swayed slightly, then moved closer towards her.

She could see each of his eyelashes in perfect detail. They fluttered as his gaze darted over her face, to rest on her mouth. His pupils widened. Katherine felt lit up from the inside like a beacon. She could feel his rough breath against her.

He closed his eyes.

"I forgive you," he said. Then he stood up. He moved slowly and carefully as if it were physically painful, then disappeared quickly down the spiral steps into the castle gatehouse. She looked after him silently, gasping air like she'd been running, and pressed her palms against her hot cheeks to cool them.

Near Turkey, Aegean Sea, 1854

"Do you need some help with that?" Katy asked, watching Matthew diligently writing notes in his hammock, which was next to hers. They were the only two in the sleeping quarters below deck. After eighteen days at sea, the room was starting to smell pungent. Katy was grateful there was only a day or two before they arrived at Varna. "I could transcribe for you."

She had been trying to read a book that had been making its way around the officers, but she'd just read four pages discussing the financial history of the main character's next-door neighbour and had reached her limit with authors who were paid by the word.

"Oh – thank you," he said, surprised. "That would be pleasant."

She leant back in her hammock, trying to decipher his tone. "Did you think that I wasn't going to earn my keep any more?"

"I actually hadn't thought about it." He adjusted his spectacles.

She rolled her eyes. "Please say that I'm not a helpless female in your eyes now?"

"Of course not! You're probably more self-sufficient than I am. Your femininity just takes a bit of getting used to."

"You aren't used to independent women? I bet all your female friends would be pleased to hear that."

"I'm not acquainted with many women, actually." He looked uncomfortable. "I don't really have many friends at all."

Katy was surprised. He seemed so charming, and he had made friends with a lot of soldiers – those who hadn't taken offence at his job title, anyway.

"Moving around so much makes it hard to keep friends. I know people all over the world, but I'm usually gone after a few weeks, and I never see them again." He looked like he was considering it as he spoke. Katy suspected that he'd never thought about his friendships before. Matthew was the kind of man who was happy with his own company. He didn't need people surrounding him to be content.

"I did wonder why you hadn't been snapped up in marriage yet," Katy replied bravely, knowing what she was implying.

"I don't think there are many women who would have me. Who wants a husband who's never at home?"

"I think some women would," she said softly.

"Really?" His cheeks were turning red.

"Clearly you don't understand anything about women. A husband who's never at home is the dream," she teased. He relaxed, smiled a little and fiddled with his spectacles again.

"Maybe the solution is to find a wife who would travel with you," she added.

He opened his mouth, closed it again. Eventually, he replied, voice strange – he sounded nervous, yet determined. "That's a good idea. I'll have to see what I can do." When his eyes fell on her, she tried not to beam too obviously.

"What will happen when we arrive at the camp?" Katy asked a little later, after they'd drafted another article. "Do you have a tent?"

Matthew shook his head. "I've got a letter from my editor saying the army has to provide accommodation for me. Hopefully the officers there will do it."

"They wouldn't abandon you, would they? Some of them really don't like you."

"I hope not," he said quietly. Matthew always took her opinions seriously, in a way he hadn't when he thought she was a young boy. It was a surprising benefit to their new situation and one she hadn't anticipated. "But if they do, I can threaten them with the full power of *The Times*. My editor would love a little scandal for the front page. '*The Times*' own correspondent mistreated by Raglan.' I'd probably get a raise."

Katy blanched at the mention of her employer's name.

"I'm sure the army will take that as a very real threat," she said weakly.

"My biggest worry right now is that we'll have to put up a tent. I've never done it before. We're going to need some help getting it up."

"As the girl said to the soldier," Katy said.

Matthew looked horrified.

Katy wasn't sure if shocking a man was the best way to charm him, but she had spent a lot of time with servant boys and they had found her lewd humour amusing. She didn't really have any other experiences to fall back on. Judging by Matthew's reaction, it seemed to be working – if mortification could be considered a more intimate reaction than keeping a polite distance, which she had decided it was.

She was going to charm Matthew with all she had.

ARRIVAL AT VARNA, BY M. GALLOWAY

Once the Light ~~Regmi~~ Regiment arrived at Varna, Bulgaria, the army marched for miles to reach the encampment. It is ~~dirty~~ filthy, lacking even the most basic sanitation. The air is hot and dusty and flies linger everywhere. Filled latrines stink in the heat and half of the camp is ill with cholera. The whole ~~camp~~ place resembles something from hell.

The army administration has failed to provide any food, water or means of transportation for the regiment. While ~~this~~ The Times' journalist has been generously provided with lodgings for his use, half of the soldiers ~~have no~~ are without tents. No rations have yet been procured.

A further controversial turn of events has almost led to a mutiny amongst the men. ~~A command~~ An order has been given regarding facial hair. The men have been told to shave off all moustaches and beards for reasons of hygiene, and many are up in arms.

Folios/v3/Time-landscape-1854/MS-5

File note: Draft of article for *The Times* by subject allocation "MATTHEW"

CHAPTER 11

12) Who are you even kidding, Katherine! I can't
    bitch about you to my mother. She likes you
    more than me. (Her own SON!)

13) Oats are in the cupboard. Sorry.

Folios/v7/Time-landscape-2019/MS-149

NOTTINGHAM, ENGLAND, 2039

Spartacus – or Tom, as Kate was still struggling to think of
him – lived off-campus in a student house. The walk there
felt a lot longer than it was, mainly because Matt was quiet,
still sulking about having to introduce Kate to his brother.

Matt knocked on his brother's front door. There were an
impressive number of free newspapers jammed into the
letterbox. Kate was a jumble of nerves. She was actually
going to meet Spartacus. Fifteen-year-old Kate would have
been giddy with excitement right now, but eighteen-year-
old Kate was a lot more mature and calm. She only bobbed
up and down on her toes once or twice while they waited.

Eventually, a tall, lean boy opened the door, mid-yawn.
He stretched, revealing a line of stomach as his old T-shirt
lifted. Kate immediately found herself staring at the skin,

thinking *That's Spartacus's happy trail, right there in front of me.* She blushed, looking away, while Matt frowned in annoyance.

"Hey. Did we wake you?" Matt asked, too loudly. "You know it's, like, four p.m., right?"

Tom peered blearily at them, yawned again and then said, "Matt! Come in. Sorry. Late night."

Kate followed them inside, barely able to contain her excitement. *This was where the magic happened.*

Tom wandered into the kitchen. After absently flicking on the kettle, he leant against the kitchen counter and scratched at his stubble, which released a few specks of glitter onto the floor. The kitchen was covered in dirty dishes. There was a plant pot in one of them, the dead houseplant inside wilting sadly into a crusty baking tray. Kate tried to hide her disgust and made a mental note not to drink any of the tea.

Tom had clearly woken up a little because he pulled Matt into a headlock. "Where've you been, bro? Haven't seen you for a while."

A muffled reply came from the vicinity of Tom's armpit. "Avoiding you, obviously."

Matt managed to escape, but a second later Tom had hold of him again. The boys wrestled half-heartedly until Matt pulled away and glanced self-consciously at Kate.

"Tom, this is Kate Finchley. Kate, this is my brother, Tom."

Tom shot Matt a significant glance.

"Yeah," Matt confirmed. "They're related."

"How did you even run into her?" Tom asked.

"It's a long story." Matt sighed, and he began making the tea while Tom looked Kate up and down.

"Hi there," Tom said.

"Hi, Tom. I've been dying to meet you for years." Kate shook his hand, politely, trying to hide a smile.

"Ignore her. She's apparently some sort of Spartacus fangirl," Matt muttered.

"Oh, really?" Tom rubbed his eyes and flicked away a lump of sleep. Suddenly, he was just a normal, kind of gross guy, and all of Kate's awkwardness disappeared. Her huge crush didn't seem so huge any more, not now that she'd met the real person behind the computer. But Matt was still pouting, and Kate decided that she could play up her admiration a little longer if he was going to be this grumpy about it.

"Yeah, I'm a big fan of your work," she said. "I didn't think I'd ever meet you."

Tom beamed. "I've never met a fan in real life before."

"Oh, you have tons of fans. You're a hero on the forums." Kate said, relaxing into teasing him.

"I'll have to check that out, when I need a bit of a confidence boost, especially if they're all as pretty as you," Tom said smoothly.

Matt snorted.

Kate mouthed, "He's sulking" at Tom, who grinned, then winked. After smoothing her face into an adoring look, she waited until Matt turned round with cups of tea and then she sidled up to Tom. "I'm pretty impressed, actually," she said. "For someone who spends all their time on a computer, you're pretty well-muscled."

Tom tried to hold back a snort and smiled seductively. "Like a feel?" He flexed his bicep. Kate gave an overdramatic sigh. She could almost feel the force of Matt's annoyed glare.

Tom schooled his face into a Faux Seductive expression as Kate ventured a hand up to his arm. She was just commenting on the raw strength he must have, when Matt finally felt the need to interrupt. "All right," he said, "enough inappropriate touching! We have important stuff to be getting on with."

"Matt's right, Kate. I really can't have a relationship with my fan base."

Kate tried very hard not to laugh. She was beginning to like Tom a lot.

"I suppose that makes sense." She released his arm semi-reluctantly – those were some genuinely impressive muscles – and Matt quickly pushed the mug into her hand, presumably so she couldn't do any more groping. He fetched his own from the kitchen counter and then came to stand next to her, slightly too close.

Kate tried very hard to hide her smile. Matt was hilarious – and easily made jealous, apparently.

Tom sipped at his tea, grimaced and then added more sugar. "So, what's happening? Have you found something? I presume you didn't come so Kate could meet me, however much of a fan she is."

"Kate and I have a job for you."

"Oh?" Tom led them through to his bedroom and sat down in his desk chair.

Matt grabbed Kate's free hand, pulling her down to sit next to him on the bed. He let go of her fingers slowly, just to make sure Tom got the message. It was probably less work than hitting him around the head with it, saying, "Look, this is a message."

As they drank their tea, Matt quickly filled his brother in on everything, including what they'd found in the loft. Tom was immediately excited about the laptop.

"Can you decode the password?" Matt asked.

"Sure! Gimme." He held out his hands eagerly, and then connected the laptop to his computer.

"So, I imagine it made the move to England a little easier, if Tom was already here?" Kate asked as they watched Tom work.

"Yeah. I missed him a lot when he went off to uni," Matt agreed.

"You seem really close."

"We are," Tom said.

"Tom's always been the adventurous one, getting me into trouble, as you can tell. He started this whole thing."

"Oi," Tom said. He was leaning back in his chair, waiting for a program to download. "I'm pretty sure you caused just as much mayhem as I did. I've probably got evidence somewhere."

He turned back to his computer and then brought up a file of old family videos. He projected the images onto the wall behind them, and while he worked on decoding the password, Kate watched the adventures of tiny versions of Matt and Tom. Kate was in rhapsodies of delight, and Matt seemed resigned to embarrassment. Matt had been a tiny little boy in comparison to his brother, and quirky. In one video, he tried to interview his entire family about what they had been doing that day, with a spoon he was pretending was a microphone.

"I wanted to be a journalist when I was a kid," Matt told her.

"Didn't you want to be a farmer for a while too?" Tom said. "Hey, don't you still listen to those farm—"

"I don't know what you're talking about, so *shut up, please*," Matt hissed.

Kate looked between them, intrigued, but then a new video started playing and distracted her.

Kate's favourite part of it was a shot of a naked boy covered so entirely in flour that it was impossible to identify him, which Matt made Tom quickly skip over.

"Was that you?" she asked.

"No," Matt replied instantly and unconvincingly, "that was someone else. I've forgotten who he was."

"Tom just happens to have a picture of him, though?"

Tom winked at her as Matt tried to distract her with a video of him wrestling Tom – the two of them were just as excitable as they had been when wrestling earlier that day. Eventually Kate found herself stretched out on the sofa, feet in Matt's lap, stifling a yawn, as, eyes half-closed, she watched video after video while Tom quietly worked. Sitting this close to Matt felt strangely natural, like she'd done it hundreds of times before.

Varna, Bulgaria, 1854

Katy had never felt such relief as the first time she managed to clean herself properly after the voyage from Southampton. It was the evening of their first day back on land, in the camp at Varna in Bulgaria. Their tent was dark and small, with only a single tiny cot, but it afforded the privacy she needed to unwrap her chest, and it felt like a wonderful luxury. She scrubbed her skin until it was pink and the bowl of water Matthew had collected from the pump was brown and soapy.

When she finally felt clean again, she went outside to where Matthew was waiting. They were sharing the tent, just as they would have been if she really was his manservant. They couldn't ask for another and, besides, Katy had been sleeping in a hammock next to Matthew and dozens of soldiers for weeks now, so she didn't think it would be awkward.

"I'll fetch you a fresh bowl of water," she said. He nodded wearily. It had been a long journey from the steamer to the encampment, which sprawled outside the city of Varna, along the edge of a huge lake. Once they had arrived, they'd had to collect their tent and erect it. They were both exhausted.

As Katy walked to the pump, she passed the campfire where soldiers were cooking the meagre rations they'd managed to get. Katy felt a pang in her stomach. They hadn't had any food since arriving and probably wouldn't until the next day.

When she returned to the tent, Matthew was inside,

shaving, having developed a layer of stubble during their voyage. She wouldn't call it a *beard* exactly.

"Thank you," he said, washing off the soap with the clean water she'd brought him.

"You're welcome." She sat on the cot and ran a brush through her hair, wincing at the build-up of tangles. She was going to need to get it cut soon. She'd kept it closely clipped ever since some of the other servant boys had teased her for her curls, saying they made her look like a girl. Now her hair was starting to curl up around her ears, and while she was androgynous enough to pass as a boy, it would be just asking for trouble to have long curly hair.

She sniffed at herself. Since she'd washed she had become very aware of the smell of her dirty clothes. "Do you think if I wash my clothes they will be dry by morning? I don't think I can stand to wear these again. They smell horrendous."

Matthew shrugged. "If they're still damp then you can borrow some of mine."

She looked up in surprise. Although she knew that he'd forgiven her for lying about her gender, this new kindness was unexpected. "Thank you," she said softly.

He nodded, and returned his attention to shaving with an air of quiet embarrassment.

She tugged at the loose hair on the brush, admiring the mix of strands, her ginger and Matthew's brown.

"Can I borrow some now? A shirt or something, to wear tonight?"

Matthew focused more than was necessary on washing

the soap off his razor. "Yes. Take whatever you need out of my bag."

Katy swapped her dirty shirt for Matthew's clean one with relief. Matthew, who was washing his face, carefully kept his back to her. When she'd changed clothes, she sniffed herself again, but all she could smell now was a lingering trace of Matthew's scent on the clean material.

Katy then tried her best to clean her clothes with just a small bowl of water and cheap soap. By the time she was finished, and the wet clothes were hung outside the tent to dry, it was dark.

Katy took a sheepskin off the cot and laid it on the floor, before making a pillow from a brown linen coat. The dirt floor didn't look appealing, but she told herself it was better than sleeping outside, or on a ship, and settled down for the night.

"What are you doing?" Matthew asked. Arms crossed, he looked like a man on a mission. He would have been quite intimidating, if it hadn't been for the way his hair curled around his face as it dried.

"I'm going to sleep?" she said.

"No. Stop it."

She raised her eyebrows at him. "We've had quite a long journey. I think I deserve at least a nap."

"I'm not going to make you sleep on the ground. Obviously you will take the bed."

"We could always … share it," she said. "Aren't people supposed to huddle together for warmth in hostile conditions?"

He rolled his eyes, but a hint of a blush rose to his cheeks and the tips of his ears. He began violently brushing out his hair, sending water droplets flying. "That's in the Arctic. I don't think you're in danger of getting frostbite here."

"Oh, I wasn't talking about *me*," she said. "Me, I'll be fine. I was talking about you. You're so thin you might freeze completely through."

"I think I can handle sleeping on the floor."

"Well, don't come crying to me if you're a cold dead corpse tomorrow morning. You're a delicate flower. I don't think you can handle the floor." Then when he didn't respond, she added more firmly, "Matthew, I'm not making you sleep on the ground. I've caused you enough trouble as it is. Besides, I bet that cot is full of bedbugs. The ground is probably cleaner."

"I'm not giving in, Katy."

He started a brief staring contest, which was apparently his new method of persuading her to agree to his point of view without the hassle of actually yelling. She always squirmed under his steady gaze, but she was determined not to be the first to look away. However, this time Matthew was even more determined. She rolled her eyes, conceding defeat by overdramatically throwing off the blanket. It actually was quite cold on the floor, though, and she shivered involuntarily.

Matthew punched the air. "I win!"

"We will alternate nights. I'll have it tonight and you can have it tomorrow. Otherwise we are both going to end up sleeping on the ground, aren't we?"

"We are going to have the same discussion tomorrow, because I'm never taking the bed from you."

"I'll have a whole day to think of arguments," she warned him.

"So will I." He smirked.

Katy felt a rush of affection for him. She usually enjoyed their exchanges, and would have replied with something cutting, but today – in their new tent with a *completely stationary floor* and a *proper bed*, and not even *one* snoring soldier in here with them – she just wanted to be nice to him. He had been so forgiving and lovely to her since finding out that she was a girl, and she had never had the chance to return the favour. She'd have to wash his clothes for him and maybe find food for them both first thing tomorrow. It didn't look like they'd be getting rations from the army any time soon. A sudden impulse overtook her and she stood up and wrapped her arms around him.

"Good night," she murmured into his ear. He was tense, but he relaxed slowly, finally pulling her tight against him and pressing his face into her hair.

"Night," he said back, a touch of something like surprise in his voice.

She stepped away, pulling down the shirt which had ridden uncomfortably high on her thighs. Then she climbed quickly into the cot and pulled the blanket over her.

"Matthew, thank you, really," she said. "You've been so good to me."

The corner of his mouth turned up. "It was a small

matter." He paused, and then added, *"As the girl said to the soldier."*

Katy let out a thrilled, too loud laugh, and Matthew settled into the makeshift bed on the floor with an unmistakable air of self-satisfaction.

CHAPTER 12

14) MATTHEW, YOUR MUM THINKS I ROCK, ACCEPT IT.
There's no need to be bitter about it. It's just because
your parents spent a significant portion of their lives without
my awesome company and have suddenly realized what they
have been missing all this time.

15) The length of time they spent without me is your own fault
for taking so long to realize you fancied the pants off me,
you know. I could have been chilling with your parents for
years by now, instead of only just meeting them. I totally
understand why they feel the need to make the most of the
time that's available to them now to tell me how cool I am.

16) WHAT HAVE YOU EVEN DONE TO MY BEAUTIFUL
LIST? LOOK AT ALL THESE NON-REGULATION
WORDS. THIS IS A HEARTBREAKING OCCURRENCE.

17) Thanks for the oats, honey.

"Kate," Matt said, rubbing her shoulder.

"What time is it?" she mumbled. "The meeting doesn't start until nine."

"What meeting?"

"The suffragettes, Matthew."

There was a long pause, and then Matt said, apparently addressing someone else, "She's dreaming."

Kate opened her eyes to see who else was in their room, and blinked. Right. They were in Tom's room, unlocking her aunt Katherine's laptop.

"Are you awake now?" Matt grinned at her, shaking his hair out of his eyes. "Tom did it! He broke Katherine's password. We've got access to all her files."

Kate sat up and rubbed her eyes. "Really?"

"Yeah!"

Kate let out a relieved whoop. "Let me see. I can't believe I *fell asleep*. Thanks for doing this, Tom."

"No problem. That's the good news. The bad news is, well ... see for yourself." Tom gestured for Kate to look at the laptop and Matt pulled up a chair at the desk for her. After she'd sat down, he leant on the back of it, to look over her shoulder.

The C-drive of the laptop was full of neatly labelled folders, of which Kate approved. She was a little obsessed with keeping her own files in order. She was clearly more like her aunt than she had ever realized. She scrolled down the list, scanning for any important ones, her eyes flicking through

REPORTS, DATA, PCR RESULTS. She tried to open one, but it came up with an error message. Then she realized what Tom had meant by the "bad news". A lot of the files were corrupted.

"I don't understand," Kate said, trying another file. It opened fine. It was only the files related to Katherine's lab work which appeared to be affected.

"I think they were destroyed remotely," Tom explained. "Someone on the same network made sure no one could open them."

"Can you fix them?"

"No. I've tried, but there isn't enough information left."

Kate rubbed the back of her neck, and then turned to face him. "So this entire laptop is useless, basically."

"There's other stuff on there," Matt pointed out. "See what's in her email account."

She opened the email inbox and then clicked through the most recent emails looking for anything relevant to her aunt's work. It was mostly filled with newsletters, except for a few with subject lines like "WHERE ARE YOU?" and "RE: Faculty meeting". She clicked the latter. Apparently Katherine had tried to set up a staff meeting days before her death, but it had been cancelled a few hours before it was held. None of the emails mentioned anything about their plans to steal from the laboratory or about releasing the bacteria, although that probably wasn't surprising.

"There's another account. Try that," Matt suggested, pointing to a subfolder of the inbox. Kate clicked on it, and it opened up the emails for a private address. There were a dozen unopened emails, all identical.

The following message to <home.news@thetimes.co.uk> was undeliverable. The reason for the problem: 1 error(s): SMTP Server <gmail-smtp-in.l.google.com> blocked sending of email to <home.news@thetimes.co.uk> due to breach of security (Error following higher command). Please do not attempt to resend this message or further action will be taken.

Final-Recipient: rfc822;home.news@thetimes.co.uk
Action: failed
Status: 5.0.0 (permanent failure)

Subject: "Research at Central Science Laboratories"
Date: "21 June 2019 18:28:53 GMT"

Dear Editor of *The Times*,

This message concerns the implications of the work being undertaken at Central Science Laboratories. We are scientists, and over the past few months we have become increasingly worried about the subject of our work.

We are drawing these concerns to your attention because when we have attempted to discuss them with our superiors, they have repeatedly stopped us. We are becoming anxious about the steps they may take to keep us silent in future. If our fears are founded, then CSL is undertaking work which may affect every one of us.

Attached is a copy of our investigations, in which you will see evidence to indicate that CSL is guiding the work of scientists in our laboratory without their knowledge. CSL is creating what we believe to be a highly dangerous and uncontrollable weapon: a bacteria which will destroy the ecosystem and kill every organism it comes into contact with. Once started, it will spread death across the globe with no way to contain it. The creation of such a weapon violates several international laws as well as obvious moral rules. The fact that it is currently being developed in secret implicates CSL in a scandal which should be stopped at all costs.

We are sending this message now because our concerns are being ignored and because CSL is about to mass-produce the bacteria. To reiterate, once released, the bacteria will not stop at international boundaries and it will be impossible to prevent its spread. We will issue more information as soon as we can. This email has been sent to all British newspapers and international news organizations.

We hope that after you read this message you will work to bring this crime to light as soon as possible, and before it is too late.

Regards,

Drs Matthew Galloway, PhD., and Katherine Galloway, PhD.

There was a moment of horrified silence.

"Well," Kate said, finally. "They definitely weren't committing treason, then."

"Whoever stopped them sending this email must also have destroyed all the files on the laptop," Tom said. "They had a lot of power."

"Do you think their bosses at CSL could do that?" Kate asked.

"I don't know."

"The real question," she said, "is *why* they did it. Obviously they wanted to stop the Galloways telling anyone about the bacteria. Yet information about it was released after they'd been killed. It was reported in the press. I've read the articles. But why? Why kill Katherine and Matthew to keep them quiet and then tell everyone about it anyway?"

"Because after Katherine and Matthew were discovered stealing the bacteria, the CSL had someone to blame," Matt said, slowly. "Before that, the focus would have been on why the CSL were making this bacteria, but as soon as Katherine and Matthew were branded terrorists, the lab could blame them for everything. CSL could make out that Katherine and Matthew had adapted the bacteria to become a biological weapon and then tried to steal it. CSL were completely innocent."

Kate stared at him in shock. "But what were CSL planning to *do* with the bacteria? Why make it in the first place?"

"They never used it," Tom pointed out. "If CSL were planning something, they never went through with it."

"That doesn't matter. We still have to find out what happened," Matt said. "Katherine and Matthew were just scapegoats. If we know the truth behind what CSL were planning, then we might discover what happened to your aunt and my uncle. We need to find out what *exactly* happened."

They worked their way through the rest of the emails in a determined silence.

From: Katherine <KitKatherine@gmail.co.uk>
To: Matthew <gallows@hotmail.co.uk>
Subject: Craaaaaaaaaap
Date: 7 June 2019 15:42:51 GMT

Matthew. Matthew, holy crap.

I asked Clare in the insecticides lab what she's working on, and it matches up, Matthew. They're doing poisons too!

Matthew. I actually cannot deal with this. You might be right, instead of just insanely paranoid, what the hell. (´°□°)´~ ┻━┻ Shit.

K

From: Matthew <gallows@hotmail.co.uk>
To: Katherine <KitKatherine@gmail.co.uk>
Subject: RE: Craaaaaaaaaap
Date: 7 June 2019 16:10:36 GMT

Talk to you at home. Can you get milk, if you have time in your giant freak-out?

From: Katherine <KitKatherine@gmail.co.uk>
To: Matthew <gallows@hotmail.co.uk>
Subject: RE: RE: Craaaaaaaaaap
Date: 7 June 2019 16:11:10 GMT

I think I have more than enough reason to be freaking out right now. Arse!! Yeah, I'll get milk. See you later. K

From: Katherine <KitKatherine@gmail.co.uk>
To: Matthew <gallows@hotmail.co.uk>
Subject: OK
Date: 19 June 2019 19:15:02 GMT

OK, so I'm going to send the email now. To everyone on staff, right? What shall I put? I reckon that keeping it non-specific is the best approach, in case we have to backtrack. I thought I'd be freaking out right now, but I'm weirdly calm about the whole thing. I'm obviously a lot more brilliant than even I realized. K

From: Matthew <gallows@hotmail.co.uk>
To: Katherine <KitKatherine@gmail.co.uk>
Subject: RE: OK
Date: 19 June 2019 19:17:11 GMT

Yeah, non-specific is good. Just say we want to meet and we'd appreciate it if everyone could attend. I think it's good that you are calm. It shows we are doing the right thing. Er, I mean, it also shows you are brilliant. Obviously… *cough* You finished yet? I'm about done for the day.

From: Matthew <gallows@hotmail.co.uk>
To: Katherine <KitKatherine@gmail.co.uk>
Subject: Um
Date: 20 June 2019 13:05:22 GMT

OK so Dr Smith came to talk to me, Katherine. He wanted to know what the meeting is about. I told him we were worried about the work in the lab and he said we should have consulted him first, because it wasn't something everyone needed to know about immediately. Told us to shut the hell up basically. Are you free at 4? He said he'd talk to us about it then.

From: Katherine <KitKatherine@gmail.co.uk>
To: Matthew <gallows@hotmail.co.uk>
Subject: RE: Um
Date: 20 June 2019 13:10:29 GMT

That sounds ominous. His office? See you there. Love you. K

From: Matthew <gallows@hotmail.co.uk>
To: Katherine <KitKatherine@gmail.co.uk>
Subject: RE: RE: Um
Date: 20 June 2019 13:11:01 GMT

I love you too.

From: Katherine <KitKatherine@gmail.co.uk>
To: Matthew <gallows@hotmail.co.uk>
Subject: update
Date: 21 June 2019 16:36:02 GMT

I started typing up the report. You are right. We have to make it public. The risk to us doesn't matter any more, and if we don't do it now, they might do something more than slap us on the wrist. K x

---

From: Matthew <gallows@hotmail.co.uk>
To: Katherine <KitKatherine@gmail.co.uk>
Subject: RE: update
Date: 21 June 2019 17:05:49 GMT

I think we should also try to do a bit of prying and get as much evidence as we can while we have the chance. You working late tonight? x

---

From: Katherine <KitKatherine@gmail.co.uk>
To: Matthew <gallows@hotmail.co.uk>
Subject: RE: RE: update
Date: 21 June 2019 17:32:59 GMT

I agree. After work? See you soon. Not planning on working past 6. K x

---

Folios/v7/Time-landscape-2019/MS-168

"So," Tom said, opening a new document on his computer. Matt and Kate turned to watch the projection on the wall as he began to assemble a timeline of events. "They start to have suspicions. They do some investigating and find out that there is something dodgy going on with some of the experiments. Then they decide to tell everyone they work with about it. They get stopped by their boss, but must not have liked his explanations because they decide to go public."

Tom went on, "They write a report. Try to email it to a load of newspapers, but it gets blocked. Somewhere around this time they go looking for more information somewhere – probably their lab. Anyway, then their family finds they have disappeared and their house has been ransacked. Then the newspapers report that they are dead and that they were terrorists."

"But before they disappear they drop some stuff off at my grandparents', including this laptop," Kate interrupted to add.

"Yeah, good point. They must have suspected they would get arrested or something and wanted to protect the evidence. I bet they had no idea that their bosses would be able to corrupt the files remotely." Tom said as he added this to the timeline.

"Then your grandmothers pestered the lab and CSL sent some soldiers to scare them into silence," Matt said, and Tom wrote up his words.

"So, what we need to know is," Kate said, mulling it over out loud, "a) what Katherine and Matthew found after they tried to send that email and b) where they found it."

"We can probably assume that it was at CSL. That's where Katherine and Matthew were when they were shot," Matt said.

"Yes, but were they really killed there like the newspapers said or at a later date?" Kate asked.

"Good point," Matt said, then added, "We also need to know c) what was done with this bacteria afterwards. If CSL, or whoever, were willing to kill to keep it a secret, then I doubt they just gave in and destroyed it when this happened. We also need to work out how the bacteria got released in the lab at CSL, and whether the Galloways did have anything to do with that."

"Do we really want to get involved in this?" Tom said, a little apologetically. "I mean, Katherine and Matthew are dead. We can't help them. And it's not as if CSL are going to release the bacteria now: it's been years. Why risk getting killed over it ourselves?"

"The fact that CSL haven't released it yet doesn't mean that they won't. The people who did this could still be out there," Matt pointed out. "If they were planning to use the bacteria before the war, then there is just as much reason to do that now as there was then. Nothing has changed since then. England is constantly on the brink of war with Europe. There's nothing to stop CSL releasing the bacteria now if they wanted to."

"And they've had years to finish making it. It could destroy the whole world," Kate added. "And Katherine and Matthew are family. We have to prove that they are innocent!"

Tom sighed. "You're right. It's just a lot more serious than my Spartacus stuff. We really could get killed, if whoever is behind this wants to keep it a secret so badly."

"We have to investigate it," Matt said, softly.

Tom nodded resolutely.

They both turned to Kate.

"Let's do it," she confirmed.

They were all silent for a moment, and then Matt let out a groan. "Where do we even start?"

"I dunno," Tom said. "Did you find anything else in the loft? Any memory sticks or anything?"

Kate shook her head. "Nothing like that. Here. This is all there was." She picked up her rucksack and took out all the documents – the diaries and some old school books – that they'd found in the attic.

Tom flicked through the least glittery of Katherine's diaries, which chronicled her life, starting with her university years. Kate hadn't had a chance to look through it properly yet.

"So what does the code say?" he asked.

Kate stared at him. "What code?"

"Code?" Matt repeated, and jumped up to look over his brother's shoulder. "Oh my God. Kate, it's in code."

The last fifty pages weren't written in Katherine's distinctive scrawl, but in a neatly written jumble of symbols.

"How did we miss that?" she said, gaping at the page.

"It has to mean something," Matt said. "Maybe it'll tell us more about what CSL were up to."

"We need to decode it. As soon as possible," Kate said.

"Well, luckily, I have a program which can do just that," Tom said, grinning. "I think we've got our next lead."

CHAPTER 13

18) Oh good God, no! My wife gets on with her mother-in-law! How could you do this to me, cruel world?!? Let me throw myself on my dagger, I can't live like this one single moment longer.

19) Don't worry, you can start a new list if you really insist on ruling my life. You do realize I've managed perfectly well for 26 years without looking to you for guidelines as to my bodily hygiene, living style and general mental & physical health, right?

Folios/v7/Time-landscape-2019/MS-149

Varna, Bulgaria, 1854

Katy was admiring the view. Now that she was out of the camp – which was a muddy, stinking area just outside the city – she could see that the landscape was actually quite beautiful. The ground was covered in wildflowers, with flocks of sheep and goats grazing amongst them, and the lake stretching out towards a cluster of hills on the horizon.

She'd slept very well last night and had woken late to find Matthew gone. She had only had a few moments' panic, though, because he had returned shortly, looking exhausted, saying, "There's no food to be had anywhere."

"That's because you are too nice, you delicate flower," she had responded fondly, and maybe a hint reproachfully. "Leave it to me."

She snuggled further into Matthew's coat, which she had borrowed because there was a bitter wind blowing from across the lake, and definitely not because it smelt like Matthew.

A small group of local villagers were hawking their wares to soldiers on the edge of the army's encampment. They weren't selling anything except junk, and her rumbling stomach was desperate for food.

She was about to give up and return to the tent when a young boy arrived, dropping off bales of straw to sell for the horses, before turning back to the village. He didn't seem interested in her at all, and wandered down the dirt road at a leisurely pace, obviously taking the opportunity for a break. A few soldiers had made their way into the village earlier in search of food, but none of them had had any luck. They had all returned to camp empty-handed.

Following a hunch, Katy trailed the boy to the village, where she watched him disappear behind a shop. She slipped in through the front entrance. It was mostly empty inside: a few dusty cabinets, containing battered boots and bowls, lined the walls. She was turning to leave when she noticed a local woman was talking to the shopkeeper at the back of the shop. Katy recognized the clink of a handful of coins and moved closer to watch.

The shopkeeper took a pipe out of his mouth and then stuck his head behind a stained and tattered curtain that hung in the doorway to a room behind the shop. He called out harshly. The boy Katy had followed came out after a moment, struggling with a large bulging bag. The woman took the bag, and left the shop without speaking, head down. Katy couldn't help smiling. There *was* food here – you just had to know how to find it.

The shopkeeper noticed Katy then. In rough English, he barked, "What, boy?"

She stuck out her chin. "I want to buy some food."

"We don't have any." He turned away from her and tapped his pipe, inspecting the end.

"You are lying."

His thick eyebrows rose in surprise, and then he grinned around the pipe, showing a mouthful of broken, yellow teeth. "Why you say that, boy?"

"You just gave a bag of food to that woman." She met his gaze defiantly.

"Clothes," he said shortly.

Katy bent down and picked up a soil-covered root that had fallen from the bag. "You sell dirty clothes?" Katy said, just as abruptly.

The shopkeeper let out a garbled sound deep in his throat, which she hoped was a laugh. "Boy, you are too clever to be English. What do you want?"

Katy clinked a couple of the coins in her pocket, partly

for the man to hear, and partly to cover the rumbling of her stomach. "What do you have?"

"Chicken," he replied instantly, then twisted his lip, thinking. "And ... the word, I don't know, but they make you…" He rubbed a hand beneath his eye.

"Onions," she guessed after a moment's confusion.

"Yes," he said agreeably. "I have bread too, and apples."

"Give me all of that," Katy said, dropping several coins into his hand.

He eagerly counted the coins, and then disappeared behind the curtain, returning a few moments later with a bag. He winked at her as she took it from him, and she smiled back, feeling victorious.

When she got back to the camp, Matthew was sitting on the ground outside their tent. There was a tin mug of coffee in his hand and his notebook was perched on his lap.

"Morning," she said, and stole his coffee. She took a sip, wincing at the sour taste. Then she peered over his shoulder at his notebook, absently brushing flat a curl of his hair that had been standing upright. Then she noticed what she was doing and pulled her hand away, embarrassed. It had been an automatic action, almost like a muscle memory.

Matthew was rewriting his latest article with the suggestions she had offered him. She felt a dart of guilt. Matthew's article had been perfectly good, but she knew that Lord Somerset wouldn't have cared for its honesty about the conditions in camp, so she had persuaded Matthew to tone some of it down. "Save them for a later article," she had said, "when we've seen more of this place."

Matthew tilted his head back and smiled up at her. "Hello. I have a present for you." The words burst out of him like he'd been dying to tell her and couldn't wait a moment longer.

"Oh! Thank you," she said. She couldn't remember the last time she'd been given a proper present.

Looking extremely pleased with himself, he handed her a brown paper package.

Katy ripped it open. Inside was a fountain pen. "Matthew!"

"I wanted to get you your own set of writing equipment," he said, looking suddenly shifty.

"It's lovely, thank you."

"No problem. You are my assistant, after all. It's practically a requirement that you have your own set." He sounded like he was persuading himself. "Also, I would rather you didn't use my pen."

"What? Why on earth not?"

"Pens adapt to your grip, and with you being left-handed, you might change the way mine works."

"What? Are you saying that all this time you've been worried I'll ruin your pen?"

"No! I … thought perhaps you might do, if you used it a lot. I love that pen."

"Matthew!"

He looked ruefully up at her, eyes full of remorse.

She wanted to be offended but instead burst out laughing at his forlorn expression. "You could have just asked that I don't use your pen!"

"I wanted you to learn shorthand," he admitted, still looking upset.

"All this time you've been watching me write while worrying about your pen? What a conflict of emotions! Did you have nightmares about it?"

He nodded dolefully and then said, completely seriously, "It was *traumatizing*."

"I don't understand you. If you are so worried about breaking your pen, why don't you just use a pencil?"

"A pencil. A *pencil*," he said, with growing horror, staring into empty space as if at the horrific vision she had laid before him. He shook his head. "Some people just want society to collapse."

She burst out laughing, and he grinned at her. "Well, whatever your reasons for giving this to me, thank you. Really, I love it." She hugged him, tucking her head under his chin and smiling into his collarbone. Now he wasn't stricken with stationery-related guilt, he hugged her back, pulling her tight against him. She sighed. Being held by Matthew felt like coming home. Eventually he pulled away, clearing his throat and brushing down his waistcoat.

"So, did you have any more luck than I did, finding food?" he asked.

She'd almost forgotten. "Oh, not really," she said casually and passed him the overflowing bag.

His jaw dropped as he pulled out the chicken by its feet, fully feathered, wings flopping to either side. He stared at it in amazement, and then at her. He hooked a hand under her elbow and pulled her towards him, looking down at her with a tender, intimate expression. "Where on earth did you find all this? I don't… You're *extraordinary*."

She tried to swallow but failed. She couldn't believe he was looking at her like that, like she'd hung the moon, all over a raw chicken.

"I have my ways," she eventually managed to reply. She tried to sound mysterious, but it came out too breathy.

His gaze shifted to her lips, and suddenly Katy snapped out of her daze and went cold. Instinctively, she pressed her face against his shoulder, hiding in a tight, unromantic hug. He had been about to kiss her, and she couldn't let him, not when she was still hiding so much from him. She squeezed him a final time, and when she released him, the soft, warm expression on his face had gone.

"So, chicken for dinner, then?" she said brightly, wanting him to stop eyeing her like she was a moving target he needed to pin down. His reply was a little subdued, but she tried not to care.

> Error in time-landscape 1854

> First objective not achieved

> Prepare for possible intervention

UNIVERSITY OF NOTTINGHAM CAMPUS, ENGLAND, 2039

Kate knocked at Matt's door, balancing two plates of breakfast in the crook of her arm. They were going to spend the morning decoding the diary they had discovered the night before. Tom had given them a program to use which analysed the text by determining the frequency with which each symbol appeared and compared the results to data tables of the most commonly used letters in English. The program then made a pretty good guess at what each letter could be.

Matt must still have been sleeping, because he took a while to open the door, finally appearing in loose pyjama bottoms. He scratched his head, then adjusted his glasses. He obviously hadn't had a chance to put in his contact lenses.

"Morning." He took the plates from her, and then let her in. He dumped the plates on his desk, where Kate arranged them. She was trying to keep her eyes from his bare chest, but the movement of his shoulders as he shrugged on a T-shirt was distracting. He dragged a woollen jumper on over the top, tucking his thumbs through the holes in sleeves.

"I brought you breakfast from the dining hall. They ran out of milk again," she found herself babbling. "The latest restriction on imports is the *worst*. They gave me *apple juice* to go on my cereal."

He grunted and settled on the bed beside her to eat.

The program would work fast, but first they had to scan in the entries and digitalize the handwritten code. It took a while for the program to learn how to pick up the handwriting, but eventually the first entry was scanned in and ready to be decoded.

The results showed that there were three symbols that appeared much more frequently than the others. According to the analysis tables, these could be "e", "t" and "a". Kate did a search and replace on the symbols for those letters. The system seemed to be working, because on a few occasions the symbol she replaced with "a" was a lone letter, which made sense.

"We can assume the other symbol that's on its own must be an 'i', then, right?" Matt asked.

"Good thinking. Where it says 't µ e', the 'µ' is obviously an 'h'."

They worked through the text, slowly revealing whole words and letting the computer make guesses to fill in the gaps. Occasionally they made a mistake, but it was easy to pick up words that didn't work. Each new decoded letter let them find several others, and soon the text was almost readable. They scrolled back to the top, so that they could read through the first entry. Kate couldn't stop grinning with excitement at their achievement.

5 JUNE 2019

I've decided to be even more fantastic and mysterious and write in code, partly because M and I have been discussing something recently which I need to write down but don't feel comfortable leaving around for anyone to read, but mainly because it's the coolest possible thing in the world. I WANT TO BE A SPY WHY AREN'T I A SPY WHEN DID MY LIFE GO WRONG

So, despite the deep injustice the universe has dealt me by making me a paltry research scientist rather than a kick-ass spy, I do have something kind of terrifying to discuss. Over dinner last night, M told me that he'd been talking to Mick from the spores lab about his work. (Shocking, I know: Save some excitement for me, guys.)

Anyway, I'd been thinking he was going to mention the baby thing again, considering he had taken me out for a posh meal and told me to wear the sexy dress he can't get enough of. But, no, apparently, he had a life-changing and dangerous dilemma he wanted to discuss instead. It looks like babies are going to have to wait until all this has blown over.

So, YEAH, I wasn't really paying attention when he

started talking about Mick, considering it was an UTTERLY
DULL TOPIC OF CONVERSATION - WAY TO SPOIL THE
MOOD, DUDE - but then he said something so serious that it
completely took me by surprise.

It turns out Mick had been telling M about his new research
proposal, which he's hoping to get funded. The research is focused
on the behaviour of the fertilizer's spores when radiated. He was
telling M about his grant proposal, and he mentioned anthrax as an
example of past research into bacterial spores.

M, who has apparently been hiding the fact this whole time
that he is some kind of genius Sherlock Holmes, suddenly realized
how similar our bacteria is to anthrax and how, with a little bit
of tweaking, our fertilizer spores would probably have a very
similar effect on mammals to anthrax. Which is, you know, a
BIOLOGICAL WEAPON.

While M was still thinking about this and doing a bit of
background research, we got an email from the Higher Ups,
suggesting that we focus our work on a specific property of
the bacteria - one which would make it even more dangerous,
according to M. That rang alarm bells for M labelled, WHAT IS
GOING ON, AM I LIVING IN SOME KIND OF CRAZYASS
SPY FILM, NO, REALLY.

He hasn't said anything to anyone else about it yet because

he wanted to ask me first, knowing that, naturally, if it was just him being a paranoid dork, I'd shoot him to the ground and then ignite the remains until his ego was thoroughly burnt to a crisp. But, anyway, I agree with him: it is actually super creepy.

Jeez, it's hard work translating my mindless rambles into code. I really need to start editing my brain-to-mouth (er, pen? Hand?) thought flow.

Why would CSL fund research into a fertilizer that was capable of producing spores which can kill mammals? Even if you give them the benefit of the doubt initially, the work has become so focused that there's no way this is incidental. They must know what they are doing.

While this whole thing is obviously the perfect experiment for any Hollywood villain with a technologically implausible lab that doesn't actually operate according to the known laws of the universe, there is a slight problem: we don't work for an evil villain with huge, fluffy Einstein hair. We work for CENTRAL SCIENCE LABORATORIES!

The Higher Ups get worryingly excited over crop protection! No, really. I have several, almost physically painful, memories of sitting with senior consultants over coffee, listening to them vomit rainbows of joy over the prospect of a bacteria that adequately protects some obscure kind of pear they only have in Sicily against some rare fly that lives in Malaysia. THEY ARE DORKS, NOT EVIL VILLAINS. They do have the charmingly fluffy hair, though.

So, yeah, assuming they aren't trying to build some kind of super-destructive weapon against humanity (which, let's face it, THEY AREN'T, HELLOOOOOOO, whatever M says), it doesn't make any sense!! What would they even do with a bacteria like that? They couldn't, like, sell it to a country as a weapon or anything.

If they released it anywhere, it would just spread and kill everyone, EVERYWHERE. Every animal and human would be killed. What use is a weapon like that? At least nuclear weapons have some kind of degree of control!

Anyway, M insists that we are going to do a bit of "digging", or as I like to call it, "KATHERINE WOULD MAKE AN AWESOME DETECTIVE. LET'S PROVE THIS THEORY WITH SCIENCE." Basically, M's going to go back over his tests and see if anything else stands out, and I'll ask around over coffee to see if any of the other projects are heading in uncomfortably villainous directions.

Sigh.

No bombs or shoot-outs or half-naked women. Not yet, at any rate.

CHAPTER 14

New text from "Katherine":

You are ridiculous and I love you.

Folios/v7/Time-landscape-2019/MS-150

UNIVERSITY OF NOTTINGHAM CAMPUS, ENGLAND, 2039

Kate woke up on a strange bed, covered with a blanket. Matt was asleep, curled in a comma towards her. They'd fallen asleep waiting for the program to finish decoding the rest of the diary. She watched him sleep peacefully, resisting the urge to stroke his hair. Then he snored loudly, and the moment was gone. She smiled, reluctantly fond, and rolled over.

She should probably go to her own room, but she couldn't bring herself to move. She checked her tablet. She had three messages from friends and a missed call from her mum. She ignored them. She'd get in touch with them later. She didn't want to disturb this moment. It was so *right* here: half asleep and listening to Matt's relaxed breathing. She felt like she belonged, like she should have been here all along.

"You're not a goose egg," he muttered as he dreamt.

"Thanks for the reassurance," she teased.

He laughed, reacting to her joking tone even while asleep. She buried her face into his pillow, muffling a grin. She'd always loved it when he did that.

* * *

A loud noise pushed into Kate's sleep and she groaned, not bothering to open her eyes. She pressed closer against Matthew, pulling the blanket over her shoulder. It was cold in the castle.

"Has it started?" Kate murmured. "It's not even light yet."

"I don't know," he mumbled, pulling her tighter against him. "But you'd think Charlie could wait until morning."

"It's very inconsiderate of him," she said, mid-yawn. "What does he think this is – a siege?"

Matthew laughed, and the sound brought her into full wakefulness.

"Oh, it was just your alarm," she said, and then caught herself. *Alarm? Castle?* Why did this keep happening, this … dislocation? Her dreams weren't usually this vivid.

Matt shifted behind her. "I don't have work today. Let's go back to sleep," he said and kissed her neck. She tilted her head, giving him better access, and then she froze. Matt had never even kissed her before, let alone done whatever this was.

"Matt?" she asked weakly.

He lifted his head. "Hmm?" he said, looking at her like he had no idea what was wrong, and she had to look around to check. Yes, they were definitely in Matt's uni room. No, they had definitely never done this before.

"I think we fell asleep here last night," she explained.

He stared at her, and then pinched his eyes tightly shut, shaking his head to clear it. Finally, *finally*, he let her go.

"Right. Sorry. I was dreaming."

"Yeah, me too."

> The build-up of memory layers seems to be causing confusion between the subjects

6 JUNE 2019

An update on our Secret and Probably Pointless Investigation:
M has gone back through the records and when you look
at the whole research set — from the very earliest stages
of development, to the final testing of the fertilizer — it's
undeniably suspicious. This is a thing that is really happening.

....yeah, so M's stupid-ass theory seems to
be holding up. WHAT IS THIS LIFE AND WHY IS IT
DOING IT TO ME IN PARTICULAR.

I hope that something turns up soon to prove us wrong
or this is going nowhere good, not only because M is going to
think he's a genius detective and get all kinds of cocky about
it, which would be a terrible thing to inflict on the world. I
love him, but he doesn't really understand quite how smart
and sexy and generally brilliant he actually is. If he got an
idea and started acting accordingly, I'd be screwed. (Literally,
metaphorically, categorically.)

I can't really take this thing seriously. It's too terrible.
I can barely make myself think about what this bacteria could
do. Imagine a world where the worst possible kind of bacterial
disease can travel across open land. Imagine it spreading across

the country, killing everything in its path, every part of the ecosystem from bees up to humans, killing whole continents.

We couldn't destroy it. There wouldn't be enough time to develop a vaccine, not at the rate it would spread. There would be nothing to do but run. Even if one bacterium is released it would have the potential to spread across the entire globe. Nothing would be left. Urgh. Why couldn't we just have become farmers like M is always on about doing? Life would be so much easier.

Folios/v1/Time-landscape-1745/MS-4

File note: Route march of the Jacobite army from their arrival in
          the British Isles to Carlisle during the invasion of
          England in 1745

Carlisle, England, 1745

Since they had made up, that day on the castle battlements, Matthew and Katherine had been growing increasingly close. Matthew barely seemed able to keep his eyes off her for more than a moment now. He would hold every gaze until Katherine looked away, unable to match his intensity. Katherine had fallen for Matthew, but she didn't know if she was ready to do anything about it yet, not when it would result in so much uproar. Even if her aunt and uncle didn't disown her, it would still cause a scandal.

Matthew seemed to understand her hesitation, even though they had never discussed it. He was patiently waiting for her to make her choice. It all depended on her. Until she had decided, they were engaged in an unspoken truce that involved just a little too much touching to be described as purely platonic and an awful lot of sleepless nights – on Katherine's side anyway.

The sleeplessness wasn't all due to Matthew, though. Katherine was also worried about the Jacobite invasion. The Rebels were rapidly approaching England, and one morning when the frost was beginning to colour the fields a soft grey, horsemen were spotted on the hills outside of the city walls. Katherine and Matthew were in the castle supply room.

"The Rebels have arrived!" a soldier called in horror. Katherine emerged to see a group of the men from the castle run up to the battlements. "It's too soon! The army aren't gathered to defend England yet!"

Katherine dashed back into the supply room where Matthew was intently focused on stacking jars of beans. With Matthew's hand in hers, her thumb rubbing across his knuckles, she followed the soldiers up to the battlements. She released Matthew's hand just as they stepped out into the dim sunlight.

Durand was looking at the banks of the river through a telescope. He was surrounded by men: the jumpy soldiers of the militia and the calmer castle garrison. Katherine strained to try and make out what they were watching. She could just see a stationary group of horses, whose riders had obviously been sent to survey the city's defences. Matthew tugged at her elbow, pulling her to a nearby step so she could see a little easier. He stood next to her, one hand discreetly pressed against the small of her back.

Katherine was just counting the number of riders when something whistled past her ear, and then a lump of stone fell from the wall just behind them with a loud crack. She let out a cry, ducking down below the parapet as dust settled on her head.

"The devils are firing at us!" Durand cried, turning to one of his gunners. "Return fire!"

The gunman was frozen with fear. He had crouched down with his hands over his head. Katherine looked around at the other soldiers. They were all too terrified to move. Without thinking, she ran forward and lifted a heavy cannonball from the pile by the cannon.

Matthew came to help her guide it into the barrel and point the weapon at the Rebels. But just as Katherine was preparing to fire, some farmers, driving a herd of cattle, wandered past the soldiers.

"Damn it," Durand muttered. "Hold fire."

Everyone on the battlements held their breath, waiting for the farmers to move out of the way. The Rebel riders made sure to keep a protective barrier of innocent men between themselves and any possible cannonballs.

Eventually, the farmers moved on, and with a nod from Durand, Katherine lit the gunpowder to send the cannonball flying across the fields with a deafening bang that made her jump. When the smoke had cleared, the Rebels had retreated, apparently unharmed.

Colonel Durand sighed in disappointment. "Good try, lads. I don't suppose they'll be back tonight. Officers, I expect more bravery from you next time! In the meanwhile, make sure the sentries keep a constant watch from now on. Ensure that there are no lights after dark, and tell the sentries not to unlock the gates in the morning – unless they want Highlanders to come rushing in."

The garrison nodded and went to do what he had ordered. Durand then turned to the sheepish soldiers, who were all standing with their heads bowed. "Now, you lot. That was appalling. A child would be braver than you men."

Katherine and Matthew grinned at each other, inordinately proud of themselves.

When it was clear the Rebels wouldn't be returning that day, they left the castle. Katherine was so jumpy with exhilaration and nerves on the way home that she practically skipped through the busy streets. Matthew was a little more collected, but even he couldn't stop talking. They discussed the brief firefight endlessly, until it sounded as dangerous as a full-on battle.

"I didn't think I'd have a chance to actually fire a cannon!" Katherine gushed, lingering at the stable door as Matthew gave the horses their evening meal. She was hopping from foot to foot, unable to stop talking.

Then she noticed the bustle of hurried activity coming from the house. She said a quick goodbye to Matthew and slipped inside by way of the kitchens. As she did so, she heard, with a wince, her aunt's voice giving a steady stream of orders. Katherine quickly dashed up the back stairs to change into her dress. Aunt Elizabeth burst into the room just as she was shoving Matthew's clothes into her wardrobe.

"Katherine, where have you been?" her aunt said. "Call a maid and pack your things immediately. The city is under attack!"

"We can't *leave*!" Katherine cried in horror.

"We are going, Katherine. I'm not sitting here and waiting for some filthy Scots to come and kill my family." Elizabeth was almost crying with fear, and anger.

"I'm not coming," Katherine said. "The city is defended. Some of the townspeople have been working for months to make sure we are ready for any attack. We will hold off the Rebels. I'm not running away like a coward."

Elizabeth's jaw was tight, her face white with fury.

"Katherine Finchley, you will stay with this family. I'm not leaving you alone in an empty house while the Scots run wild. You will be … attacked!"

"I'm staying, Elizabeth," she said firmly.

Elizabeth replied in a quietly serious tone, "I have given you the freedom and space to mourn your grandmother over these last few months. I have tried to support you and not stifle you, by letting you oversee the clearing of her house in privacy, but I will not let you do this. You are coming with us, even if I have to drag you into the carriage myself."

> Subject allocation "ELIZABETH" may cause delay in time-landscape 1745

> Request intervention

  >> Request denied

CHAPTER 15

KitKat 16:11:33	I want you to do the leg flick.
Gallows Humour 16:13:28	What's the leg flick?
KitKat 16:13:56	Like in films. The girl flicks her leg and waves it in the air and that shows how good a kiss it was. Next time we kiss, I think you should do that.
Gallows Humour 16:14:11	Why don't you do it? You're the girl.
KitKat 16:14:36	Boys can leg flick too! GENDER EQUALITY.
KitKat 16:14:46	(╯°□°）╯︵ ┻━┻
Gallows Humour 16:15:01	Stop using that emoticon on everything. I swear it's not even remotely funny.
KitKat 16:15:27	ANYway, the point is that then I'd get to say my kiss is leg-flicking good. I can't make my own leg flick.
Gallows Humour 16:15:52	Mmm, now that's an image.
KitKat 16:16:10	NOT AT WORK AGAIN.

Folios/v7/Time-landscape-2019/MS-155

Varna, Bulgaria, 1854

Katy stared in horror at the unwashed patients lying on straw pallets in the hospital tent in the soldiers' camp at Varna. The place was filthy. The floor – a foul-smelling mess of reeds, with open sewers running beneath them – combined with the stench of illness. She and Matthew were waiting for the doctor who had agreed to be interviewed about the cholera outbreak spreading through the encampment.

"If this is what it's like *now*," she whispered, looking around the hospital, "imagine the conditions when the fighting starts and the place is inundated with injured soldiers." She had never imagined that the hospital tents could be this bad.

Matthew nodded. "I hope to improve it before then."

"How? By writing about it in the paper?"

"Yes." Matthew looked at her steadily. The uncertainty she'd felt at having to spy on him suddenly tripled. Matthew was only trying to help, and judging by the state of the place the army needed it desperately.

Katy had been surprised that morning when he had asked her to come with him to the hospital tent. "You're still my assistant," he'd explained when she asked why, "even if you did turn out to be … unexpectedly female."

Standing in the hospital tent, she wished more than ever that Matthew would leave her behind when he did his reporting. She didn't want to spy on him any more.

"Most of the problems are caused by a lack of equipment," Matthew went on. "I can change that by bringing it to the public's attention, to raise funds."

"Oh." That sounded perfectly reasonable. Why had Lord Somerset been so against Matthew coming here?

"Where are all the doctors?" Matthew asked.

She looked around, suddenly realizing that, aside from all the patients, the ward was completely deserted. "There should be nurses on duty in here at the very least," she replied.

"Nurses aren't allowed," Matthew said, sounding resigned. "Before you say it, yes, it is ridiculous. The French are allowed female nurses. I intend to fix that as well."

"I hope so. Well, we should make ourselves useful while we wait for your doctor," Katy said, rolling up her sleeves.

"Shall we take around food and water?"

For a moment she thought he was angry with her, but then he said, with a hint of exasperated fondness, "You are … you're…" He stopped, bit his lip. "Yes, let's do that. I think the stores are next door."

They returned from the storeroom with some meagre rations, which had been reluctantly provided by the soldier in charge, to find that a doctor had appeared.

"Good morning," he said, straightening up from examining a patient. "What are you doing?"

"We thought we'd make ourselves useful while we waited for you," Matthew explained.

Katy turned to Matthew and said, "Let me take those supplies. I'll hand them out while you're talking."

Three hours later, they left with several pages of notes on problems with the hospital and some ideas for simple improvements that could be made.

"You should definitely pass them on to your editor," Katy told Matthew. She didn't care about Lord Somerset any more. Those men needed help. Many of them hadn't been fed since the night before. The army should be thanking Matthew for helping them, not trying to stop him.

That evening Katy came back into their tent from the latrines to find Matthew lying on the makeshift bedding on the floor with his eyes closed. He was trying to get out of the argument about who was to take the bed by pretending to be asleep.

"That isn't going to work, Matthew."

He stirred, turned over onto his stomach and then

pulled the blanket over his head like her mere presence was disturbing his sleep. "Shush…" he slurred. "I'm sleeping."

She rolled her eyes and prodded him with her foot. "I don't believe you."

When he made no reply, she said archly, "Fine. If you're asleep, I won't have to leave the room to change into my nightclothes, then, will I?"

He opened one eye. "You are already wearing your nightclothes."

"And you're *awake*."

He yawned dramatically, throwing a hand over his face. "I'm too tired to move. Please don't be so cruel as to make me get up now."

"Because it would be so terrible of me to make you sleep in the bed?"

"Exactly," he muttered into his arm. She had a suspicion that he was hiding a smile.

She looked between him and the soft, cosy cot that had been so comfortable last night. It had a proper pillow and everything. She couldn't resist climbing into it. "You can't expect to get away with this every night," she warned him.

"You can make it up to me with a cooked breakfast," he mumbled sleepily.

She let out a loud, obnoxious yawn in reply and then stretched out. "I've had a long, hard day providing food for my family, Matthew. I've been *hunter-gathering*. I probably won't be able to stand up in the morning."

He laughed, despite being almost entirely asleep, like it was a reflex.

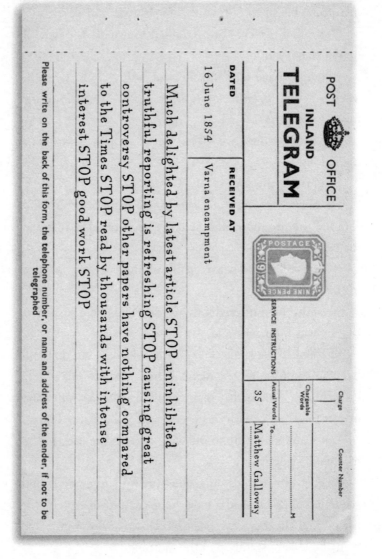

POST OFFICE

INLAND

TELEGRAM

	Charge	Counter Number

| Chargeable Words | | |
| 1 | | |

| SERVICE INSTRUCTIONS | Actual Words 35 | To......... Matthew Galloway ......M |

DATED

16 June 1854

RECEIVED AT

Varna encampment

Much delighted by latest article STOP uninhibited
truthful reporting is refreshing STOP causing great
controversy STOP other papers have nothing compared
to the Times STOP read by thousands with intense
interest STOP good work STOP

Please write on the back of this form, the telephone number, or name and address of the sender, if not to be telegraphed

Folios/v3/Time-landscape-1854/MS-6

Kit—

The first copies of <u>The Times</u> have reached me and I have to say that I am disappointed in your work so far. I've already had several letters from concerned officials. I hired you to make sure I didn't have to worry about this.

I thought I had made it clear what I wanted from you: a series of articles with no detailed information, that paints the army administration in the best light possible.

I hope I didn't put my trust in the wrong person. Don't let me down again.

Lord Somerset

UNIVERSITY OF NOTTINGHAM CAMPUS, ENGLAND, 2039

Kate returned to Matt's room to find him still reading diary entries. They had been working on it all morning. She handed him a plate of toast for lunch. "I got you peanut butter," she said.

"Ooh, thanks! That's my favourite."

"I … know," she said and shrugged. She was getting used to just knowing things about Matthew. "What does the diary say?"

"Nothing we didn't know already. Katherine is talking about telling the other staff what's going on. She must have written this shortly before they decided to send that email asking for a meeting." He took the mug of tea, gulping it down. "We need to hurry up and read the rest, though. We're meeting Tom in half an hour."

"I'm already looking forward to it," she joked.

Matt's expression froze into a polite smile, and she grinned, ducking her head to look at his downcast eyes. "Hey," she said softly. "You know we're teasing you, right? Matt, I'm not interested in Tom." She gulped nervously. "I'm interested in *you*."

He didn't speak. She took a bite of toast to fill the silence, trying to appear casual and not at all as if her insides were tearing themselves to shreds.

"Kate," he said quietly, almost inaudibly.

She didn't reply, suddenly panicked. Had she read all the signs wrong? Had she just made a massive fool of herself?

"Will you go on a date with me?" Matt asked.

Kate couldn't help her huge smile. "Yes!" She felt lit up from the inside out.

Matt just looked at her, pleased.

"This counts as me making the first move, you know," she insisted, watching him with bright eyes.

"You can think that if it makes you feel good," he agreed easily, pulling her towards him. He dipped his head to press a smudge of a kiss on her lips and then kissed her more firmly, like he was unable to help himself.

```
> First objective achieved in time-landscape 2039

> System progressing as desired
```

Kate suddenly shivered as a feeling of déjà vu swept over her. All at once the saying "someone walked over my grave" made a whole lot more sense. She could suddenly see everything, oh, so clearly. She had done this, *exactly* this, before.

Matt had kissed her, just the way he was now. Except – it had been different. *He* had been different, slightly taller than her, and he had cupped her chin to tilt her face upwards. She leant into him now as she had then, her body boneless and utterly open. He pulled back, his lips parting from the kiss. It had been too short, but achingly sweet. She wanted more. Her mouth pressed closer to his, closer, closer, reluctant to part.

Her eyes fluttered open to meet his. He pushed a strand of hair from her face, and she was momentarily distracted from the kiss. *Her hair was short. It hung down across her eyes in a way it hadn't since she was a child. Matt's clothing felt rough against her skin in a way synthetic fabric never usually did. There was a smell of smoke in the air around them, the scent of old tobacco. She barely recognized it: cigarettes were banned and almost impossible to find.*

"I bet Lloyd George doesn't kiss like *that*," Kate said, cheerily.

"I'll take that as a compliment," Matt replied.

She pulled back quickly. They stared at each other.

"What did you say?" he asked.

"Nothing. What did you say?"

"I don't know…" He paused. "It made sense at the time."

Kate couldn't think of anything to say to that. In her mind, she kept picturing Matt dressed in old-fashioned clothing and looking dashingly handsome. They stared at each other, both lost in their own thoughts. Eventually, he looked away, frowning at the ground. He had obviously decided not to discuss it any further.

She thought it best to follow his example. At least, she reflected, it had detracted from the inevitable awkwardness of a first kiss. She hoped it wouldn't happen next time, though. She'd completely missed the actual kiss.

"Shall we, uh, read the rest of the diary?" Matt asked.

"Yeah," she agreed in relief.

As they reviewed Katherine's diary, Matt kept shooting glances at her, but she couldn't look at him. Her mind was full of crazy ideas. Why had that kiss felt so familiar? Why did she keep seeing Matt in different periods in history, both in her dreams and when she was awake? She was so close to blurting out her suspicions of magic and reincarnation and time travel that focusing on Katherine's diary was the only thing keeping her grounded. She really hoped that something was going to be explained soon, because this was what going mad must be like.

The feeling didn't get any better. As they read more and more of the entries, Kate felt like she had seen the end of a film early. She seemed to know what Katherine had written before she read it.

Then Matt kissed her again, leaning into her like he couldn't wait any longer. It was quick, barely a peck. She tensed, waiting for another vision to overtake her. Matt seemed to be waiting too, and after a moment he kissed her again, properly this time, cupping her cheek and pulling her against him. His lips were soft and he tasted of tea.

She relaxed against him, enjoying the moment. It still felt like they had done this many times before, despite the fact that this was almost their first kiss. But then, everything they'd done had seemed like a repeat of something they'd done many times before.

They kissed for a long time, discovering – or, rediscovering – each other's mouths. Finally they parted, pressing their foreheads together and just breathing each other in.

"I've been wanting to do that for so long," he said, biting her bottom lip gently, a brush of his teeth against the tender skin.

She gasped, dazed, trying to remember anything except the shape of his mouth against hers.

"Me too," she said when she had regained the power of speech.

11 JUNE 2019

M has been a bit busy since I last wrote — by which I mean I can't even remember what he looks like any more — and because I'm ridiculous and co-dependent I miss his stupid face more than I should after only about six days of clashing schedules.

And there has been no sex whatsoever! None! We both just kind of grunt at each other at night, collapse face down on the bed, fully clothed and refuse to move until the alarm drags us from our almost coma-like depths of exhaustion the next morning.

Six days! It must be some kind of terrible, never-to-be-repeated record.

IF THIS IS WHAT BEING MARRIED IS LIKE THEN I WANT A DIVORCE. And then sex.

But we actually found time to have a chat today about the repercussions of This Thing. (The Thing at CSL, not our lack of sex.) I don't think it needs saying that we can't let this research carry on there, even if it's accidental, but the question is whether we confront the Higher Ups or assume it really is serious and inform the police. But if we go public and we are wrong about this, everyone in the entire country will hate us, won't they? We will have started an actual national crisis because of M's stupid stupidface paranoia! There's already enough panic at the moment with the latest bombing scares, without adding a false alarm to the terrified hive mind of the general public.

Either way, we are going to have to tell someone. Although we kind of know what is going on, I think we need to do some illicit investigating in the offices. Which, now I'm actually going to be doing it, isn't as exciting as it sounds. I'm mainly just scared, to be honest.

Anyway, that's what life has been like recently: going over everything we know and double-, triple-guessing ourselves and then trying to decide what to do in endless roundabout conversations until my poor, sex-deprived body gives in to unconsciousness. Then I spend all night dreaming about dying in dramatic ways involving shotguns and possibly torture.

I have gone over all the research in the lab so many times I feel like I could run the whole place myself, which, while I do enjoy my job and all, would actually be my idea of hell, OK. I do like to keep my brain intact, surprisingly, and if you want a job that sends you completely insane, then look no further than trying to control a few dozen independent, obstinate, foul-mouthed research scientists. (Trust me on this – I'm one of them.)

The thing that is worrying me the most is that we really need to take our time before acting on this, but I've noticed that all the current projects are finishing imminently. I don't know if this means the bacteria will be ready soon, but from the research timeline, I'd say there is a possibility it could be.

Holy crap, what a terrifying thought.

CHAPTER 16

Katherine Galloway commented on **Matthew Galloway**'s status "I think Katherine has thrown me over for a slice of chocolate cake. She hasn't spoken a word for the last fifteen minutes except to the icing."

Like • Comment • Share

Katherine Galloway You have to resign yourself to the fact that you are now essentially the cuckold in my great romance with cake.

9 hrs • Like

Folios/v7/Time-landscape-2019/MS-156

Carlisle, England, 1745

Katherine sat in the carriage, next to her uncle and opposite Elizabeth and her young cousin, as they approached the edge of the city. They were all silently looking out of the windows at the dark sky and the eerily empty streets. The only sound was the echo of horseshoes on the cobblestones. Everyone who hadn't already fled the city was safely barricaded inside their homes.

Katherine shifted in her seat anxiously. She couldn't flee at the first sign of danger like this. It went against everything she'd been working towards. What was the point of having defences if you immediately left them at the first sign of danger?

She folded her arms, while her mind desperately worked on a way to avoid having to leave with her family, to avoid abandoning Matthew. He had stayed behind in Carlisle with the other servants when Katherine's aunt and uncle had decided to flee the city.

Their carriage joined a queue of several others waiting to be let out of the gates of the city in secret. It seemed that there were plenty of other citizens who weren't brave enough to stand and defend their city.

When it was their turn, her uncle handed the guard a large bribe, and the gate slid open soundlessly. Their carriage was the last to pass through into the open countryside. Katherine could hear the relieved sighs of the guards as the gate began closing behind them. The citizens had escaped and the Rebels had not been alerted to the open gates.

This was Katherine's last chance. Once those gates were closed, the soldiers would not open them again. She couldn't leave the city now, at the moment when everything was happening. She hadn't even had a chance to say goodbye to Matthew. She had to go back. Resolve hardening, she flung open her door and leapt from the carriage. She squeezed between the closing gates and dashed back inside the city. The guards were too shocked to react, and she ran past them, skirts held above her ankles, shooting straight down the road.

"KATHERINE FINCHLEY!" her aunt shrieked from behind the closing gates, but it was too late. Katherine was gone, already weaving her way down Carlisle's narrow back streets, and the gates wouldn't open again.

Katherine ran until her lungs were bursting and a

stitch had developed in her side. When she stopped, she looked at the darkened buildings around her. Now she was alone, the impact of what she'd done hit her, and she suddenly couldn't breathe. She'd left her family, in the dead of night, and her home was on the other side of the city. The lane was deserted. She brushed her skirts flat, trying not to panic. She just had to walk home. She had walked across the city every day to the castle – except then she hadn't been wearing a dress, and it hadn't been the dead of night, and she had been with Matthew.

She took a deep, calming breath. She was perfectly all right. It was only a ten-minute walk from here.

When she reached the gate that separated the drive of her aunt's house from the street, Katherine's heart sank. It was locked. Of course it was. She rattled the chain hopelessly. She was stuck outside. What a fool she had been. She dropped down onto the ground, her back against the gates, head in her hands.

"Hey!" a voice shouted, making her jump. "What are you doing?"

A lantern was making its way down the drive, and she could make out the candlelit features of the man who was carrying it.

Matthew.

She stood up. "Matthew! It's me!"

"Katherine?"

"Please let me in," she begged, half-choked up with relief.

"What are you *doing*? Did you…? You *idiot*!"

"I needed to be here. I couldn't leave."

"You're so ... *urgh*!" he said, running a hand through his hair in frustration. "Why did you do that?"

"I had to," she said quietly. "Please let me in."

He unlocked the gate silently. Katherine bit her lip, worried he was angry with her. As soon as the gate opened, though, he tugged her inside and pulled her close to him. He tucked his head against her shoulder and let out a noise that was almost a sob.

"Anything could have happened to you in the city in the dark," he mumbled into her neck.

"I'm sorry," she whispered. "I just couldn't leave after all our work." Silently she added, *I couldn't leave you.*

She shyly touched her hand to the small of his back and then leant her head against his. They didn't pull apart for a long time.

BUCKINGHAM PALACE

My Lord Raglan,

I have received notice from Her Majesty Queen Victoria to instruct your lordship to initiate measures for the beginning of the attack against the Russian army, unless you should be of the opinion that it could not be undertaken with any reasonable prospect of success.

It is the belief of Her Majesty's Government that the difficulties of the attack appear to be more likely to increase with time. As there is no prospect of a safe and honourable peace until the Russian fleet is taken or destroyed, it is most important that nothing but insurmountable impediments should be allowed to prevent the battle from beginning.

The longer the delay, the more intelligence the Russian army will gather from information published daily in The Times, most of which had not been communicated to Her Majesty's Government through any official channels, prior to its publication in the paper. Time is of the utmost importance for success in this endeavour.

The army should prepare for departure from Varna to the Crimea without due delay.

On behalf of Her Majesty,

Victoria

Queen Victoria

Folios/v3/Time-landscape-1854/MS-8

File note: Orders from England that began the invasion of the Crimea

Folios/v3/Time-landscape-1854/MS-9

File note: Journey of the British Army through the Ottoman
Empire to the Crimea. By the time the army set sail
from Varna, Bulgaria, its number had been reduced,
largely as a result of a cholera outbreak, to 27,000
men. The French army was severely depleted too, to
around 30,000 men, and the Turks had 7,000. The
Allies were in a desperate situation, with inadequate
food supplies and tents that were not waterproof

Crimea, Ukraine, 1854

Katy leant closer against Matthew, trying to muffle her shivers in his collarbone as they waited in a queue to get a tent. She didn't care what the other soldiers thought. She needed the warmth. She could barely feel the extremities of her body from exhaustion and bitter cold.

They had waited weeks in Varna for orders to arrive from England. Finally they had come and the regiment had left Varna for the Crimea, where the battle against the Russian army would take place. The ship had been full of drunken soldiers, cheering and hollering along to the national anthem. There had been a lot fewer of them than had set out from Southampton all those months ago. Cholera had killed hundreds of men. Aboard the ship, Katy and Matthew had stuck together, talking quietly and avoiding the rowdy men.

The voyage had lasted a week, and much of it had been spent waiting for scouting ships to decide where the troops should land. Eventually, they had all disembarked and then marched to the temporary campsite in the wind and rain. Katy was worn out now. She felt at the end of what she could handle and the war had scarcely begun.

The next day the British troops would march to meet the approaching Russian army and then the fighting would begin. They had already had their first sighting of the enemy: a group of Russian officers on the clifftop had been counting the number of English and French troops.

"Not long now," Matthew whispered. "We're nearly at the front of the queue."

She nodded, trying to keep her eyes open. They just needed to get their tent and then she could sleep. She swayed as Matthew moved away from her to speak to the soldier assigning tents. She regained her balance quickly and then made more of an effort to look like she was at least partly conscious.

"I'm Matthew Galloway, of *The Times* newspaper," Matthew told the soldier. "I've been promised accommodation while I travel with the regiment." Matthew handed over the letter from Lord Raglan, which the soldier stared at blankly for a moment, and then handed back.

"I don't know anything about that," he said. "Go and talk to the general." He pointed vaguely in the direction of a larger tent, which was obviously the centre of operations.

"Thank you for your help," Matthew said politely, and turned towards the tent, looking a little nervous.

Katy followed him with apprehension, knowing they were probably going to have to fight to get accommodation. In Varna it had been easy to get a tent, but as more of Matthew's articles had been published in *The Times* he had begun to be treated with increasing distrust and even aggression.

"Matthew, wait," she called, dropping her bag and pulling him close. "It's going to be fine. You can do this."

He held on tight to her as if she was the only thing keeping him upright. His breath was hot against her throat.

"What would I do without you?" he replied.

She shivered against him, and bent her face into his hair, smiling as she absorbed the heat of his skin. "Probably shrivel up and die, like the delicate little flower that you are."

"Most likely," he agreed easily. After a moment, he drew back. She took the hint and pulled away, even though she felt like she could hold him for ever. A strand of hair had fallen into his eyes, and she was unable to resist brushing it away. She didn't care that the soldiers would think her behaviour odd.

He turned and walked over to the tent. He held up a hand as if to knock, then stared at the canvas, at a loss. Katy, who had followed him, cleared her throat noisily. A soldier poked his head out. "Yes?"

"We, er, we were told to report to the general," Matthew said. "Is he here?"

The soldier exhaled through his teeth. "He's very busy. Do you have an appointment?"

"No. I need to speak to him about accommodation. I'm a journalist for *The Times*: Matthew Galloway."

The man grunted as he gestured for them to follow him inside.

"The general is in a meeting now," the soldier said, pointing to a man with his back to them who was with a group of officers gathered around a table. They were probably discussing supplies, or lack of them, Katy thought.

The soldier indicated a bench along the side of the tent and they sank down on it gratefully to wait. It was the first time they'd sat down since they'd left the ship. Katy watched the backs of the soldiers with curiosity, admiring how neatly pressed their uniforms were despite the dirty surroundings.

Eventually the meeting ended and the general turned to face them. Katy stared at him in horror.

It was the officer who had caught her reading Lord Somerset's library books.

He knew who she was.

Katy closed her eyes tightly and supressed a disbelieving groan.

> ALERT: Crisis imminent in time-landscape 1854

> Actions of subject allocation "KATY" may soon become known to subject allocation "MATTHEW", which will be detrimental to the progress of the objective

> Intervention recommended

  >> Intervention denied

CHAPTER 17

From: Katherine <KitKatherine@gmail.co.uk>
Subject: Can you print this? My printer's bust

From: Matthew <gallows@hotmail.co.uk>
Subject: Katherine, this isn't even work. It's a comic strip

From: Katherine <KitKatherine@gmail.co.uk>
Subject: STOP QUESTIONING MY SCIENTIFIC METHODS YOU ARE
A TERRIBLE HUSBAND

From: Matthew <gallows@hotmail.co.uk>
Subject: I will be your printer bitch if you bring me coffee

From Katherine <KitKatherine@gmail.co.uk>
Subject: Coffee isn't the only hot thing waiting for you in my office

From: Matthew <gallows@hotmail.co.uk>
Subject: Someone hot? What's Mick doing in your office? (JOKE
JOKE I'M ON MY WAY)

Folios/v7/Time-landscape-2019/MS-159

21 JUNE 2019

We are going to break into the CSL offices tonight! We've written an email to be sent out this evening to all the media outlets we can think of, in case we don't return. The worst-case scenario is that we are arrested, and this way we can still get what we know so far out there to the public.

I'm taking my laptop with all our research over to Mums' in my lunch hour today so we will have a reliable record, just in case. I'm going to take my diaries too. There's this loose brick in the chimney in the loft where I can store it. It will be good to have a backup of our research if they ever confiscate our work computers. Or if something happens tonight.

I'm not really sure what else to say. If we find out anything useful and don't get caught, I'll write again. If not, I guess we've done all we could to make the situation public, and this diary shows that. I'm scared. But I don't have any doubts. Only that all of this has made me realize one thing — I want to have children now, not wait until I've built my career. I want a baby so badly. I want to teach it to be foul-mouthed and inappropriate and show it all of the awesome things there are in the world until its brain explodes with glee. But there is still time for that, I hope. If we can find a way to fix this awful mess.

Anyway, our plan is to take photos on my phone of anything we find and upload them to a storage website as we go along. I've put some of the most incriminating research on there already, as well as the research proposals by DEFRA that we were working from. Hopefully it'll be enough to show that something suspicious is happening.

This way, even if we get caught, we've already got the evidence out there and they can't do anything about it. The address and login are as below. If you are reading this ... well, I guess you know what to do.

UNIVERSITY OF NOTTINGHAM CAMPUS, ENGLAND, 2039

Kate read the final diary entry from 2019 while Matt was out getting them a snack. She immediately checked the storage website to see if there were any photos, but the URL led to an error page. The website was defunct – unsurprising, after twenty years. They'd have to find a way to access it somehow, though. Maybe Tom could find a cached version. She sighed, resisting the temptation to send Matt urgent messages until he returned.

Eventually he appeared, and she burst out, "You need to call Tom right now!"

"Kate," he replied, in a long-suffering tone, "do you remember me telling you that I have to be present for the entire conversation? You can't just filter me in at the end."

"Sure, of course," she said, not really listening. She read him the last diary entry impatiently.

Matt called Tom.

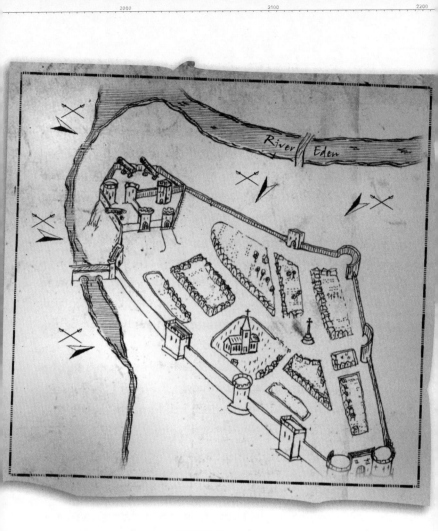

Folios/v1/Time-landscape-1745/MS-5

File note: City of Carlisle during the 1745 Jacobite siege

Carlisle, England, 1745

Katherine shivered, wrapping her thin shawl more tightly around her shoulders. It was just before dawn, and there was nothing to see from the castle battlements but a dense white fog, stretching across the countryside. Yawning into her palm, she leant against the wall. It felt strange to be in the castle in her dress, but now that her aunt was gone, there was no longer any reason to dress as a boy. Today she was just another curious bystander, getting in the way of the garrison's watch. The battlements were lined with others just like her. The citizens of the city, both men and women, who had not run away, were tensely watching for the enemy to appear out of the fog.

"Tea?" a low voice murmured in her ear, and she jumped, turning to face Matthew.

"Um," she said, sounding the height of eloquence. She corrected herself hastily. "I mean, please. Where did you get that?" she asked, accepting the warm tin cup gratefully.

"I returned to the house. I thought you might be cold."

"Thank you, Matthew. You're very thoughtful."

She breathed in the steam rising from the tea and leant close to him. Then she saw how the people near them were staring, and took a step away again. She'd momentarily forgotten that she was dressed as a lady, and that Matthew was her servant. She couldn't talk to Matthew in the way she was used to. Instead she turned back to look at the fog, hoping for cannon fire, a battle, *something*, to stop her from embarrassing herself. There was nothing but the harsh sound of crows cawing to each other across the farmland.

"Did you know," Katherine said into the quiet, "that Genghis Khan had a special method of scaring the enemy that he used when he laid siege to cities? The first day his army would erect a white tent, which meant that if the city surrendered the inhabitants would be spared. The second day, it was a red tent to show that the men would be slaughtered when they were defeated. The third day – if the city was still being stubborn and holding its defences – they would erect a black tent. The black tent…" Katherine cleared her throat. She was scaring herself. "The black tent meant that everyone would be killed. There would be no mercy."

Matthew was silent.

"I'm sorry. That was less comforting than I expected it to be."

"It's all right. It is better to be prepared." Matthew shifted, tapping his fingernail against the stone, thinking. "First, the prince will send Durand a message to surrender, saying we won't be harmed – white tent. Durand then has to calculate how long he thinks he can hold out. He can't wait for ever, but he can try to defend the city until the army arrives. But I don't think Durand will go down without a fight. If we don't surrender, then the Rebels will prepare to attack. After that, the battle commences, and there is no guarantee of safety if the Rebels get into the city. Charlie will let his Highlanders pillage as they see fit – red tent." He paused. "Sorry, that was not very comforting either. Perhaps I will stop there. It is unlikely Charlie will kill everyone. No black tent."

Katherine swallowed nervously, looking out over the

fog and desperately trying to catch sight of the army. She knew they were out there, lurking just out of view. She even thought she could hear the echoes of their bagpipes in the distance. All they could do now was wait – and hope that Matthew was right and there would be no black tent.

Katherine awoke to the sound of cannonfire. She opened her eyes to find herself pressed against Matthew's shoulder, his arm curled around her. It scared her how *right* it felt. They were resting against the barricade wall. The townsfolk who hadn't left the castle for their homes were all sitting on the battlements, and any one of them could turn around and see her sitting like this with a servant. She dislodged Matthew's arm, flushing, and stood up.

In the encroaching darkness, it seemed that the Rebels had been trying to approach the city. The castle's cannon fire, which had woken Katherine, had sent them into retreat. As they returned across the fields, to the river, a victorious chant of the national anthem echoed through the castle. *"Lord grant that Marshal Wade, May by thy mighty aid, Victory bring. May he sedition hush and like a torrent rush, Rebellious Scots to crush. God save the king!"*

Katherine and Matthew beamed at each other. The Rebels didn't dare attack the city.

An hour later a lone rider came to the city gates. There was dead silence as the rider was given entry. "A farmer has come with a letter from the prince!" came the cry as the message he carried was passed along the battlements from the gates.

Having come to recover the King's Rights, we are sorry to find that you should prepare to obstruct our passage. To avoid the Effusion of English Blood, we hereby require you to open your Gates in an immediate surrender of both the city and the castle, and let us enter in a peaceful manner. We shall take care to preserve you from any harm or insult and set an example to all England of the Honour with which we intend to fulfil our Duty.

If you shall refuse us entry, we are fully resolved to force it by Any Means Necessary and then it will not be within our power to prevent the dreadful consequences which usually follow a town being taken by Assault. Consider this seriously and let me have your answer within two Hours, for we shall take any further Delay as a peremptory Refusal and take our Measures accordingly.

Charles P R

Charles, Prince of Wales
Regent of the Kingdoms
of England, Scotland and Ireland

It felt like it took an eternity for Durand to make his response, but in reality it was probably only half an hour. Eventually another cannon shot sounded. The message of the cannonfire was clear: *We will not surrender.* Katherine gave a cheer, proud that her city was standing up against the enemy where others had surrendered.

Matthew let out a wolf-whistle. "Well, that was to the point." He was bright with pride, and she couldn't take her eyes off him.

Later they walked back to her aunt's house in silence. Matthew had his head bent down and Katherine paused at the front door uncertainly. The house was dark and silent. They were surrounded by quiet – the whole city seemed deserted, and she was very aware that they were utterly alone, in a way they had never been before. They were unlikely to be interrupted, whatever happened. She drew in a stuttering breath, and said, "Do you want to come in for dinner?"

He watched her for a moment, and then nodded slowly and followed her inside.

"Where are all the servants?" Katherine asked Matthew.

"Your uncle sent them home to their families. I said I would stay with the house, as I can't return to Scotland."

"Where is your cousin, then?"

"She had to leave," he said, a little sadly.

She touched his arm. "The siege can't last for ever. It won't be long before she's back again."

He nodded, but he didn't seem convinced.

"As we are the only ones here I suppose I should find some food for us," Katherine said.

She'd never prepared a meal before. She ventured into the kitchen. The stone surfaces were empty. She walked down the steps into the cellar, investigating the cool pantry until she discovered a joint of cold ham, hanging from the rafters. She found plates and carefully cut up the ham and then served it with some apple chutney and beans.

Meanwhile, Matthew sat at the kitchen table, watching her. She had been planning for them to eat there, but it was freezing cold without the fires. The stone floor seeped ice into the soles of her feet.

"Shall we go into the parlour?" she asked.

"I think your aunt would be outraged to find out that her servants ate in the parlour while she was away."

Katherine grinned. "I know. Somehow I can't bring myself to care. It's probably the threat of death. It makes social conventions seem a little less ... important." She took a step closer to him. He bent his head minutely towards hers. He blinked once, twice, and then she leant in and pressed a soft, quick kiss to his lips.

> First objective achieved in time-landscape 1745

> System progressing as desired

She pulled back immediately. What was she doing? How could she be so improper?

Matthew was pale and shocked too. "Katherine—!"

She could feel herself flushing with mortification. She'd spoilt everything. Matthew wouldn't want anything to do with her now. She fought back tears. Then, with a sudden rush, he bent his face down towards her again, and kissed her. It was a long, intimate touch.

She pressed herself into him. She knew she shouldn't, but it felt so right, like they had done this a hundred times before, like they were meant to do this. Matthew wrapped an arm around her waist, pulling her tight against him as his thumb rubbed gentle circles into her side. Katherine felt as if her happiness was inexhaustible.

He pulled back with a shudder, their lips breaking apart.

"We can't," he said despairingly. "It isn't right. I'm taking advantage of you, Katherine. I can't take you away from your family, your life. We can't be together."

"Yes, we can. We'll run away. I don't care, Matthew. Take me back to the Highlands, where we can steal cattle with the best of them! I love you."

"Katherine, you don't know what you are talking about. You have no real idea of what life is like if you live in poverty. You'll regret this decision."

Katherine pressed a hand against his cheek. She could feel the beginnings of stubble against her palm. He leant into the touch, but his expression was closed.

"I have no inheritance, you know," she said, voice soft and loving. A tone she didn't recognize. It was so full of warmth and happiness. "I told you, my father was a servant. I wouldn't even be living here but for the grace of my aunt and the stubbornness of my grandmother. I should have grown up a servant, like you. My cousin will inherit the family fortune. I'm not a golden egg to be stolen away by a servant. I'm a goose egg."

"Well, if you have no money, I'm not sure I want you any more," he said, grinning widely.

She snorted and kissed him again. She couldn't help the giggle that escaped from her. It vibrated against his lips. She was overcome with giddiness. He kissed her more deeply, and her laughter melted away. She sighed into his mouth, shivering.

After a long moment, he stepped back, parting their lips almost reluctantly again. His eyes were dark, soft; hers caught on the flushed line of his neck.

"We could elope. Start a farm, a family," he said, achingly hopeful.

"That sounds wonderful."

He kissed her again. It was soft and filled with promise. Katherine tried to hold in the groan that was threatening to escape. Matthew's lips were pressed to her neck and his fingers were wrapped in her hair. His fingertips caressed her scalp, before moving to rub her neck at the base of her skull.

Shocked at her audacity, she pulled his bottom lip into her mouth and sucked. His hands brushed her hair behind her ears, thumb rubbing along the length of her neck. He pressed into the hook of her jaw and she shivered again, helplessly opening her mouth to him.

After a while he groaned.

"*Shh,*" she murmured into his mouth. She took a moment to finish the kiss in her own time, firmly, insistently, and then pulled away. She'd wanted to touch Matthew for weeks now. She was going to make the most of her every chance.

"Am I allowed to speak, now?" he asked, smirking.

"You may," she said, laughter in her voice.

"Will you marry me, Katherine? I want us to spend this life and the next together."

"Yes," she said. "Yes. What did I do to deserve you?" she asked, pressing soft fingertips to his cheekbones.

"What did *I* do to deserve *you*?"

"We can be equally blessed."

CHAPTER 18

<u>Several rules for one Katherine "I am the</u>
<u>worst ever to exist" Galloway</u>

1) NO MORE "SECRET" LUNCHTIME MAKEOUT
SESSIONS IN YOUR OFFICE. We are never going
to live this down. You are a terrible, terrible
influence on me. I was a perfectly respectable
gentleman before you forced your way into my
life and got us caught kissing on a desk!

2) You can wipe that stupid grin off your face right
now! This is so not funny. At all. You do realize
we have to work with these people, right? EVERY
DAY, FOR THE REST OF OUR LIVES.

Crimea, Ukraine, 1854

His meeting over, the general crossed the tent towards them with a clear expression of recognition. Katy winced, hoping against hope that he wouldn't say anything about her and give away her secret. She squared her shoulders and prepared to interrupt him if he mentioned Lord Somerset. To her surprise, though, he turned to Matthew, saying in delight, "Matthew Galloway!"

"George!" Matthew exclaimed, shaking him warmly by the hand. Katy watched with a mixture of horror and amazement. "How are you?" Matthew went on. "I feel rather stupid, not realizing I was waiting for my old friend."

George laughed. "What are you doing in this neck of the woods? Please say you aren't a soldier, or I'll have to speak to your superior about uniforms."

Matthew chuckled. "Ah, no. But I am here in a professional capacity. I'm reporting for *The Times*."

George's expression dropped. "That's you? Oh, I am sorry to hear that. I wish you weren't involved in this."

"Why's that?"

"You won't be made welcome, I'm afraid. A lot of my comrades don't approve of bringing a journalist to the front. Security, you know. I spoke to Raglan last week, and he's furious with you. Apparently, the Russians got hold of one of your articles and it has caused a lot of trouble at home."

Katy held back a wince. She felt on the verge of fainting.

"I've heard the same ever since I arrived," Matthew

confirmed glumly. "But I have to carry on regardless. What I'm doing is too important."

"Important?" George offered them a seat, watching Matthew intently.

"People at home are concerned about the organization of the army. Contrary to what your superiors believe, I am not here as a spy for the Russians but to help the British soldiers. I've sent back accurate descriptions of the administration here, and my efforts have set in motion several urgently needed reforms. My editor tells me that there has already been a huge amount of progress since we arrived."

George looked doubtful. "Well, I'll keep my opinions to myself. Anyway, how can I help you today?"

"Accommodation, George. I have a letter from Lord Raglan, promising assistance. He signed it several months ago as a favour to the editor of *The Times*, though it seems his opinion of me has changed since then." Matthew passed over the letter.

"You're lucky you were sent to me. Anyone else and you would have been refused. Raglan has issued orders not to help you. But I think I can find something for an old friend, even if our opinions on what you are doing here do differ."

Matthew grabbed George's hand again, shaking it gratefully. "Thank you, George. It means a lot to me."

"No trouble at all, my man."

They beamed at each other, and then Matthew seemed to remember himself. He turned to Katy, who was doing her best to imitate a chair and sink into the background.

"Sorry, Kit, this is my old friend George. George, this is my assistant, Christopher Russell. I've known George my whole life; he's a family friend. Sadly, we've rather lost touch and I don't see old George as much as I'd like any more."

"We are rarely in the same country," George chided, and then he turned to Katy. "Pleasure to meet you, son."

She tilted her head in a weak kind of nod while trying to hide her face. "And you," she murmured.

She could feel his gaze on her, but she kept her own firmly on the ground and only when she heard him speaking to Matthew again did she relax. Then, to her horror, she looked up to find that George's eyes were still firmly fixed on her. There was a slightly perplexed frown creasing his brow.

"I'll arrange for a tent to be found for you," he said. "In the meanwhile, please make yourselves comfortable here. I'll have some water brought in for you. I can't offer much in the way of tea or coffee, I'm afraid."

"Thanks again, George," Matthew said.

"My pleasure," George said. He was still looking at Katy. Then his expression cleared. "Oh, yes. I remember you. You're Raglan's boy, aren't you? The one I found reading books in the library instead of working. You've found yourself some honest work, I see. It was good of him to provide you with a servant for your journey, Matthew. And one from his own house too. I bet he regrets that now he's so angry with you, doesn't he?"

Matthew stared at Katy like he had never seen her before. Her face must have told him everything he needed to know, because he said, "Excuse me, George. I'm feeling a little ill. I'm just going to get some air." Then he left the tent without waiting for a reply.

George stared after him in confusion.

"Well, I do hope Matthew is all right. I'll go and arrange your accommodation. Please help yourself to refreshments while I'm gone."

Katy nodded shakily. After George had bustled off, she pressed her hands to her eyes, unable to hold back the tears.

Matthew didn't come back.

UNIVERSITY OF NOTTINGHAM CAMPUS, ENGLAND, 2039

Kate went to her final lecture of the day, since they were waiting to see if Tom could access the online storage. It felt strange, though, carrying on with real life, with everything that was happening. It all seemed so unimportant now. After her lecture, she went straight back to Matt's room. She found him waiting for her with a hot meal and a glum expression.

"Tom can't access the website," he said in a monotone. "He says the servers are completely lost. There are no backups, or anything. There's no way to see the photos."

Kate scrubbed her hands over her face, suddenly exhausted. *"Crap."*

Matt pushed a plate of food towards her, as if she could possibly be hungry right then.

"Eat," he said, "and I'll tell you the plan."

"Plan?" she croaked, in a rather pathetic voice.

He just nodded towards the plate. "Plan," he agreed.

She grabbed her fork and began gulping food down without tasting it and without taking her eyes off Matt.

"We have to go to the lab," he said. "To CSL."

She swallowed quickly. "What? It was quarantined after the bacteria contamination! We can't!"

"The quarantine must have ended by now. It's been twenty years."

She looked down thoughtfully at her plate. "OK. Say we risk going there, which is still a *really bad idea*, what's the point?"

"If we can find the last place the Galloways were, then there's a chance we can find Katherine's phone – especially if the building has been left untouched and in quarantine pretty much ever since," Matt said.

"I guess there's a chance. But wouldn't they have destroyed all the evidence? They wouldn't just leave it lying around the lab for anyone to find. They were trying to keep the whole thing a secret. Not that we know who 'they' are yet!"

"I'm hoping that Katherine and Matthew managed to hide the phone, just in case. That's what I'd do, anyway – leave as much backup information as possible, like they did at your grandmothers'."

"Yeah, I'd do that too," she said slowly. She was starting to think that anything she would do, Katherine would have done the same. They were similar – too similar.

"At any rate, this is the best plan I've come up with, Kate, and I'm so desperate for this not to be a dead end. If you have any better ideas, I'd love to hear them."

He looked hopeful, but she shrugged, at a loss. All she could see in Matt's plan was all the things that could go wrong. It was so chancy.

She put down her fork. "We could go tomorrow, if you want," she said quietly.

Matt nodded. "Tomorrow."

> Time-landscape 2039 progressing as planned, however the
  safety of the subjects may be at risk

"I can't believe we're going to CSL," he went on. "We're actually going there!"

She cupped his cheek. "Let's not talk about that now. Can we just be us?"

He nodded, his expression softening and becoming more intimate. He kissed her. Her toes curled in her socks. She slid a hand under Matt's shirt.

"Let me know if this is too fast," she told him. "It's OK if you want to slow down."

"No," he said. "This feels … right. Like we've done it before."

"Hmm," she said. "In my imagination."

He grinned wickedly at her, tugging off her top. "Oh, yeah? What else do we do in your imagination?"

"Well, usually you aren't wearing any trousers," she whispered in his ear, hooking her thumb into his belt and pulling him closer.

"Let's see what we can do about that, shall we?"

CHAPTER 19

3) Hey, dude, you're the one who forgot to lock the office door! It's not my fault you were so utterly distracted by my fabulous breasts you lost all mental functions! Just be glad Clare walked in on us and not Mick, otherwise this would be all over the internet by now. There are enough saucy pictures of you out there to last a lifetime. ;)

4) Anyway, chill. They are all super jealous of us and our lunchtime antics. WE ARE THE COOL KIDS IN THE LAB.

Folios/v7/Time-landscape-2019/MS-160

Crimea, Ukraine, 1854

Katy sat in their newly provided tent, waiting without hope for Matthew to return to her. She wasn't expecting him to come back. She couldn't blame him for staying away – although she also couldn't help but wait for him. She kept replaying the scene with George in her mind. Matthew had just shut down completely when he found out that she was working for Lord Raglan. She could still picture the blank apathy on his face. He wasn't going to come back. She'd betrayed him.

Nothing she said was going to make this better.

Finally there was a movement at the entrance of the tent, and she looked up, heart pounding and stomach clenching.

It was only a soldier.

"Kit Russell?"

She nodded.

"I've come to take you to your new assignment."

"Assignment?" Her voice cracked.

"Your employer has transferred you over to work with the medical officers. He doesn't require your services any more."

> As predicted, the actions of subject allocation "KATY" in time-landscape 1854 have become detrimental to progress

> Chances of mission completion becoming increasingly unlikely

> Intervention recommended

  >> Intervention denied

UNIVERSITY OF NOTTINGHAM CAMPUS, ENGLAND, 2039

Kate was dreaming about Matt kissing her against her desk when an alarm went off. She blinked herself awake. A radio soap was playing on Matt's clock radio. They were in his room in halls.

She pulled his arm over her waist more firmly, before bringing the duvet up to cover her eyes. Then she lay in the confined darkness, sleepily listening to the sounds of talking until it resolved itself into a discussion on crops. Then she sat up.

She pointed a finger at Matt, and exclaimed, *"You!"*

Matt rubbed his eyes, and frowned at her. "What?"

"You listen to farming shows!" she announced. "Oh my *God*, you loser!"

"Shut up. There isn't anything wrong with a healthy interest in crop rotation."

She choked on her laughter. "No one listens to farming shows except *farmers*. It broadcasts at *four a.m.*! That means you record it *to listen to later*," she said, amazed at his dedication to listening to farmers discuss fields.

"They have interesting sections on badgers and stuff too."

She couldn't help shaking her head at him. "I thought you were cool," she said accusingly, sadly. "You misled me. All this time. With the retro haircut and the mismatched clothes, I thought you were being ironically hipster, but really you are just an *old man*! I can't date someone who listens to this. It will utterly ruin my street cred!"

"Street cred," Matt repeated under his breath, and then pulled her down on top of him, silencing her outraged rant with his mouth. She smiled against his lips and kissed him back, already preparing her next jibes.

"Tom said you wanted to be a farmer when you were a kid," she remembered suddenly. "You still kind of do. That's so … *adorable*."

"Stop talking about my brother when we are in bed together," he said.

She wrapped an arm behind his neck, kissing him, to

show just how focused on him she was and not any of his relatives. In a voice she hoped was sexily husky and not just reminiscent of someone suffering from a bad cold, she murmured, "Are you sure you wouldn't rather just listen to the rest of the episode?"

Matt removed his lips from her collarbone and looked up at her. "All right." He said it with such sincerity that she almost fell for it. After reaching across her, he flicked up the volume on the radio. Then he leant back and crossed his arms behind his head, a picture of contentment. She let out a cry and pulled him back over her immediately. He claimed his victory with a kiss.

"I win," he said, low and quiet.

Kate shivered. That was what a husky voice was supposed to sound like.

"I think we can both win," she decided. "We're definitely both the coolest people in the room."

"Not exactly hard, is it?"

"That's what she said," Kate interjected.

Matt shook his head. "And this is where I chose to lay my affections," he muttered, like it was just the latest in a series of bad life choices he'd made.

"You're *awesome*," she said contentedly, sighing as he kissed her neck.

He snorted at her. "'Awesome'? That's the word you choose? Really? So romantic."

"You're *radical, dude*," she intoned, pushing his head back down into her neck. "Get back to work. We don't have much time. We have to make the most of it."

CHAPTER 20

5) Matthew hereby declares that Katherine Galloway is retroactively responsible for all embarrassing and painful incidents that have occurred in his life to date. Including but not limited to that time he broke his own nose with a tennis racket in year nine. KATHERINE'S FAULT.

6) There are no naked pictures of me on the internet!! None!! That is a barefaced lie!!

7) WE AREN'T THE COOL KIDS IF WE GET FIRED FOR SEXUALLY HARASSING A DESK.

Folios/v7/Time-landscape-2019/MS-160

Crimea, Ukraine, 1854

Katy was crossing the camp on an errand for her new employer when she saw him.

"Matthew," she choked out.

Katy hadn't seen him for days, not since he had found out about her connection to Lord Somerset. She had been working alongside the doctors in the hospital tent, tending to the soldiers ill with cholera. The army was still camped on the shore three days after landing, waiting for orders to march to battle. The closest Katy had come to Matthew in that time was in her dreams, which were the same, every single night. Each night he died in her dreams, and every morning she woke, covered in sweat, bile rising in her throat. However much she told herself it wasn't real, she couldn't escape the sense of foreboding. The memory of being utterly alone and staring down at his dead blank face ached in her very bones; she couldn't bear it.

Now that he was here, alive and well, like she'd hoped for constantly, she couldn't think of a word to say. She tried to summon up the speech she'd prepared, the apologies she had rehearsed countless times in her head, but her mind was utterly blank. Soon, though, the battle would begin and she might never see him again. This was her last chance to tell him why she'd done it.

"I can explain everything, please—"

"Kit Russell," a voice said, interrupting her.

Katy spun around to find a bored horse staring intently at a yellowing patch of grass; its rider was staring intently at her.

Lord Somerset.

He had found her at the worst possible moment. She shifted on the spot, looking between her employer and Matthew, who still hadn't spoken.

"He knows," Katy burst out.

"Ah." Lord Somerset – or Raglan, as Matthew knew him –

looked regretful. "That explains why your articles were so revealing, despite Kit's presence. When did you find out?"

"A few days ago," Matthew said bitterly. "I can't believe you've been spying on me, Kit, all this time."

"Days?" Lord Raglan said. "But that means… Kit, I must say I am disappointed in you for not exerting more pressure over Mr Galloway before he discovered where your true loyalties lay. Did you not work closely enough together? Did he never trust you?"

"Actually, Sir, I did have opportunities to change his articles." Katy held her head high. "I decided not to take them."

Somerset tilted his head enquiringly, hands tightening on his reins. "Why is that?"

"After seeing the true conditions in the hospitals and the lack of attention given to the soldiers' welfare, I decided that something needed to be done, despite your concerns."

"You were sent here to make sure that no information was leaked to the Russians. How do we know that they won't be better prepared for the battle because of you? You could lose us the war!"

"I don't know if that is true or not, Sir. I sincerely hope it is not, because I believe in what Mr Galloway has been doing. He is a brave and honourable man, and his editor tells us that his articles have led to a series of much-needed reforms. Already women are journeying to the front to volunteer as nurses – you may have heard of Florence Nightingale. There's also a train track being built to the front, all because of the information in Matthew's articles.

More supplies and ammunition will reach the front and the men too, because of him. The advantages of progress outweighed the possible risks of the articles. I'm sorry to disappoint you, Sir, but I utterly stand by my choice – and Mr Galloway."

Raglan looked furious. "I see. In that case, there is nothing more to be said. I release you from my service." He pulled his horse's reins and galloped away.

Katy didn't care about him. When she dared to look at Matthew, he was watching her intently, a complicated expression playing across his features. He looked nervously hopeful, but he didn't venture a comment on her confession. Then suddenly he ducked his head and disappeared back into the crowds in the encampment. She stared after him. He knew everything now. She couldn't do any more to get him to forgive her. It was up to him.

Carlisle, England, 1745

Katherine and Matthew sat curled under a blanket, watching the Rebels dig their trenches in the fields below the castle walls. They were just visible through the fog, digging tirelessly in their shirtsleeves, muskets propped up beside them. It was a strange sight, with the snow melting all around them.

The young men of the militia had become all aflutter with panic at the sight. They had abandoned their posts and begun to argue frantically over whether to surrender.

Katherine and Matthew were among only a few civilians to remain in the castle, instead of fleeing the city or barricading themselves and their families in their houses. They watched the terrified soldiers with a kind of serene curiosity. They had each other and at that moment, it was all that mattered.

Eventually, the whispering gang of militia boys pushed forward a representative. He tentatively approached Colonel Durand, who was eyeing the Rebels' work through a telescope. The soldier handed the colonel a letter. As he read, his face turned an impressive shade of puce.

We, the militia, whose names are hereunto subscribed, are of the opinion that the castle is not strong enough to hold off our enemies, and we absolutely refuse to defend it.

The threat posed by the Rebel Army is too great for any force to withstand, and the damage will be much greater if we resist their demands than if we surrender.

Folios/v1/Time-landscape-1745/MS-7

"What is the meaning of this?" the colonel spluttered in outrage.

The wide-eyed soldier stuttered out a response, stumbling over the words so quickly that it must have been memorized. "Sir, we're too exhausted to continue the guard. We had expected relief from the British Army by now and we can't carry on holding the defences alone. We're going to surrender."

"No!" Durand said firmly. The boy opened and closed his mouth several times. His eyes darted beseechingly back to his friends, who were clustered together at a safe distance, listening intently.

"We're perfectly capable of defending the city," Durand insisted. The boy was so terrified that he didn't even seem to be listening. "The Rebels' trenches are terrible, and too far away to be useful. They don't even have any cannons!"

"I'm sorry, but we're going to surrender before we're all killed, Sir. We're going to speak to the mayor." The boy ran back to the group.

Durand tried to stop him, but it was too late. The militia marched out of the castle, leaving Durand with only the elderly men of the garrison to defend Carlisle.

Crimea, Ukraine, 1854

The Russian army were a stain of burnished metal on the other side of the river. At first Katy hadn't understood what she was seeing. It looked like their enemy was a giant, armoured creature, crouching in the foothills, waiting to pounce. Then she realized that she was seeing the helmets of the soldiers, who were spread in a long line across the horizon. After a long and hot day of marching, they had reached the battleground.

The British troops were spread out across the plain in a

wave of red coats, their bayonets flashing in the sun. They were a thin red line, marching towards the enemy. To the right of them were the French, a smaller group in dark uniforms, and beside them were the tartan kilts and tall black bearskin hats of the Scottish regiment.

Katy began to climb down the crumbling slope to join a group of civilians gathered at a village on the plain. It was no more than a smudge of wooden outbuildings in the vast desert. They made a dull group against the startling brilliance of the soldiers.

The air became saturated with noise as the artillery began firing. Katy automatically ducked in shock, expecting to be hit. She could feel the air vibrating around her, as though the bullets were touching her as they passed. A shell exploded in the buildings ahead. Its wooden walls caught fire and the air filled with white smoke that spread quickly through the village. The people she was with screamed and ran for cover. Katy blinked away the soot as she tried to see through the dense air.

She should have stayed on the hill, where the whole battlefield was visible. Now she was in the centre of the chaos and couldn't see a foot in front of her. She wished she could find Matthew, just to make sure he was safe. She hadn't seen him since the encounter with Lord Somerset the day before.

She'd watched Matthew die four times in her dreams now. Every morning she woke up screaming his name, the image of him dying burnt across her retina in vivid, putrid colours. It had felt so real; each of his deaths had ripped out another part of her heart. It wasn't like any other dream she'd ever had. It felt like a memory.

Why was she so upset by something that hadn't even happened? Matthew was here somewhere – avoiding her, but well and healthy – and yet she felt as lost as if he were long dead.

> Time merging is creating mental suffering in subject allocation "KATY" in time-landscape 1854

> This may affect the chances of the objective being achieved

> Time is running out and the subjects have still not made progress towards the desired outcome

> Intervention recommended

>> Intervention denied

CHAPTER 21

Matthew, you need to watch out. You're starting to sound like me. You realize you used MULTIPLE EXCLAMATION POINTS in your last note. What happened to "Excessive use of punctuation is for idiots and chavs. Please don't email me if you can't control your typing, Miss Finchley" and "Stop shouting at me in capitals, Katherine. It's weird and doesn't make your point any more valid. The data still doesn't fit the hypothesis"? I've trained you so well. :')

One day you might even be cool!

Folios/v7/Time-landscape-2019/MS-160

CENTRAL SCIENCE LABORATORIES,
WEST MIDLANDS, ENGLAND, 2039

The sky had turned a dark orange by the time they walked to the laboratory from the train station. A rusted sign announced that they had arrived at Central Science Laboratories, but they would have known even without the sign. The fence was covered with fluorescent warning boards which screamed DANGER: QUARANTINE ZONE.

"The gate's locked," Matt said, lifting the padlock.

"I bet we can find a hole in the fence. This kind of place

is like catnip for rebel kids. They'll have made a way in years ago."

"And you would know all about rebel kids?" he said, following her as she walked along the perimeter.

"I'm sure I don't know what you mean," she said lightly. "I was a perfectly well-behaved child."

He snorted, but she chose to ignore him, having just found a reasonably large hole in the wire fence.

"Told you!" She ducked through the hole into the brambles on the other side. She pushed her way through the spiky branches until she found a way out to the safety of a tarmacked car park.

She was pulling out the leaves that had caught in her hair when Matt appeared from the bush, looking windswept and harassed.

"You OK?" she asked.

"I think my elbow is bleeding."

"You're fine," she told him, and grabbed his hand.

They picked their way cautiously through the empty, weed-covered car park towards the building beyond. The complex looked untouched, its huge windows unbroken, though green with mould. It didn't look anything like Kate had imagined, and was more like a library than the quarantined site of the outbreak of dangerous bacteria. She couldn't believe they were risking everything to chase down a long-forgotten mystery that had happened a lifetime ago. But she felt like this was her whole reason for being – her whole reason for living. She couldn't stop. She had to do this for herself, for Katherine.

They approached the building cautiously, but there was no sign of life. Kate peered through the dusty panes of glass, while Matt tried to open the doors. The security system had obviously stood the test of time, because they wouldn't budge.

"Why don't we just break a window?" Kate suggested, interrupting Matt's musings on messing with the wiring in the locks. He looked shocked at the idea.

"Matt, it's an *abandoned building*. Who cares?"

"But it's such a waste of glass!"

"You have such a warped sense of morality. I really don't think it matters, you dork. Here, I'll do it." Kate prised a sandstone rock from the border of a long-overgrown flower bed and threw it at one of the windows. It bounced off with a reverberating thud.

Matt winced. "Congratulations," he said dryly.

She rolled her eyes and picked up the rock again.

"Good idea, Kate. I bet it works perfectly *this* time."

"I've been a bad influence on you, Mr Galloway. Less of the sarcasm, young man. Cynicism doesn't suit you," she said.

"I hardly think sarcasm is the worst thing you've brought into my life," he muttered.

"You're welcome," she said, carefully aiming the stone at one of the corners of the large glass panes of the sliding doors. The glass smashed, sending a satisfyingly majestic spray of shards across the floor of the reception. Kate glanced smugly at Matt, but he was too busy staring inside to notice.

"How are we supposed to know if the bacteria is still alive?" he asked.

They regarded the building apprehensively.

"You know, I'm pretty sure the bacteria outbreak wasn't real, anyway," Kate decided. "Look at this place. It seems that they had plenty of time to shut everything up neatly. I think CSL made the outbreak up, to make sure people stayed away. I think we should risk it. Besides, wouldn't the bacteria have already been released through the window I just ... er ... broke?"

Matt nodded and stepped through the gap in the door, glass shards crunching beneath his feet.

Kate followed him and then turned on her torch, illuminating the reception area. She picked up a brightly coloured leaflet from the floor. On the front there was a picture of Matthew and Katherine Galloway, posing in lab coats and holding test tubes, beaming at the camera.

Funded by DEFRA

Welcome to

CENTRAL SCIENCE LABORATORIES

Leading partners in agricultural chemical development

Read about our work in an interview with two of our leading young scientists Matthew and Katherine Galloway.

"Ready?" Matt asked, bumping his shoulder against hers.

She dropped the leaflet, mouth dry, and nodded. "Ready."

Carlisle, England, 1745

"It's hard to believe we're in the middle of a siege," Katherine said. "Everything is so peaceful."

Tomorrow there was going to be a meeting to decide whether the city should surrender to the Jacobites, but for tonight the town was silent.

"Can you come up to my bedchamber?" she continued, a little nervously. The request felt scandalous even though they were now betrothed. "I was freezing cold last night, because I couldn't light the fire."

Matthew nodded, an odd look on his face, and followed her upstairs. Their hands met on the banister, and they both jumped away from the touch, looking shyly at each other.

Once in her room, she sat at her dressing table, unpinning her hair, as he built a fire. He kept darting glances at her. When the fire burnt steadily, he got up and came to stand behind her. She leant back against his chest and pressed a kiss to his forearm. He stooped to run his lips along her neck: soft butterfly strokes down to her collarbone.

The sound of a moan echoed around the room. It took her a moment to realize the breathless, wanton noise had come from her, and she closed her eyes in embarrassment. She sounded like that, and all he had done was kiss her neck! He began pressing soft kisses onto her eyelids. The expression on his face was reverent when she opened her eyes.

"Could you help me take off my dress?" she asked quietly. "It's a struggle doing it alone."

His gaze dropped to the line of her bodice and she shivered.

As Matthew's hands began to carefully undo the buttons of her dress, Katherine thought how much more romantic the elaborate undressing was when Matthew was doing it, instead of a maid. When he had untied the ribbons of her chemise, she stood up and eased the dress down to the floor. She already felt naked and there were still several layers to go. Matthew undressed her slowly, savouring each moment like she was an elaborately wrapped present. He kissed each new length of exposed skin with wonder.

Eventually he had peeled her clothes away from her and she stepped out of the pile of abandoned garments. His breath came out in a rush, and he quickly drew her into a kiss. His fingers were cold against her back, and she gasped.

He smiled. "Sorry."

"Don't be."

He helped her into her nightdress, spending a long moment tying the ribbon. Then he pressed a kiss against the base of her neck.

She turned to him with a grin. "Now it's my turn."

She began unbuttoning his waistcoat and shirt, kissing the newly revealed skin down his chest.

"Much faster," she murmured against the skin. "Maybe I should go back to dressing like a boy."

"I wouldn't have a problem with that," he replied. "As long as it wasn't in public."

She could quite happily spend the rest of her life kissing him. Katherine's hand found his waist and slipped under his shirt to touch the smooth, bare skin.

He jerked in surprise. "We have to stop. We should wait until we are wed."

She let out a sigh, closing her eyes to the feel of his hands rubbing circles into her scalp. She wasn't ready to go further than this. It all felt too good to be true.

```
> Time-landscape 1745 progressing as planned
```

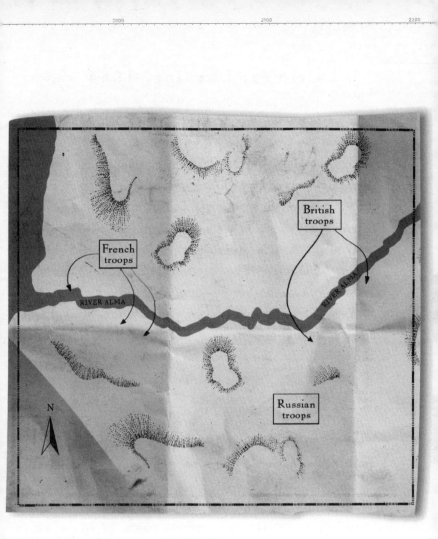

Folios/v3/Time-landscape-1854/MS-10

File note: Plan of regiments at the Battle at the Alma River.
　　　　　 The French and British marched on the Russians by
　　　　　 fording the river

Crimea, Ukraine, 1854

The battle was raging and Katy had lost track of where she was. The air was thick with smoke from the village's burning buildings and every shadow made her blanch with fear that she had somehow wandered over enemy lines and was surrounded by Russians. She stumbled forward again, feeling a squelch beneath her feet. For one sickening instant, she thought she had stepped on a body, but then a fruity scent made its way up through the smoke. Grapes. She was in a vineyard.

From somewhere near by came the sound of shots and men calling out to each other. She could feel the heat of fire on her skin. A shape suddenly fell towards her and Katy ducked, thinking it was a shell, but at the flapping of wings she realized it was a panicked bird trying to escape the battle. A shot went past Katy's head, and she shuddered to see it hit the wall of a building, shards of brick exploding from the hit. The noise terrified her, but it helped her sense of direction. She now knew that the front line must be at the river. She ran until the smoke cleared and suddenly she could see it. The neat, ordered palette of colours of the regiments had dissolved into a mass of brown, the vivid reds blurring with the blues.

Then Katy reeled back in shock. There were several *ladies* standing on the crest of the hill, their dresses flying around them in the breeze. The Russians were having a *picnic* during the battle! She gaped in awe at their arrogance – to view war like an evening's entertainment.

After a moment, she remembered herself and checked the progress of the soldiers. The British were swarming over a wooden bridge, with the Russians firing down on them from the other side of the river. Men dropped into the water and swam to the bank, before clambering up the slope of the hill, pulling at the stringy grass to get onto land, only to be shot down by the Russians.

Her plans were vague, but she couldn't stop the feeling that she had to find Matthew, that he needed her help. She aimed for the river. Soldiers were wading through the deep water, rifles held above their heads. She was amazed to see that several held bunches of grapes in their teeth – they'd obviously passed through the vineyard too, and made the most of the opportunity.

The battle was getting fiercer all the time, and a screeching rocket now flew over her head and landed on the opposite bank. It exploded among the Russian men in a flush of bright fire. She heard a scream and saw an injured soldier clinging to the riverbank just downstream from her, blood flowing from a wound on his head. And then there was Matthew, as she'd known he would be, right in the middle of the danger. He was knee-deep in water as he tried to push the injured man onto the bank.

Carlisle, England, 1745

Nearly everyone in Carlisle had gathered in the cathedral for the meeting to discuss whether to surrender. Durand

and his garrison were busy trying to persuade the terrified townsfolk to keep fighting the Rebels.

"I'm on Durand's side," Matthew told Katherine firmly. "We can hold out against them. We can't trust them to keep their promises, not now we've refused their original conditions. We have to keep them out."

Katherine "hmm"ed thoughtfully.

The meeting went on a long time, but even though the civilians were initially willing to hold the defence, the militia refused to help.

At this, a wave of panic spread through the cathedral.

"We have to surrender!" a gentleman cried. "We can't defend ourselves without soldiers."

A vote was taken and nearly all of the civilians voted to surrender. Durand stood up to address the crowd. His booming voice echoed around the high ceilings of the building. "Ladies and gentlemen, whatever the city decides to do, the castle and its garrison are going to remain firm. Anyone who wishes to join us in the castle will be welcomed. We are well defended and have enough provisions to hold out for as long as the siege continues."

He paused and then went on, "The castle gates will be closed at dusk and will stay locked when the Jacobites enter the city after your *surrender*." He said the word pointedly, clearly disgusted with the militia for giving up so easily. Katherine understood the feeling. After a firm nod, he began to walk swiftly towards the exit.

A soldier blocked his path. "Sir," he said, "Prince Charlie's conditions require that the castle surrenders with the city. I'm going to have to insist you give up your arms."

"The garrison will not surrender," Durand replied. "The city should refuse to give in to threats of violence, regardless of the reason. Carlisle can't cave to Charlie's threats, especially when we're perfectly capable of holding our defences. Carlisle is better than that. *We won't surrender.*"

"Sir, I am afraid I must insist. We already have a document for surrender drawn up… If you would just sign it, then all of this can be over. If you don't, Carlisle is going to have to face the wrath of the Highlanders. We won't allow that. I'm sorry. I have no choice but to ask you to sign."

"I refuse, you cowards," Durand hissed.

The soldier silently lowered his musket and pointed it at Durand. After a moment of shock, everyone began to shout. Then everything happened at once. The garrison and the militia aimed their weapons at one another, throwing angry threats into the sea of noise.

Durand stood frozen.

"No!" Matthew shouted, frantic. "He can't die!"

Katherine ran forward, not sure what she was planning to do but knowing she had to help. But Matthew pushed her back and moved to pull Durand out of the line of fire. The soldier holding the musket jerked forward in surprise – and then, without any warning, the gun went off.

A bang echoed around the room.

"No!" Katherine screamed. She couldn't hear anything except the ring of the recoil in her ears, couldn't see

anything except the blood spreading quickly across the back of Matthew's shirt, soaking the fabric in seconds.

Matthew had been shot.

```
> ALERT: Subject allocation "MATTHEW" in time-landscape 1745
  is compromised

> Situation critical

> Intervention recommended

  >> Intervention in progress
```

CHAPTER 22

Katherine, I'm cool! Just because I don't communicate like a drunken teenager doesn't mean I'm not hip. Or "epic", or "gangsta" or whatever the kids are saying these days, because I know you are laughing at me for using the word hip, don't lie.

Maybe you are rubbing off on me a little bit, though. It's kind of fun, messing around with notes on the fridge.

(Also, did our relationship really start with me telling you off for your grammar? Why did you even go out with me?)

Folios/v7/Time-landscape-2019/MS-160

Crimea, Ukraine, 1854

Matthew had almost succeeded in pushing the injured man onto the bank by the time Katy made it down the hill.

"Matthew!" she cried out, her words inaudible over the sounds of battle and the rush of water. She dropped down on the bank, grabbing the injured soldier and heaving him the rest of the way onto dry land. He was a Highlander. His tall, fluffy bearskin tilted to the side and was damp and seeping water.

"Matthew, we need to get out of here," she said.

Matthew struggled up onto the bank. Before he could reply, someone fired at them.

Katy knocked him down, and threw herself on top of him. This was it: he was going to get shot. She had to stop it, even if she was hit herself.

"Katy!" he cried out, trying to squirm out of her grasp, but she held on fast. She couldn't let him die.

> ALERT: Time-landscape 1854 in imminent danger of timing out

Katy gasped for breath, the panic rising in her as if she were drowning, and then suddenly the Highlander was covering them both, hiding them in the dark safe space below his body. She had no idea why he had decided to sacrifice himself, but she gritted her teeth and closed her eyes as the shots increased. The soldier above them was shaking. Warm liquid dripped down onto her face. He was crying out, writhing as the impacts shook him, and then it was suddenly silent and Katy stared into Matthew's eyes. The Highlander had saved them; he had saved them both.

Matthew was *alive*, staring at her with horror and panic and disbelief, and quiet filled every corner of her mind. She couldn't remember how to breathe or think or do anything except close her eyes and clasp the relief that he was alive, that she didn't have to watch him die again like at the cathedral. He was still here; he was still hers.

It was then that the memories came, opened up inside her as if they'd always been there. All it had taken was a brush with death to remind her of them. They blossomed in her mind in vivid stains, and she remembered everything – and Matthew was everything and she loved him and always had.

She had done this before. She had held Matthew's blood-soaked body and gasped for breath through her tears. It wasn't just déjà vu, because she remembered it so clearly, like it had happened only the day before. But that was impossible.

She could see it all with perfect clarity, their previous lives together. Her vision went black and she blinked away the blur of her tears. The world came back into focus, new and different.

> Time merging has reached 100% completion in time-landscape 1854

> It is highly unlikely that these subjects will achieve their objective, considering this hazardous landscape

Carlisle, England, 1745

With blood pouring from the wound to his chest, Matthew stood still long enough that Katherine had the sudden hope that his injury wasn't serious, that it was going to be fine, he would be all right. And then all at once he fell to the floor, as if his strings had been cut. There was a deafening silence.

The soldier who had shot at Durand and hit Matthew by mistake dropped his musket and stepped back in horror. Katherine pushed her way, shakily, through the crowd, her legs on the verge of collapsing beneath her.

"Everyone get back!" a soldier called. "Give her privacy." Suddenly the cathedral was clear of everyone except Matthew, Durand and Katherine.

Katherine couldn't believe this was happening. She dropped to the floor beside Matthew, pulling him onto her lap.

"Matthew!" she cried, her voice sounding hollow.

His head fell back on her shoulder. "I love you."

She closed her eyes, pressed her cheek against his. "I love you too, Matthew. *Please*, please don't go."

Durand was standing near by. He was covered in Matthew's blood.

"Please don't surrender," Matthew begged him. "You can't. Please, you need to hold fast. Promise me."

Durand nodded, face white. "Nobody else will die – I promise."

Matthew turned back to Katherine, running his eyes over her face like he was memorizing her features. "Katherine, please look after – Anise for me. Please."

She nodded and tried to force a smile, as she watched the light fade from his eyes. A resigned stillness was sweeping through his body. Everything was blurring before her. She blinked away tears as she stroked the hair out of his eyes.

He didn't blink, and she realized it was because he couldn't take his eyes off her.

"I love you," he mouthed, and then he closed his eyes, and didn't open them again, even when she begged him not to leave her. She wept great racking sobs that tore from her chest and shook his lifeless body. She couldn't stop. Her voice was a rough choke and her cheeks burnt from the salt of her tears.

```
> Subject allocation "MATTHEW" timed out

> Intervention in progress

> Mission failure

> Searching for the closest match

> … searching …

> Male match found in adjacent space thread

> Transferring male candidate

> File loading …
```

He gasped. Matthew's eyes fluttered open and he focused on her, breathing hard.

"Matthew?" she asked, heart in her throat. He had *died* – she had *watched* him die – but here he was, alive in her arms. She could feel his heart stuttering as his chest pressed against hers.

"K-Ka—" he choked, coughing up blood. He cleared his throat. "Katy? You died… What's happening?"

She stared at him in shock as he struggled to stand. There was no rip in his clothing, and no wound on his chest.

Crimea, Ukraine, 1854

Katy was standing on the riverbank in the midst of the Crimean battle, with the dead Highlander at her feet, and she remembered everything – every moment throughout history that she and Matthew had been together and then been torn apart. She couldn't fathom how she'd ever forgotten it. It was so obvious and clear, including the way Matthew had come back when he had died in 1745. Panic rose inside her, and then arms were wrapped around her, pulling her back to reality.

"It's all right," Matthew murmured. "You're safe – it's over. I'm here."

"You died," she bit out, shuddering against him, and he brushed a hand down her spine.

"Not this time. You've got me – it's all right. I'm fine."

"Do you remember? Please – tell me you remember too, that it's not just me. Tell me that I'm not going mad or…!"

"I remember." His voice was quiet. "I died. I was shot. In the cathedral. I remember."

She sighed, felt steadied, and pulled herself back together. She could do this. Matthew was with her, and all her imaginings were real, but they were going to be all right, so long as they got out of danger now.

"We need to run," Matthew said as though reading her mind. "As fast as we can. Can you do that, Katy?"

"Yes."

"One, two, three," he murmured, and then Matthew was pulling her along and away from the river and the battle to where the air was clear and the ground wasn't soaked in blood.

She paused, orienting herself. They headed towards a stone outhouse. Inside, it was empty. Dust had settled over everything like in a long-deserted tomb. She barricaded the door behind them and then dropped to the floor with a sigh of relief.

Matthew was safe. He was alive.

> Time-landscape 1854 out of danger

> Threats still remain

> Surveillance will continue until subjects are safe

CENTRAL SCIENCE LABORATORIES, WEST MIDLANDS, ENGLAND, 2039

Inside CSL, Kate and Matt stared silently at the small metal sign that labelled the office as belonging to K. GALLOWAY, JUNIOR RESEARCHER. For once Kate couldn't think of anything to say – not even a trace of witty banter.

She had been here before.

She knew she had, except she definitely hadn't.

Either she was going crazy or something else was going

on. She opened her mouth to ask Matt if he was feeling the same way, but the words wouldn't come out. She couldn't say something that would make her sound insane.

Matt twisted the handle and pushed the door open with a long creak. The sun had set and the room beyond was dark except for their narrow torch beams. Dust motes floated as they disturbed the air.

Kate's gaze was focused absolutely on the cardigan on the back of the desk chair. It had faded to a pale cream from the force of twenty years of sunlight, but the knitted pattern was still obvious in the fabric. She brushed her hand over it, feeling the threads beneath her fingertips. Her breath caught. This was Katherine's. She had been right here, working in this very room: emailing flirtatious comments to her husband, writing lab reports, worrying about the bacteria, shrugging off her cardigan and leaving it behind at the end of a busy day.

She forced herself to look away, to where Matt was pulling open the desk drawers.

"There's nothing here," Matt said.

Kate peered over his shoulder. The drawers and filing cabinets were all empty.

"Someone must have destroyed all their work after they were killed," Kate said.

They looked at each other, horrified. Their whole trip had been for nothing. There was nothing in the room that told them anything more about the death of the woman who had signed the documents they had read.

"Matthew's office should be near by," Matt said, trying to

be optimistic. "There might still be something there."

"Wait," Kate said. She gently wrapped a fox ornament from the desk in the cardigan and then put both of them in her rucksack.

When they found Matthew's office, the door was locked. Sighing wearily, like a man preparing himself for imminent death, Matt rammed the door with his shoulder to try and break the lock. Surprisingly, it was successful.

"Wow. I thought that only worked in films," she commented as he rubbed his shoulder gingerly.

"I think it was a pretty cheap lock. It's only an office door," he said. "*God*, that hurt so much more than I thought it would."

"Matt, you delicate flower, this was your chance to show me how much of a man you are. Why are you spoiling it?"

He grinned. "After you, my dear."

It was a wreck inside. Papers were scattered everywhere, along with the splintered remains of a desk and chair. Worst of all, there were dark black stains on the walls. Kate drew in a horrified breath. They were unmistakably blood splatters.

"Matt…"

He took her hand. "I guess this is where it happened, then."

Kate closed her eyes, feeling dizzy. She could picture the moment they had died, so vividly. She felt sick. "This is where we – they – died. They really were shot."

CHAPTER 23

Matthew, our relationship started because I wouldn't leave you alone until you took me out for dinner. You were all determined to keep it purely platonic because we worked together and everything, but I pestered you until you gave in. How can you have already forgotten that? YOU DIDN'T THINK YOU HAD ANY CHOICE IN THIS, DID YOU?

<u>A dramatic re-enactment of how it went down:</u>

K: Hey, sexy, nice to meet you, I'm Katherine!

M: You used too many commas in that sentence.

K: Let's make out now.

M: No. Please leave me to die alone and miserable in a pit of despair.

K: But look at my charming sense of humour! My fabulous breasts! How good I am at error analysis! We should make out.

M: But we work together! I'm reserved and no fun!

K: Did I mention my fabulous breasts?

M: Sure, let's make out.

CENTRAL SCIENCE LABORATORIES,
WEST MIDLANDS, ENGLAND, 2039

Kate hadn't actually believed that Katherine and Matthew had been shot in 2019 until she saw the bloodstains. She had hoped to find that they had secretly escaped, or even died in some freak accident at the laboratory.

"We have to hope they managed to get some evidence and leave it for us to find before they were caught," Matt said, squeezing her hand before releasing it. "Something that will help us to prove they were innocent." He picked through the wrecked office, shoving the broken furniture into a pile.

"You think they might have hidden something here?" Kate asked.

"Why else would they be in Matthew's office? It's not near any exits." He rummaged through the destroyed desk drawers in quick succession.

"I guess that makes sense…" she said, and then shook herself. She had to help. "We want a phone, right?"

He nodded. "Or a camera." He was still moving quickly, scanning through the filing cabinet drawers before hurriedly moving on.

"Matt, slow down. We don't have to rush. You aren't going to find anything like that."

"No," he said distractedly. "I'll find it. I just need to work out where I – he would hide it. When I see the place, I'll know. It's not anywhere here."

She watched him thoughtfully, remembering how she'd

felt in the loft, how she'd gone straight to the hidden laptop. "Close your eyes. Think. Where would you hide it, if it were you? You've got barely a minute. Someone is outside the door, forcing their way in. Where do you hide something small, something precious?"

Matt stood still for a moment. When he opened his eyes, his gaze went immediately to the printer. He flicked up the lid. Then, looking like he had forgotten to breathe, he reached inside and carefully pulled out the ink cartridges. In the last slot, hidden in the shadows, was a mobile phone. He let out a giddy breath, before turning to Kate with a look of such triumph that she almost couldn't meet his eye.

"You went straight to it!" she said. It was happening to Matt, too. It wasn't just her with an eerie sense of déjà vu.

He shrugged. "It just felt right, you know?"

"You are brilliant." Kate kissed him, hard and determined, not letting go for long seconds. When she pulled back, he looked a little stunned, and she kissed him again, just to see the expression once more. He wrapped an arm protectively around her waist and pulled her closer.

"That was leg-flickingly good," he murmured, pressing a kiss below her ear. She collapsed against him, and then pulled the phone out of his hands.

"All of my kisses are leg-flickingly good," she said.

She examined the bulky phone curiously, before pulling off the back of the casing. Behind the long-dead battery was a memory card. After pulling it free, she slid it into place in her tablet and projected the footage, which was blurry and pixelated, onto the bloodstained office wall.

INT. CAR – NIGHT

Silence. An opening shot of the inside of a car roof. The camera twists down to show the darkened road, streetlights momentarily turning the image white before it focuses.

KATHERINE
(softly, close to camera)

All right, Matthew. Tell our dedicated audience the plan.

The car pauses at the traffic lights. It is the only vehicle on the deserted street. MATTHEW clears his throat, and the camera shifts to him. He is concentrating on driving, the streetlight flickering in the hollows of his cheekbones.

MATTHEW

We start in Dr Smith's office. Test out your new lock-picking skills - which I'm sure are expert by now—

KATHERINE
(interrupting, slightly disgruntled)

Hey, I did practice on the front door earlier!

MATTHEW shoots a fond, exasperated look off-screen.

MATTHEW
(wryly)

Using instructions you read online. Anyway, if that works, we start looking for anything compromising—

KATHERINE

If we can get into the computer, that is.

The traffic lights turn green and MATTHEW looks back to the road, releasing the handbrake.

MATTHEW

I think it'll work. Everything I read online said that if you reboot with a different operating system, you can still access the hard drive.

KATHERINE
You've got the OS on a memory stick?

MATTHEW
(nods)

We're here.

Both are silent. The car turns into a long driveway, and the headlights briefly light up a sign saying CENTRAL SCIENCE LABORATORIES, DEFRA. *MATTHEW flashes his ID at the security guard, who lifts the barrier. They drive through and park. MATTHEW stares out of the window before turning to KATHERINE. His face is scared. He leans in to kiss her.*

FADE OUT.

INT. DR SMITH'S OFFICE – LATER

A computer screen is visible over KATHERINE's shoulder. The text on the screen is blurred and jolting in a rainbow of colours. The camera moves back until the image resolves into a densely worded email.

KATHERINE
(reading aloud)

"In reference to our previous correspondence, I confirm that approval has been given for Central Science Laboratories to proceed as directed. Preparation of the bacteria has been undertaken on the assumption that the date of release will be 15/08/19 and it is essential that this estimated timeline is maintained as closely as possible, with full detailing of the effects of the bacterial spores on human health. There is a limited period of time available to allow the weapon to be manufactured ready for distribution to troops at the onset of war.

Funding for testing has been approved, and test subjects from Wakefield Prison have been sent to your site. Arrival is expected within the hour. Please provide regular reports of the progress made. It is imperative that you inform the MoD immediately of any changes, so the relevant actions can be taken." It's signed by someone from the Ministry of Defence.

KATHERINE's face, slack with shock, turns to MATTHEW. The camera catches her chin and the dark outlines of her eyes.

KATHERINE

It isn't CSL that are doing this. It's the army! The bacteria's going to be used in war, in two months. It is a weapon.

MATTHEW

They are testing it on human subjects. That can't be legal.

(pause)

What else is there?

The camera pans back to the computer screen. KATHERINE clicks through several documents, skimming them before moving on to the next. Then she stops on a saved email.

KATHERINE

(gasps)

There's an email from the prime minister. Oh my God. It says...

(reading aloud)

"Dear Dr Smith, Dr..." Blah blah... "As agreed in our last meeting, please consider this communication as confirmation that the bacteria's effect on the test subjects met with our requirements and receives full approval for use as a destructive weapon. However, since then it has been decided that more information is required on its waterborne properties. It is essential that the bacterium is not able to survive for extended periods of time in aqueous conditions, to avoid cross-contamination of the British Isles during exposure in Europe. Funds have been released for further study on the lifetime of the bacteria in aquatic wildlife, with a report expected within three weeks. This is the final requirement for the project from the council before .the bacteria will be passed on to the Ministry of Defence for use." Then there are a load of figures and calculations for costs.

MATTHEW

Are you kidding me? What the hell? The prime minister knows about this? He plans to release the bacteria in Europe and just hope that it doesn't spread to the UK because it doesn't travel in water? How is that allowed? How is this ethical? Our country is run by idiots!

The video cuts off.

INT. DR SMITH'S OFFICE – SEVERAL MINUTES LATER

KATHERINE

Is that thing recording again? Good. This is a report from Marge, dated two weeks ago. She was working on a vaccine for the bacteria to give to farm animals. It should work on humans too, right?

MATTHEW
(calmer now)

Well, at least if the bacteria does spread to the UK - which I still can't believe is something they are just hoping doesn't happen - they can vaccinate everyone so no one dies. Even if our government decides to completely annihilate the rest of the world, we'll be fine, right? Obviously! What the hell is the matter with these people?

We have to release the formula for the vaccination, so countries can counteract it, wherever it's released. Can you full-screen that so I can get a close up of it, Katherine?

MATTHEW zooms in on the screen and focuses on the vaccination's details.

> OK, now scroll across so I can get the rest in.
> Slower. We're going to have to transcribe this
> so we can give people the cure.

There is a DNA breakdown of a vaccination, and instructions for creating it on screen. The recording ends abruptly.

INT. BASEMENT – HALF AN HOUR LATER

The camera is focused on a grey concrete floor.

MATTHEW
(shakily)

I can't – I can't – no. No.

The camera travels up to an internal window, with blinds half closed. The words DANGER: QUARANTINE ZONE are printed on them. The camera zooms in past the blinds into the room beyond, which is dimly lit with fluorescent bulbs. There is a line of steel tables in the room; a black body bag sits on each. The nearest bag is unzipped, an arm, bright red with oozing sores, is dangling over the edge of the table. The fingernails are yellowed, peeling away from the skin. The sleeve is bright orange. A prison serial number is printed in black on the shoulder.

KATHERINE

I'm going to be sick.

The camera shuts off.

INT. FREEZER – TEN MINUTES LATER

KATHERINE is pulling vials of bacteria off the shelf of a freezer and dropping them into a box. Her breath clouds in the cold air.

MATTHEW

This is all the samples, right?

The camera bobs in MATTHEW's hand as they take the box to a lab benchtop oven, setting the temperature to 200°C. The oven begins to hum.

KATHERINE

Yeah, I think this is the last freezer load.

> Assuming someone doesn't find out and turn
> off the oven immediately, the heat should
> kill all the samples. All the research will be
> destroyed.

KATHERINE pours the contents of the vials onto the top shelf of the oven.

MATTHEW

> It's the middle of the night. No one will find
> out until morning. We can stop it all.

As he finishes speaking, there is a noise from outside the lab, and the camera swings round just as the lighting in the hallway flicks on. There is the sound of the oven door closing. The camera jerks up and down as KATHERINE and MATTHEW run for the door at the other end of the lab.

INT. MATTHEW'S OFFICE – LATER

KATHERINE holds the camera. The view of MATTHEW shakes as if she is trembling violently.

KATHERINE

> Next time, we're moving somewhere hot and
> quiet before any of this happens.

MATTHEW
(Kissing her)

I like Spain.

MATTHEW kneels down to fumble with the printer.

KATHERINE
(voice cracking)

Hurry, Matthew.

MATTHEW

Tell them.

KATHERINE
(whispering directly into the phone's microphone)

> We've been caught. They've put the building
> in lockdown and are searching for us. There's
> no time to upload the videos, so we are going

to leave this one recording so you can—

(gasping, trying to catch her breath)

—can see what they do to us. We've tried to destroy all of the bacteria. But - but if there's more ... if they use it, please make the vaccine. Copy it down from this video and then use it. Please.

Footsteps echo down the corridor.

Matthew, did you hear that?

The camera turns to the empty doorway. More footsteps.

MATTHEW

Give me the phone.

The image drops to show the floor and then the swapping of hands. Then the phone is pushed inside the printer. A close-up of MATTHEW's frantic face fills the screen before he closes the lid. Grey, then black. The sound is muffled but still audible. Footsteps get louder. A guard calls out indistinctly.

MATTHEW
(fiercely)

I love you. In every life. I love you. I love you so much.

KATHERINE
.(pained, desperate)

Matthew —!

There are several loud gunshots. Then silence followed by the sound of the guards giving orders and reporting to superiors. After several minutes, the voices quieten. The video plays on, the screen dead and black.

Carlisle, England, 1745

At the back of the cathedral, away from the meeting, Katherine stared at Matthew's skin, at the smooth place where the wound should be. His skin was unmarked. When she looked up, Matthew was crying.

"Matthew?"

"You died," he said, tears streaming down his face. "I'm sorry. I'm so sorry I left you. I thought I'd lost you. I forgive you. I forgive you for everything. I can't lose you."

"I never died, Matthew. Why do you think I died?"

"We were in the Crimea. You were hurt when the rocket hit. I watched you die."

"Crimea?" she gasped. "What *rocket*? There haven't been any rockets. The city is under siege and you were trying to protect Durand and *you* were shot. Matthew, you've been hurt. You're imagining things."

He stared at her. "I don't know who you are, but you aren't my Katy. Who are you? Where am I?"

"What? We're at home, in Carlisle." There was no flicker of recognition in his eyes. "*Carlisle.* You've had a terrible shock. I don't know what happened, but you somehow escaped death. I think you should sleep. When you wake up, everything will make sense."

As they left the cathedral, it was clear that Durand and his supporters had won the argument. They were preparing to retreat to the castle, to barricade the entrance and prepare for the Rebels' attack.

Katherine couldn't bring herself to care as she led

Matthew away. When they arrived at her aunt's house, he looked nauseous, so she left him sitting on her bed and went to fetch some water. She returned to find him bent over, clutching his stomach.

"Are you all r—?" she began, but before she could finish he had thrown up on the floor. She stayed still, watching him heave until there was nothing left to come up. She knew she should comfort him but couldn't bring herself to touch him. Eventually he sat back, looking exhausted. She passed him the water. He gulped it down gratefully, before collapsing back on the bed while she stooped to clear up the mess on the floor. By the time she had finished he was asleep.

He was curled in a ball, a pained expression on his face. She didn't know what to think. Matthew had been shot – the blood proved that. He'd died in her arms. Then suddenly he'd healed, but he thought they were in the Crimea. Katherine didn't even know where that was.

Now she had the chance to look at him more closely she could see that there were small changes in Matthew's appearance. He looked slightly older – there was a definition to Matthew's face that hadn't been there before, like he'd grown into his features. His hands were smoother and free of the calluses that always made Katherine shiver when they brushed against her skin. He looked *fragile* compared to earlier in the day and softer, like he'd spent his life indoors, not working with horses. His hair was shorter too and cut in an unfashionable hairstyle that she had never seen before. When he had spoken, his accent had been different. It was still Scottish, but seemed less thick, more relaxed and English.

They were all subtle changes, but they still made the hair on the back of her neck rise. She didn't know what they meant, but she knew that this wasn't her Matthew. It was something else. Something had taken his place, pretending to be him. The thought scared her.

She fled from the room in horror. She couldn't let herself think about what this meant for her Matthew. She couldn't think that he had died, not yet. But where was he? How had he just ... vanished? And how had *this thing* taken his place?

She went to one of the spare bedchambers, leaving the creature to sleep, and laid under the cold blankets stiffly, her mind running endlessly over the way she'd watched the life disappear from Matthew's eyes and then reappear in a horrifying, unnatural way. She lay awake for a long time, but eventually morning came and she knew she had to move. She had to go back to the thing that was lying in her bed. She felt more nauseous and terrified with every step she took towards the room. She pushed open the bedroom door slowly, not sure what to expect. The thing was still sleeping, so she placed the palm of her hand against its shoulder, shaking it. It opened its eyes and peered up at her, blinking.

"Kit?"

"My name is Miss Finchley." Her voice sounded hollow. The thing with Matthew's face looked hurt for a moment. Then it sat up, rubbed its eyes and pressed its fingers to its temples as if it had a headache. It was watching her carefully, and her cheeks hurt from keeping her feelings of repulsion off her face. Her stomach clenched in fear. The thing smiled at her hopefully, but she ignored it.

"Katherine…" it murmured in a voice that was so close to Matthew's she couldn't stand it.

"Don't call me that," she said fiercely. "I don't know what you are, but you aren't my Matthew. What are you?"

It didn't answer, just stared at her incomprehensibly. "I'm Matthew Galloway. I don't know what's happening."

"If you're here … where's my Matthew?"

It didn't reply, just looked at her. She knew what the look meant, though. He'd gone. Her Matthew wasn't coming back, and she was left with this thing that appeared to be him but wasn't. She turned and ran. The tears were streaming down her face. She dropped onto the bed in the guest bedchamber, barely able to stop herself screaming into the pillow.

> Intervention in time-landscape 1745 may not have had the desired effect

> Although there is still a subject allocation "MATTHEW", the progression of the relationship is now increasingly unlikely

CHAPTER 24

Katherine, I love the way you describe things you've made up in your head like they are facts. That isn't how it happened, at all. The actual truth:

K: Excuse me, DUDE, I know you are right in middle of a very important and delicate experiment, but I'm new here, and from now on I will take up all of your attention and you won't ever escape me, so get used to it! So, yeah, if I ever give you a chance to speak, could you show me how to requisition new chemicals, yo?

M: Wow. Did you even pause for breath then? Sure, I'll help you. I'm Matthew, a fool who doesn't know what he's letting himself in for.

K: Nice to know, I'll be sure to pester you almost incessantly for the rest of your life. Where's the best place to buy alcohol around here? I've only been here four hours, but I really need to get drunk!

M: .... um, what?

K: Never mind! So, requisition forms? That's an interesting cupboard. I can't wait to have sex in it!

M: .... what

K: So, why are you working here? I applied because some girl told me the cafeteria did great nachos, and it turns out she was right!

M: Uh ... REALLY?

K: Oh, and they funded my PhD. But, you know, mainly the nacho thing.

M: I've never had the nachos here, actually.

K: Come on, let's go and get some.

[Cut to a few months later, when I had got used to your ... Katherineness]

M: Hey, Katherine, I know you are weird and have no brain-to-mouth filter and think you are a teenager and everything, but somehow I find it oddly charming. I don't know why – maybe you've brainwashed me – but it's too late to do anything about it now! So, yeah. Drink?

K: We've been going out for, like, a year. What is wrong with you?

M: What?!

Carlisle, England, 1745

It was late afternoon before Katherine found the courage to face the thing again. It was staring blankly at the ceiling when she entered her bedroom. It turned to her, eyes brightening, and she couldn't help but freeze. She was surprised to see that its skin was red, dark with an unhealthy shininess like it had a fever. The room smelt strongly of vomit.

"Hello," it said, uncertain and a little afraid.

"Hello. Do you need anything? Any food or water?"

It hadn't eaten its breakfast. It shook its head. "Just… Can you tell me where I am?"

"You're in Carlisle. On the border of Scotland and England. We were in the cathedral, and you were shot. Then you weren't. That's all I know. What do you remember?"

"I remember being in the Crimea with my – my friend Katy when she was shot in a battle and died. Then everything went black and I woke up in a cathedral on the other side of the world, and a woman with Katy's face is treating me like a monster."

She couldn't even process what he was saying. She swallowed. "What do you think happened?"

After a long pause, the thing closed its eyes, frowning heavily as if in pain. Then it replied in a heavy tone. "I was hoping you'd know. It seems such a coincidence that someone who looks like me should be in Carlisle with someone who looks so much like my Katy. And surely we'd have run into each other before now? My family is from near Carlisle, just across the border."

"You look so similar to Matthew, like you are brothers. Twins! But even if you were twins, that wouldn't explain how you suddenly appeared. Do you think it was magic?"

The thing that wasn't her Matthew rubbed its head. "I don't understand why anyone would want to pull me across the world to replace a dying man."

"Maybe they were trying to be kind. Your Katy died; my Matthew died. They bring us together so we aren't alone?"

"It's possible. I'm not sure I'll thank them for it, though."

Katherine agreed. There was no possible way this man was a replacement for her Matthew. She didn't know what to say. "How are you feeling?"

"Bad. I was vomiting all morning and I have a terrible headache. I think I have a fever."

"Do you need anything? I could get a doctor?"

"No. Thank you. Hopefully it'll pass soon."

She nodded, and they were quiet again. After a moment, to break the silence, she said, "You told me you were in the Crimea?"

"I'm a journalist for *The Times*. I'm reporting on the war."

She gaped at him. "In the Crimea? I didn't know the Jacobites were attacking anywhere other than England."

"Jacobites? What have they got to do with it?"

"We are at war with them, like you said." She frowned. "That's why Matthew was shot, because the Rebels are attacking the city."

"I meant the war with the *Russians*."

Katherine stared at him, open-mouthed. She hadn't heard anything about that. "Are you sure? You aren't just confused, after the shock?"

He nodded decisively. "I'm sure. We've been at war with Russia for months now. I don't know how you haven't heard about this." After a moment, he asked, "Did you say the Jacobites are attacking England? *Again?* What does the king want *this time?* And what a time to choose, when England is at war with Russia? First the Scots refuse to help in the war, leaving England alone, and then they attack us? *Really?*"

"The *Russians*," she said, startled. She felt like they were each having a different conversation.

Slowly, he asked, "Katherine, what year is it?"

"The year of our Lord seventeen hundred, five and forty."

The thing – the man – stared at her in shock and then began to laugh, a weak sound that ended with him coughing. She watched in confused dismay, until he recovered enough to explain.

"Let us start from the beginning." He held out his hand. She shook it reluctantly.

"Hello, Katherine Finchley. My name is Matthew Galloway, and I come from the year eighteen fifty-four. I'm very pleased to meet you."

Crimea, Ukraine, 1854

Matthew leant against the wall of the outhouse, gasping for breath, his eyes closed. It was almost quiet inside the building, which provided a small haven in the middle of the battle. Katy scarcely noticed. She was still trying to reconcile the Matthew beside her with the one in her memories – to unite the two versions of him that she'd known.

"Tell me what you remember?" she asked eventually.

He considered her for a moment. "I was a servant in your house during the Jacobite rebellion. You were spying on me *again*. We helped to improve the city's defences, and when the Rebels attacked, the soldiers panicked and wanted to surrender. There was a vote, and an argument and I was shot. That's the last thing I remember."

"So you don't remember coming back?"

He stared at her, uncomprehendingly.

"After you died, you woke again, fully healed," Katy said slowly, remembering what had happened in Carlisle, all those years ago and in another lifetime. It was strange, remembering things from a century ago that hadn't happened to her. But the memories were all crystal clear and too vivid to be anything but real, even if she didn't understand how that was possible.

"What do you mean?" Matthew asked. "I woke up *healed*? How?"

"You – he, the other Matthew – said he came from the future. We decided you must have been brought back by a witch, but we were just guessing. Neither of us had any idea what could have happened. I still don't." She tried to think what else he'd said, and suddenly it clicked. "You came from now! I remember you saying you'd been reporting on a war against the Russians. That's *now*. It must be a battle that's *going to happen*."

"I travel through time," Matthew repeated. "At some point during this war, I go back into the past."

"Yes. You said that your ... that – I died. In the war. I *die*." She swallowed. She had watched Matthew mourn some other version of herself, and at the time it had been sad, in a surreal kind of way. But now she knew that he had been mourning her, *Katy*. She was going to die, and Matthew was going to be left all alone, until he went back to 1745, pulled to another person who had been left alone. "That's why you went back – because I lost my Matthew back then, and you lost me now."

Katy was going to die. Neither of them knew what to say for a moment.

"What else can you remember?" he asked. "We have to make sure it doesn't happen again. You have to remember. What else did he say?"

"I don't know!" she said. "It didn't mean anything to me at the time. I wasn't paying attention."

"You have to try, Katy. You're going to die, otherwise."

She growled, annoyed at herself. "I can't remember all of those details. Why can't you remember it happening? *I don't understand*."

"It hasn't happened to me yet. It's still in my future."

She paused for a moment. "Maybe it's a good thing you

can't remember that life," she admitted. "It didn't go well."

He looked at her, terror in his eyes. "How can it get any worse than this?"

"Trust me," she said. "It can." She took a deep breath and then asked, "Does all this mean you're forgiving me now?"

"I suppose it does." He didn't seem pleased about it.

"I know it doesn't make much difference at this point, but I'm sorry. I regretted my decision to spy on you almost as soon as I met you, and I hated myself more and more every day. I'm sorry I made you trust me when I was lying to you." She moved her foot back and forth, digging an arc into the dusty soil. "I did – I do – like you, Matthew."

"I thought that was a trick too – a way to get more information out of me."

"No! I wouldn't… That wasn't what I was doing at all."

"Well, I get that now," he said grumpily. "The fact that we were … friends in another life makes that clear. There is obviously something between us. We are clearly meant to be together."

She paused, awestruck by what he was saying. She couldn't process it, but she knew it to be true. "Good," she said in relief. "I definitely wouldn't want you to think that I was pretending to like you, because I really do – like you. More than I should."

"Are you only saying that because you're afraid you're going to die?"

She regarded him carefully. "Just because this would have taken longer, that doesn't make it any less true. I love you." She blinked. She hadn't meant to say that.

Matthew froze. His lips parted slightly, and for a moment she thought he was angry, but then he broke into a radiant smile. Without another word, he pulled her towards him, gentle and cautious. She let him, watching him with wonder.

He leant close to her, his eyes dropping to her lips. "I love you too." She could feel his breath on her face. "I forgive you."

She used his lapels to pull him down so she could kiss him squarely on the mouth.

> First objective achieved in time-landscape 1854

"Finally," he groaned, tangling his fingers in her hair. "I keep remembering what your mouth tastes like and I've been desperate to see if it's the same now."

"Is it?" She pulled his lip into her mouth. He let out a guttural sound deep in his chest, and she swallowed the noise, making him melt into her. She shuddered, overwhelmed with the sensation.

They kissed heatedly – not at all like a soft first kiss, but greedily, as if they knew that they might not get another chance. Katy lost herself against him as she re-learned what would pull a groan from his throat and what made him smile. She ran her tongue across the ridge at the top of his mouth, making him grin against her and break the kiss.

He said in a deep, raw voice, "It's exactly the same," and for a second she didn't know what he was talking about. "Kissing you."

"You too," she replied weakly, running a finger along the

wing of his collarbone. He curled his hand tightly around her fingers, like he was scared she would leave him.

"I'm going to marry you," Matthew said. "When this war is over, we're going to get married. We're going to buy a farm in the countryside and start a family and never have to do anything like this again."

"You said that before," she joked. "A century ago."

"It's still what I want more than anything. I'm going to marry you one day."

"Is that your proposal?" she replied, teasing him to hide the happiness that was twisting in her stomach. "So romantic."

He began to reply, but she muffled the words with a warm, deep kiss.

"Katherine, will you marry me?" he asked when she eventually let him pull away, his voice softly serious, the words pressed against her cheek.

"I will," she agreed, and pulled him back into the kiss.

CHAPTER 25

Wow, Matthew, you make me sound insane. Regardless, I think everyone would conclude from this that I am awesome and you are a little bit oblivious. You seriously didn't notice when we started going out? What did you think was happening every time we went out for dinner or to the zoo or ice skating? You came to a wedding as my plus one! Twice! Dude. I can't believe I actually tricked you into dating me, that's a little pathetic!

Folios/v7/Time-landscape-2019/MS-160

CENTRAL SCIENCE LABORATORIES,
WEST MIDLANDS, ENGLAND, 2039

The video they'd found on the memory card from 2019 ended, leaving Matthew's words reverberating through Kate's mind: *I love you. In every life. I love you. I love you so much.* She touched her face and found it wet and tearstained. She'd forgotten for a moment that they were watching a video. It had felt like they were about to be killed themselves – that it was their blood covering the walls.

"Matt, can we get out of here? I can't be in this room. Please."

He wrapped an arm around her shoulders. "Let's go back to your office," he said against her hair.

She nodded, searching for his hand and holding it like a lifeline.

Once inside Katherine's office, they sat down against the wall, trying to decide what to do next. Kate couldn't stop herself from listening for the sound of footfalls, expecting guards to chase them even now.

When she tried to speak, her voice came out in a croak. She cleared her throat. "Katherine and Matthew destroyed the bacteria. They destroyed it and stopped it being used in the war. They saved the world!"

"Yes," Matt said. "They did it. It's over."

Kate sighed. He didn't understand. "Matt, it's not over. Nowhere near. They've had twenty years to make it again."

"*Shit!* That's why this building has been in quarantine all this time. So that CSL could work on it in secret."

"We need to destroy it," she said, reluctant and terrified. "Again."

> Subjects in time-landscape 2039 will be in danger if their actions continue

> Intervention recommended

>> Intervention denied

Carlisle, England, 1745

"How can you be from the future? That's not possible. It's witchcraft, and witchcraft isn't *real*," Katherine said. She was exasperated. They had been having the same conversation since Matthew had revealed that he was from the year 1854.

"I think we have evidence that it must be," he replied, quietly.

"Why should I believe you, anyway?" she said, suddenly angry. "You could be making all this up."

"I'm not, Katy."

Katherine flinched. "Don't call me that."

He grimaced. "Sorry."

She picked at a callus on the palm of her hand.

"I promise I'm not lying to you," Matthew said. "I'm from the future." She didn't look up, and he carried on talking, voice slow, almost inaudible. "The English and French armies have been fighting the Russians. When I left, we had won the first battle. Before a rocket killed all of our leaders, we were probably going to win the war. I can't see how that is going to happen now."

"Rocket?" she asked in a soft, unsure voice.

"That's what was happening when I came here. The first battle was over, and we had won. We were in the encampment. The commanders were having a meeting to discuss their next tactics, and the Russians had managed to shoot a rocket from the river, into their tent. I saw it happen. I tried to help, to rescue them, but I was too late.

Their tent caught fire, and everyone died." As he rubbed his hand through his hair, he looked like a real person mourning his friends, not the monster she'd imagined he was at all.

"All of the generals died," Matthew continued. "My friend George was killed. We – we don't have anyone else to lead the army. There is no one in the English or French armies who has been trained – no one who has experience in war. Everyone in charge was in that tent, and now they are all dead, because I was too slow. I couldn't save them, or Katy."

"Katy? What happened to her?"

"She had died earlier that day. In the battle by the river. She was shot. I couldn't save her either."

They were both silent.

"I'm sorry," she said. "I'm sorry that you had to live through that."

He nodded.

She ran through the situation in her head, trying to rationalize it. "So, someone, some … witch? Some witch noticed that in seventeen forty-five a man called Matthew Galloway dies. They find an ancestor of his in eighteen fifty-four who has just lost his … friend and who looks startlingly similar and has the same name. An extraordinary coincidence. They decide the best thing to do is to bring them together, ignoring the laws of the universe, logic and morality."

"It is impossible. How, why, and who did it."

"Don't forget 'when'. She – or he – could be from eighteen

fifty-four or seventeen forty-five or even the year nineteen hundred for all we know, however far off that sounds."

"If it is possible ... just *if* ... then I'd like to know why they *care*. What's so special about us that they can mess with magic like that?" Matthew tried to stand up then, but he was dizzy and fell back onto the bed. "Help me up, please. I need to move around. I feel very unwell."

"Perhaps you should rest."

He insisted that he would stand, so she helped him up. The redness extended all over his skin, and he felt hot, dangerously so, when she ran a hand over his arm.

His hair was standing on end from his nervous messing and she had to stifle the impulse to flatten it down. This wasn't her Matthew. She might know him in another life, but for now he was practically a stranger. She didn't know anything about how he lived or what kind of a person he was. The things she loved about her Matthew could be completely different in this man. Even worse, what if she wasn't the same Katherine he knew? What if he didn't like this version of her?

Matthew pulled away from her to support himself on her dressing table. He tugged at his shirt.

"My skin itches," he explained. "My clothes are scratchy."

Katherine tried to hide her concern by making a joke. "Are you a delicate flower?"

Unexpectedly, his face dropped and a crease spread across his forehead. He almost looked like he was going to cry.

Katherine pressed a hand to his shoulder. "Are you all right?"

"Yes, sorry. I just… I miss Katy."

Katherine dropped her hand awkwardly. "I'm sorry for your loss," she said eventually.

He nodded.

"Does it make it worse…? That I look like her, I mean."

He took a long time to reply. "No. I think it helps. It makes me think of the happy memories, rather than the sad ones. She was wonderful, and she made me laugh so much. She wouldn't want me to cry over her. She'd probably tease me incessantly about it if she were here."

"I can tease you incessantly about it if it helps."

The resultant smile was watery, but it was a start. "Perhaps later. I'm not sure I could handle that at the moment."

> Subject allocation "MATTHEW" in time-landscape 1745 has
  still not recovered from the transfer

CHAPTER 26

Katherine, you didn't trick me so much as ... actively instigate a relationship I wasn't ready for. It all worked out well in the end, though, so it's fine. I forgive your slight sexual harassment. Plus, it's not like you proposed to me or anything! I still did that part right.

Although, you know, thinking about it, I'm not sure I really remember how we got engaged... I remember the next morning and the ring we chose. Katherine, please say you didn't torture me until I proposed or do something so equally terrible that I erased it from my memory?

Folios/v7/Time-landscape-2019/MS-160

Crimea, Ukraine, 1854

"You told me that the rebellion of seventeen forty-five was successful," Katy said suddenly. They were sitting leaning against each other inside the outhouse. "The second Matthew said that the uprising ended in a Jacobite victory.

In his … world, plane of existence – whatever you want to call it – Carlisle surrendered to the Rebels and they marched on through England. Charlie won the right to rule Scotland and so it had been an independent country since seventeen forty-five, but you said that it was awful. There was a huge famine and half the population of Scotland died because there wasn't any work and hardly any food. You – he – said that their king kept trying to invade England. He refused to support England in this war."

"But … that's not what happened. I know my history. That's definitely *not* what happened. The Jacobites were defeated."

Katy shrugged. "That's just what the second Matthew said. I don't think I've remembered it wrong."

"So he is from a place where the Jacobites won? Some kind of different version of history?"

"I suppose."

"But, Katy!" He sounded so relieved that she looked up in surprise. "That means that it doesn't happen! If Matthew Two wasn't from this world, then none of the things that happened to him will happen to me, and I won't get sent back. You won't die!"

"Matthew, the Scots being independent probably won't make a difference to how this war goes."

"How do you know that? It might make all the difference in the world! If the Scots weren't fighting with us, we'd have fewer soldiers. They have a truce with France, so France might not have fought either. And that man who saved us at the river was a Highlander. If he hadn't been there, we would have been killed! Already things have happened in new ways because of that one difference."

"What are you saying? That *all of history* changed because of a single uprising? That if one little siege – the siege of Carlisle over a hundred years ago – had gone differently, it would have changed the outcome of everything that came after?" She stopped talking. She needed to think. Matthew began to speak but she shushed him quiet. "It was *you – us,*" she said eventually. "We changed the outcome of the siege. Durand might have surrendered if we hadn't been there. You made him promise that he wouldn't."

"*No.* That … we can't… This isn't *real.* You can't possibly be suggesting that us just *being there* changed the whole course of history!"

"I think it might have," she admitted, "although it sounds awfully big-headed. But it makes sense. Maybe we weren't in Carlisle in this other world, so Durand surrendered straight away and the Rebels carried on their invasion of England. Maybe they managed to get to London before the English army had a chance to get there to stop them."

"So, in our world we delayed the surrender of Carlisle long enough for the army to be mustered to defend England?" he asked, a little sceptically. "So that meant the Jacobites didn't win and Scotland remained a part of Britain."

"Exactly."

He threw his hands up in exaggerated disbelief. "But that's *ridiculous.* We aren't… We didn't *know* any of that would happen. It was all just chance!"

"I wish I had a better explanation, but I don't."

He was silent, resigned.

Katy tried to remember what else Matthew had told her in 1745. "You told me about the war – this war – and how it went," she remembered. "Something was happening when you were sent back. Something big." She bit her nail, deep in thought.

"Can't you remember what it was?" Matthew stroked the hair off her face. His touch was distracting.

"I can't remember," she said, frustrated. She hadn't taken too much notice of what Matthew had been saying at the time. She hadn't known it would be so important. "Does it matter? We're living in a different version of the war. It might not even happen here. Those things happened in a world in which the Jacobites won the uprising. Everything might be different this time."

"But there's a chance it might happen. Lots of things are still the same. Any information about where even a single Russian rocket might drop is better than nothing."

"A *rocket*," she said. "There was a rocket! All of the generals were killed at once. You tried to stop it and couldn't."

Matthew drew in a horrified breath. *"All of them? All of the generals were killed? There would be no one to command the soldiers or plan the tactics. The army would have no chance of fighting and winning. Are you sure? How did it happen?"*

Katy paused, trying to pull the memory from the back of her mind. It had been in a different life, and she had been so scared and upset that she hadn't been focused on what

Matthew was telling her. She had been in the middle of a siege and had just lost the man she loved – she hadn't cared about the details of a war a century in the future. It *hadn't been important*.

She closed her eyes and tried to picture 1745. They had been in her bedchamber. Matthew had been toying with a slice of bread. She could see him picking crumbs off the crust. But what had he said? What had happened?

She opened her eyes suddenly and stared in horror at Matthew. "They were in a meeting. In a tent. A rocket hit it. It caught fire. Everyone was killed before they could escape. All of the commanders – English and French."

"Yes, but *when*? When does it happen?" Matthew sounded desperate.

"I don't know, Matthew. You didn't tell me anything like that back then. You said I'd died – shot during a battle by the river. Then later a rocket hit a tent full of the commanders." Katy knew she sounded irritated, but she couldn't help it. "The Russians managed to get close enough to the tent by going up the river."

"A river? But … that's where we are now. You didn't die, not here. It must be a different river. A different battle."

They were silent.

"The Highlander," Matthew said suddenly. "He saved us by the river. You would have been shot if he hadn't been there."

"So?"

"In that other time, that other version of this war, the Highlander wasn't there to save you. Because the Scottish hadn't fought alongside the English."

"He saved my life," Katy said. "I would have *died*."

"But you didn't! You're alive. And that means this rocket – the rocket that killed the commanders – is coming today. It's going to happen *now*!"

```
> ALERT: Subjects in time-landscape 1854 in danger

> Intervention recommended

  >> Intervention denied
```

CENTRAL SCIENCE LABORATORIES, WEST MIDLANDS, ENGLAND, 2039

Kate and Matt searched through half a dozen identical, desolate labs trying to find any trace of the bacteria before they reached the basement. It was cold – too cold for a building that should have been without power for decades. Kate pressed a hand against the wall. She felt the hum of a generator and knew they were in the right place.

"Look," Matt whispered. "The floor. It's clean."

Almost every other surface in the building had been covered in dust. Wherever they went they'd left a trail of footprints in the grime like tracks in the snow. But here, in the depths of the basement, the floor was immaculate. There was even a broom propped against the wall.

"Someone comes here. A lot." Kate swallowed, shining her torch down the pitch-black corridor. It illuminated a bolted metal door, with a sign that read BACTERIAL STORAGE ZONE. DO NOT ENTER.

"Oh, no. No, no, *no*," she muttered. "They really do have it. They can't, they wouldn't…"

"Let's find out," Matt said, catching her shoulder and rubbing a thumb into the muscle. "We need to find out."

"I can't," she said desperately. "This isn't *happening*. This was supposed to have ended twenty years ago."

"Kate, it is happening. We need to go in."

She nodded. They moved towards the door.

"The freezer is still running," Kate said. "They've kept it going all this time."

Matt turned the large handle and the seal of the door pulled free with a long, slow hiss. Lights came on inside, flickering weakly on and off before settling into a dull glow that revealed rows of shelves that were packed tightly with vials, each one neatly labelled with a bright-yellow sticker stamped with a skull and crossbones.

"*Shit.*"

"How much do they *need*?" Matt asked, voice hovering somewhere between horrified and awestruck.

"They could destroy the entire planet in a *day* with this stuff. If the contents of this room got released…" Kate stepped into the freezer and carefully picked up a vial. It was labelled with an expiry date and a stock number as if it was any normal lab chemical instead of a deadly weapon.

"Kate, look," Matt called. He was holding a blue folder that had been dangling from a piece of string attached to the wall by the doorway. "It's a logbook of the stock. Look."

She ran her eyes down the page. Columns, filled with dense handwriting, listed the quantity and stock number of vials that had been taken out. The dates showed that almost every week for the last few months at least five vials had been checked out. The last log was only two days ago, when fifteen vials had been removed.

"They're taking it somewhere. This isn't over."

A sound echoed down the hallway that led to the freezer. Footsteps.

CHAPTER 27

Oh, look, Matthew, we've run out of notepaper. I guess this is the end of _that_ discussion! Can you remember to buy bread, please?

K

Folios/v7/Time-landscape-2019/MS-160

Carlisle, England, 1745

Matthew was lying back on the bed. He looked very unwell, but Katherine still pushed him to tell her everything he could remember being taught about the 1745 uprising in his version of history.

"I know that when the Rebels marched to England the army wasn't ready to defend London. The government panicked and signed agreements allowing Prince Charles to rule over Scotland just to stop an invasion. His descendants carried on his rule – causing as much trouble as possible. The current king keeps trying to conquer England, when even Bonnie Prince Charlie was content with just Scotland. He refused to help fight the Russians, so we're struggling to manage with the men we have. I know I should support my country, but, really, the king is a spoilt brat. The Scottish kings have ruined Scotland in lots of ways, through carelessness and greed. There was an awful famine, for years and years. Nearly half of the population died. I think that for ordinary people like me, it would've been far better for Scotland to have stayed as part of the British Empire."

"So you are saying the English need more time – here and now – because they are not ready to fight back against the Rebels?"

"I suppose. I don't know. I'm sorry. I wish I could give you every detail of the Scottish rebellion, but I can't remember exactly what happened. I suppose we'll just have to wait and see what happens now."

"Do we, though? I mean, if we know that the English need more time to gather troops, then perhaps we can make sure the Rebels' march is delayed. We've already managed to stop Durand surrendering, with my Matthew's death. If we can stop the soldiers leaving Carlisle for just a little longer, we can make sure the English have more time to gather their army and defend England."

"How do you suggest that we stop a whole city surrendering if it wants to, and for long enough that it makes a difference?"

She grinned at him. "Well, you could sacrifice yourself again? That might work."

"Perhaps not."

"If you are feeling up to it, shall we go and see what's happening at the castle? We can improvise."

"Matthew? What would you want for your Katy?" Katherine asked, as they walked to the castle. "I mean, if you died, what would you want her to do? Would you want her to find someone else?"

He looked at her searchingly. "Were you *with* Matthew here, in this time? Were you together?"

She looked back, surprised. "Yes, of course. Weren't you with Katy?"

"No. I – I think we would have been, eventually. But she'd betrayed me, and it took me a long time to forgive her."

"What did she do?"

"She spied on me, for the army. To make sure I wasn't reporting the wrong things."

"Oh." Quietly, she admitted, "I spied on my Matthew too. I thought he was a Rebel and I followed him to make sure he wasn't revealing secrets. It's the only reason we really became friends, I suppose. I wouldn't have taken the time to get to know a servant otherwise."

"Was he revealing secrets?"

"No. I was wrong. He forgave me."

Matthew didn't reply, and they walked on in silence. Katherine thought about the similarities and differences between their lives until Matthew surprised her by answering her original question.

"Yes, I think I would have wanted you to move on after I'd died. I'd have wanted someone to take care of Katy after I was gone, if she hadn't died. I'd want that, rather than have her go back to being a servant, alone but loyal to me. I think your Matthew would have wanted the same. I know it's different for you because you have a family and a home, but I still think I would want you to have a happy life. It doesn't do any good to mourn for someone who is gone. They don't care. Their story has finished."

"Except in this situation, where I can't seem get rid of you," she teased. She wasn't good at serious discussions and she didn't know how to tell him what his words meant to her. She felt guilty for so quickly replacing her Matthew, even if it was with a different version of him. That actually made it seem worse somehow, like their past together meant so little that just a man with the same face as him was enough to please her. But she couldn't find the words to explain that, so instead she made jokes.

Matthew seemed to understand because he didn't laugh. Instead he said, "I would never have left my Katy if I could have found a way to stay. I promise you. If this had been the other way around - if I had died and your Matthew had replaced me in my world - I would have wanted my Katy to love him and live with him. I think your Matthew would want the same for you."

"Thank you," was all she could say.

He turned away and they began to walk again. After several steps, he added in a light, casual voice that didn't fool her at all, "What about you? Would you want your Matthew to find someone else if you died?"

Katherine thought about it and found to her dismay that she had very strong feelings on the subject. She wasn't as good a person as Matthew. She wanted him all to herself. Luckily, the circumstances seemed to oblige.

"I'd be far too selfish to let you find happiness with

someone else," she eventually replied, cheerfully. "Sorry, but you have no choice in the matter. You're only allowed to be with me."

He laughed, quietly. "Well, I think I can find it in myself to forgive you for that."

"As for finding happiness with a different *version* of myself – if that is what is going on," Katherine continued, "well, I have one condition."

"Ah. And what is that?"

"She isn't allowed to have better hair than me. I'd want you to always look at her stupid slapdash hairstyle and remember mine with longing. I'd be content with that." Matthew peered at her hair speculatively. "Bear in mind that I currently have no maid to set my hair," she added hastily.

"I see. I shall consider your condition most carefully."

"So?"

"I think the diplomatic response is silence. I can't offer an opinion without offending *some* version of you. Knowing my luck, ten different Katherines would immediately appear out of thin air and demand that I rank their hairstyles in order of preference."

"That is, of course, the correct response. I thank you for the compliment."

"I never said a word, and anyone who says otherwise is lying most terribly," he intoned, but his eyes were twinkling.

She leant against his side, biting at her lip to hold back a smile. Matthew immediately stopped walking, swaying slightly as if he couldn't handle the extra weight. She stood upright again. She had been trying not to pester him about his illness, but he definitely looked worse.

"I'm not sure how I didn't notice anything before," he said. "It's completely obvious that we aren't in the nineteenth century. Look how *rural* everything is."

He obviously didn't want to discuss how he was feeling.

"Well!" she objected, mildly insulted on behalf of Carlisle. "You've hardly caught us at our best. Things are usually a lot tidier – fewer barricades and piles of weapons, that kind of thing. Besides, I thought you said you were living in a tent in this *glorious future* of yours?"

"I didn't mean it as an insult. I'm actually quite impressed – given how much time has elapsed – how similar life is. Mind you, if you look at it the other way, it is a little discouraging how little progress has been made in a whole century."

"You mean there aren't any horseless carriages yet?" She raised an eyebrow, and he ducked his head, grinning.

"Hah! No, I doubt there will ever be a way to stop using horses for travel."

"I guess flight is also out of the question?"

"Oh, no," he said. "Have I not shown you my wings?"

Her mouth dropped open and then she caught sight of his face. "*Matthew!* That isn't funny!"

"It really is. You believed that so easily!"

"Well," she blustered, "a hundred years is a long time. What do you think life is going to be like in *nineteen* fifty-four? If someone told you there would be a way to fly then, would you believe them?"

"Of *course* not! Don't be ridiculous."

She sniffed, unconvinced. "I'm sure that's true, dear."

He looked startled at the pet name, and she mentally winced. She'd relaxed with this Matthew far too quickly. She shouldn't be acting like this when they had only met yesterday. There was an awkward silence.

CENTRAL SCIENCE LABORATORIES, WEST MIDLANDS, ENGLAND, 2039

The footsteps were dulled and still some distance away, but getting quickly closer.

"Hurry," Kate said, in a violent whisper.

Matt nodded. After tugging the folder free from the wall, he followed her out of the freezer. She shoved the door shut behind him, not bothering to push down the bolt.

"They'll have seen the entrance," Matt said, with dawning horror. "The broken glass. They know someone's here."

"Come on." She looked down the corridor. There was no sign of anyone yet, but the footsteps were getting louder. "This way."

She ran in the opposite direction, further into the basement, turning corners at random through the endless series of corridors. She tried to tread softly, quietly. Matt followed behind her, his breath warm against her neck.

Their torchlight made looming distortions of the hallway, sending Kate into skitters of panic. She held onto the hope that there was another exit, inwardly pleading that they weren't running into a dead end.

She clutched the vial tightly, to keep it from slipping in her grasp. There was another heavy metal door up ahead. It was padlocked. She thought it was the only exit, but then she saw the turn in the corridor and spotted, with shuddering relief, the steps leading upwards.

She took them two at a time. The door at the top was locked. She turned back, watching the hall behind Matt disappear into darkness as he reached her, torchlight shuddering across the walls.

"Locked," she said, panting.

He didn't hesitate, but leant into the door and hit it with his shoulder. It didn't give as the door to Matthew's office had, but screeched and held firm. She looked down the steps into the blackness of the basement and saw the growing light of a torch beam.

"They're coming. Try again."

Matt rammed the door a second time, letting out a low gasp of pain. This time it gave, and he fell through the doorway, nearly tripping. Kate caught him.

"Come on," she hissed, and then they were running again, down another long corridor and the footsteps behind them were finally, *finally*, receding into silence.

Matt paused to get his bearings, and then carried on. Kate followed him, too relieved at their escape to pay attention to where he was taking them.

Then they were in the foyer, skidding to a halt with a crunch of shattered glass, and looking straight into the headlights of a car parked outside the door. Neither of them moved. When there was no shouting or gunshots, Kate made herself walk towards the car.

"It's empty," she said in relief. "There's no one here."

"It belongs to that security guard, I guess. He must be alone," Matt said, stepping through the empty door frame and heading towards the car. "Come on."

Matt pulled open the car door and slid into the driver's seat. Kate stared open-mouthed at his audacity. This was a military vehicle! Then he jerked his head, impatiently. She hurried forward, climbing into the car. He turned the key in the ignition, reversing just as their pursuer appeared in the foyer, blinded by the headlights.

The man, dressed in neat military uniform, pulled a gun from his holster. Gunshots followed the car as they drove towards the open gates, and there was a loud ping as a bullet hit the boot, but they turned onto the main road and sped away.

Matt let out a huge sigh and Kate couldn't help but whoop in relief.

"I really hope we don't get pulled over," Matt said nervously.

"Yeah, this is a military vehicle. We'd get into a lot of trouble for stealing it."

"Not just that. I don't actually have my licence yet."

Kate didn't stop laughing until they were on the motorway and tears were streaming down her face, and then she wasn't sure if she was in fits of laughter or hysterics.

CHAPTER 28

Folios/v7/Time-landscape-2019/MS-161

NOTTINGHAM, ENGLAND, 2039

They were nearly back at the university before either of them spoke again. Kate kept staring down at the vial that was still tightly clasped in her fist. She carefully released her grip, putting it in the cup holder.

"How are we going to reveal this? What if they stop us, like they did last time?"

Matt had been staring fixedly at the road, but he risked darting a glance at her. His hands had remained firmly at the ten and two positions for the entire journey. She'd never seen anyone use an indicator with such determined terror before. He shrugged, and then winced when it jolted his shoulder, injured from ramming the door.

"Last time we didn't know how seriously they would take it," he said. "We can be more careful now, and this time we've got Tom to help."

"Excepting that this time we've stolen a military vehicle and probably have a whole army squadron after us. And they are going to be ready this time. They've had twenty years to prepare for another leak."

He paused. "We'll go to Scotland," he decided abruptly. "We can't trust anyone here. Wherever we go they'll find us, but we have a better chance if we are out of the country. They'll try to kill us to keep this a secret, but we don't want to make it easy for them."

Kate nodded, tense. "I'm scared," she admitted, quietly. "I don't want to die for this, not again." Again? What was she saying? It wasn't them who had died twenty years ago. It was Katherine and Matthew.

Matt hadn't noticed her slip-up. "Me neither," he said. "But I don't regret this – even if we are going to die – because it led me to you."

She stared at him, wide-eyed. "Nor me. I can't imagine my life without you, Matt. You are ... everything."

"I love you," he said in an undertone and actually released a hand from the wheel to take hers, pressing the words into her palm with a kiss.

"I love you too," she replied, her breath catching in her throat. She realized then that she always had. She couldn't remember falling in love with Matt. She hadn't had the butterflies in the stomach, the giddy absorption of falling in love. It hadn't been like that. She'd just seen him, and suddenly it had all clicked into place.

She'd always been in love with him, and had been quietly, patiently, waiting for him to turn up. Perhaps once there had been a time when she wasn't tied to him with every molecule of her being, but it was so long ago it was impossible to remember.

Carlisle, England, 1745

The castle was heavily guarded. Katherine had to talk their way inside using a degree of slyness that surprised even her. She made up an excuse for why they hadn't joined the defence with everyone else the day before, saying that Matthew had been injured and hadn't been well enough to re-join the fight. Once the soldier had recognized him as the man who'd been shot, they were allowed in and taken to see Durand, who wanted to meet him. The soldier kept giving Matthew sideways looks, as though he couldn't believe his eyes. Most of the crowd from the cathedral had been too far away to see Matthew's miraculous recovery, but clearly word had spread among the soldiers.

Durand, too, looked shocked. "But your injuries..." he stammered.

"I'm quite all right," Matthew replied. "It looked much worse than it was. It was just a flesh wound. I've only got a slight fever. It's nothing to worry about. We came here to tell you that you were right to hold out. The city and the castle can still give a good fight to the Rebels."

"Thank you for your support, although I don't know how much longer it will be of any value," Durand admitted. "The city is determined to surrender, and more and more of my garrison think we should join them."

"But I heard that the English army isn't prepared for an attack," Katherine interjected.

"It's true that the army hasn't arrived from the continent yet, Ma'am," he conceded, smiling weakly.

"So surely the best thing to help England is to delay the Jacobites and make sure the English army has enough time to prepare," Katherine said. "Even if you eventually surrender, the longer we hold the Rebels here, the more likely the army is to win any subsequent battles."

Durand nodded thoughtfully. "That's a good point, Ma'am. I'll take it into consideration. I don't believe the consequences would be hugely negative if I were to think for a few more days before coming to a decision over whether to surrender to the Rebels or not."

Katherine sighed. "Thank you, Sir. I know you're much better informed than us, so I appreciate you taking the time to consider my advice."

Durand held out his hand to Matthew. "I am glad to see your injuries are not as bad as I expected." Durand still looked dazed, as though he couldn't believe what he was seeing. "And thank you again for your support. Will you be staying in the castle?"

Katherine spoke once again, seeing how exhausted Matthew looked. "Mr Galloway is still a little weak, Sir. He needs a proper night's rest, so we will return home."

Durand nodded again and turned away with a final goodbye.

The minute Katherine and Matthew were outside the castle, Matthew vomited into the gutter. He rested, gasping for air, eyes closed tightly against the light. She stroked his hair back from his forehead, testing how hot his skin was. It practically burnt.

It was only when they were walking back to the

house with Matthew leaning heavily on her arm that she noticed the clumps of hair twisted around her fingers. It took her a moment to realize they were Matthew's. She looked at him, his eyes half closed as he focused all his effort on walking, and back at the hair, a thick mass of lifeless brown twisted against her skin. She swallowed, and quickly pulled the hair off her fingers and then threw it away. What kind of sickness did he have? Why was his hair falling out like that?

> ALERT: Subject allocation "MATTHEW" in time-landscape 1745 in critical condition

> Effects of radiation were not considered. Subject may not be able to survive the transfer between space threads

> Similar interventions not recommended in other time-landscapes

> Advice requested

> … waiting …

> … waiting …

> Advice not received

> Surveillance will continue without intervention until input is given

CHAPTER 29

Three missed calls from "That Man Why Won't He Leave"

New text from "That Man Why Won't He Leave":

> **How did we get engaged? Please just tell me. It can't possibly be worse than what I am imagining right now. M x**

Folios/v7/Time-landscape-2019/MS-162

UNIVERSITY OF NOTTINGHAM CAMPUS, ENGLAND, 2039

They drove the whole way back to campus in nervous fright, certain that the next set of headlights that flashed past would be accompanied by sirens. At two in the morning they arrived at a lay-by just outside the campus, where they had arranged to meet Tom. He was waiting for them. They quickly jumped into his less conspicuous Mini.

To Kate's relief, Tom drove a lot faster than Matt, and they were soon speeding down the motorway at an almost dangerous velocity. Kate ignored the concerning creaks the old car made and caught Tom up on what had happened.

"So we want you to help us release the videos we found on my – I mean, Katherine's phone and set up a press conference to show people what the government has been doing, and the weapon stock they've got ready to use," she finished. "We've got a sample of the bacteria to prove it's real."

Matt turned to look at her. He had been staring fixedly

out of the window, watching for police cars. "Actually, Kate, we should hide the vial. We don't want it to get confiscated when we cross the border."

"Just hide it in your pocket," Kate said. "They aren't going to do a full body search."

Matt nodded.

They drove until morning, when the sun was a thin red streak rising into the sky. Kate spent the journey worrying: not about the bacteria, but about her and Matt. She felt sure she going crazy. She still couldn't find a rational explanation for what was happening to them. Since leaving CSL, they had been talking as if it had been them caught and killed twenty years ago – but that was impossible.

They were getting close to Scotland. The latest sign had said that the next turn-off was for the international border, as well as listing the nearest cities.

Kate stared at it. "Wait!" she shouted, looking back at the sign as they passed it with growing certainty.

"What?" Tom asked.

Matt just sighed, like he already knew what she wanted to do.

"Can we stop for a bit? In Carlisle?" she asked.

It had all become clear in her mind. She had to see Carlisle. She needed to find out whether all the things she remembered were real or not. She'd never been there, but somehow she had all these – *memories?* – of the city. If she could prove they weren't real, that they didn't match up with the true city, then it must be all in her head and she was crazy.

However, if the Carlisle she remembered was accurate, then she'd have to finally pluck up the courage to talk to Matt about it, once and for all.

"But we're only a couple of hours from home?" Tom said.

"I know. I'm just… I'm really hungry. Please?"

"We can just go to a drivethrou—"

"I'm hungry too," Matt interrupted. "We've been up for almost twenty-four hours. I need a break."

"What's going on? Guys! We can't just *stop* for *breakfast.*"

"Please, I need to!" Kate said, panicky, unable to explain herself, but knowing that they needed to stop.

"Just do it, Tom!" Matt shouted.

Tom muttered his disapproval, but took the turn-off.

Kate tried to breathe around the panic rising in her chest. Everything was going to make sense when they got to Carlisle: she knew it. She would work the rest of it out there. She had to, because she couldn't keep going if she didn't make sense of what was happening in her head.

Carlisle, England, 1745

"How do you feel?" Katherine asked when Matthew finally woke up after almost twelve hours of sleep.

"Dizzy. My chest hurts." He struggled to sit up. He was in her bed again. She'd spent the night in the armchair, watching him.

"What do you think is wrong? I've never seen a disease like this before. Is it something they have in the future?"

she asked, sitting beside him on the bed and pressing the wetted cloth against his hot skin.

"No. I don't know what this is. I wasn't ill before I came here."

Katherine winced at the blistering ulcers covering his body. She wondered if he had smallpox, but it didn't look right. Perhaps she should get a poultice to put on him? "Do you want me to get the doctor?"

"I'll be all right," he said. "Trust me. This is nothing eighteenth-century doctors can help me with. They probably still believe in humours."

"Of course they believe in humours – they're doctors!"

He somehow found the energy to give her an indignant lecture. "Humours don't exist. Treating people based on a mythical explanation like humours usually does more harm than good. Bloodletting is barbaric!"

She frowned. "Are you trying to fool me again? Bloodletting helps people. My grandmother would have died a lot sooner if she hadn't been bled once a day."

"Bloodletting wouldn't have harmed your grandmother as long as it wasn't done too much, but it didn't help her in any way. There are no such things as humours."

She was quiet, trying to take that in. She'd never even questioned the existence of humours. They were an explanation of the world that made sense. What else did she think she knew that was completely wrong?

CHAPTER 30

New text from "Katherine":

> So … there may have been a little plotting involved in our engagement. Nothing particularly harmful, I promise. You like being married to me, right? So it all worked out perfectly in the end! Can we stop talking about this now?

Folios/v7/Time-landscape-2019/MS-163

CARLISLE, ENGLAND, 2039

The moment they arrived in Carlisle, Kate knew she had been there before. It was larger and more sprawling than she remembered, but there were still traces of the Carlisle she knew in the old buildings that had survived the years since she'd last been here in 1745. The town square had a department store, a pharmacy and a cafe instead of the dressmaker's and greengrocer's and butcher's of her memories, but the cathedral was still there, ancient and immovable as always.

"Can we – can we just drive past the castle?" she asked, a little desperately.

"This is *crazy*," Tom said. "Someone could find us any minute. What are you doing?"

"Please, Tom," she said. "It's important. We'll be quick – I promise."

"You have ten minutes. Then we have to leave," he ordered.

She nodded her agreement. Matt was still watching her,

worried, and she knew that he was experiencing the same sense of déjà vu that she was.

It was the castle that had changed the most. The moat was gone and instead neat lawns bordered the crumbling walls, and a busy duel carriageway thundered past the entrance. But it was still a military facility, with tanks parked in the car park as tourists wandered along the retired castle battlements.

Tom waited in the car, ready to drive off as soon as they were done, while Kate and Matt went inside. The castle was just opening for the day, and Kate impatiently bought tickets from a half-asleep attendant.

Matt was silent beside her. As they entered the castle courtyard, he grabbed her hand, holding on like an anchor. She shivered slightly, pulling him close.

They went straight up to the battlements, which were wider than she remembered and neatly paved and fenced. Kate took a deep breath, suddenly hearing the cannonfire that had echoed around the stones all those centuries ago.

> Time merging has reached 100% completion in time-landscape 2039

Matt let out a shuddering gasp beside her; she could feel him trembling.

Now she looked closer, she could see that much of the castle was exactly the same. She led Matt silently to where they had stood watching the Rebels digging trenches in the snow in 1745. Now it was a playground, and the sound of laughing children filled the ancient battlefield.

"It really happened, then," she said, stroking a hand over the cold stone, worn with another three hundred years of weathering. The cannons were still there. She touched one of them, wondering if it was the same one that she had repaired with Matthew.

"I don't understand," he said hopelessly. "It was all real?"

"It was," she confirmed. "We were here."

"And … and other places. The Crimea?"

"And Bletchley Park. We were there too."

He nodded. "Why? Why did it happen? Why do we keep coming back?"

"The closest we ever got to an explanation was witchcraft. Even now, three hundred years later, I don't have a better reason."

"There must be a reason. *Why?*"

"We keep helping," Kate remembered. "We stopped the murder at Bletchley Park, saved Alan. We keep *helping.*"

"And now? Now we do what? Make sure the bacteria is destroyed? Stop an apocalypse before it starts?"

"Apparently." She tried to push away the swells of a panic attack. They couldn't do this: it was too much responsibility. They weren't anything special.

"It's really important, then," he said, quiet, resigned. "If we're here, if we were brought back again, it must be a huge, pivotal moment. It has been every other time, even if we didn't know it then."

"What if we fail?" Her voice was almost inaudible, breath misting in the cold morning air. "What happens next time? We come back and the world is a wasteland?"

"We won't fail," he said, determined. "This is what we're here for. We can do this."

She turned to him, pressing her face into his shoulder and breathing in deeply. He wrapped his arms around her, held her until they both stopped shaking. "We can do this," he repeated.

Crimea, Ukraine, 1854

The encampment was quiet, almost peaceful, as Matthew and Katy rushed back from the front line to the tent where the generals were meeting to discuss the battle. A soldier stood on guard at the entrance, dozing on his feet as the generals inside planned their next move.

"I don't think we should wait," Matthew said. "It could happen any time."

"Shall we just *barge in*?" Katy asked doubtfully.

"Yes?" Matthew took a hesitant step forward, eyeing the quiet horizon. "There isn't any sign of rockets yet."

Katy straightened her shoulders, cleared her throat and, regardless of anyone watching them, she leant up to kiss Matthew, quick and soft. "We can do this," she promised. "It's going to be fine."

"See you on the other side." He cupped her cheek, then pushed a curl of hair behind her ear.

She shivered. "Don't say it like that. It makes it sound like you mean in the *afterlife*."

He blinked once, twice, and it looked like he was going

to cry, but then he smiled. "If that's what it takes to find you again."

"Oh, trust me. You aren't getting rid of me now." She kissed him again, and then finally pulled away. "Let's save the world."

Carlisle, England, 1745

When Katherine brought Matthew his dinner, she was shocked at how much worse he had become in the hour she had been away. His skin was redder, blistering, and he was trembling badly. She shook him awake gently, and he sat up shakily. He managed to eat only a little of the meal before he threw up once again. She chattered as she tucked in the blankets, trying to distract them both.

"So you say I was a servant in a war in eighteen fifty-four? That other me sounds very brave. I'm not sure *I'd* be able to do that. I must seem so dull in comparison. I don't even know how to boil potatoes properly!"

Matthew blinked blearily, rubbing a hand across his forehead. "You were amazingly brave. But you aren't dull now. You've just lived a different life. I am sure there are lots of things that you can do that the Katy I knew couldn't."

"So the minute you saw me I swept you off your feet with my sparkling wit and personality? You proposed on the spot and we were wed within the hour?" She was trying to make him smile, but he just answered seriously.

"Not precisely. Actually, I thought you were a boy."

When he saw her outraged expression, he hurriedly added, "You were dressed like a boy. You introduced yourself as Kit."

"Oh." She lay down next to him, turning to face him and making herself comfortable. "So how long did it take for you to find out I was a woman?"

He turned his head on the pillow to grin cheekily at her. "You're a woman?" He broke into weak laughter at her unamused expression. "It's a long story and not one I'm very proud of. I got angry and treated you badly. I'm quite ashamed of myself, so I'd rather not give you all the details. But eventually I got to know you as a woman."

"And you fell deeply in love?"

Considering she'd been teasing him almost incessantly since she'd met him, it surprised her when he actually blushed, his cheeks reddening even more than they already were.

"I was in awe of your determination to survive at all costs. When I met this tiny little girl, who'd found a way to carve out an existence when the whole world was against her, I felt as if I'd been mollycoddled my entire life. She was fiery and funny and challenged me in a way no one else had. So, yes, I fell in love."

She gazed at him, filled with utter amazement that this was how he saw his Katy. Then she folded her arms. "What do you mean, a tiny little girl? I'm not tiny!"

"What? Oh, well. Katy was a lot shorter than you. She was very skinny. I don't think she had a consistent food supply growing up." He paused, looking sad. "I wonder if she would have grown as tall as you if she'd been raised properly. It's horrible to think that just the way people live can change so much about them – not just their memories, but their physical appearance too."

"Katy's a lot braver than me."

"I'm sure that isn't true. When I … *arrived* … you were in the middle of defending your city. You could have chosen to leave Carlisle with your family, but you didn't, you stayed to fight. You could even have just waited at home to see what would happen, but you've been on the battlements, assisting the garrison with the cannons. That sounds wonderfully brave. If anything, I'm the weak one. In comparison to both versions of you, I'm a coward."

"I think you're very brave. You went to a battlefield as a journalist. That takes a lot of courage."

"I think that was an anomaly," he admitted in a low tone. "I was caught up in the glory of it all."

"I don't think there are any true heroes. Just people who ignore their survival instincts long enough to do something incredibly foolhardy."

"That sounds about right. Although even with hindsight, I think I made the right decision – or the version of me that lives in this century did. Defending Carlisle was worth one life."

There was a silence, and then Matthew smiled brightly, trying to reduce the tension. "Wait … you don't know about dinosaurs, do you? They weren't discovered until my century."

She shook her head. He grinned. It was the most excited

she'd seen him since his arrival. "You're going to be utterly amazed. Do you know what a fossil is?"

They talked for a while longer, and once Katherine had got past the shock of *giant spiky lizards that roamed the earth*, she was very interested. But he was growing more exhausted, so she let him sleep. By morning she was wrung out, having spent the night in a light doze, worrying dreadfully. Matthew had woken up several times to throw up, and she made sure she was there to care for him.

CHAPTER 31

Katherine Galloway invited **Matthew Galloway** to join the closed group *"Help get Matthew to ~*~propose~*~ and think it's his own idea in four easy steps"*

Members (35) • Posts (250)

Folios/v7/Time-landscape-2019/MS-164

CARLISLE, ENGLAND, 2039

Kate was waiting with Tom in the car while Matt picked up breakfast — and coffee. Her tablet buzzed and she stared at a text that Matt had just sent her: "I've just remembered Clove." He must have sent it from the cafe.

She stared at it, trying to decipher his meaning. *Clove?* What was Clove? Had he misspelt "love"?

"Tom, do you kno—?" She was interrupted by the sound of sirens. Kate peered out of the rear window in horror as the wailing tone got closer. A police car was pulling into the car park of the fast-food restaurant.

"*Shit,*" Tom hissed, starting the engine.

Two officers burst out of the car, guns in hand, and ran into the restaurant.

"What?" Kate said. "*No.* What's happening?"

There was an explosion of noise from inside the restaurant. Kate watched in horror as people began running outside.

> ALERT: Subject allocation "MATT" in time-landscape 2039
  in danger

> Based on previous results, intervention not recommended

"They must have sent out an alert for you two," Tom said, reversing the car too fast. "Your faces were probably caught on CCTV at CSL."

"What?! Stop. Where are you going? We need to help him." Kate went to open the car door, but Tom reached over and grabbed her shoulder.

"Kate, *no*. We need to go."

"*Matt*. We can't just leave him. We need to—" A series of gunshots sounded from the building, and Kate froze.

Tom squeezed his eyes closed, took a breath. "We need to leave."

He didn't stop to explain. He drove out of the back exit, checking left and right for more police cars. "Kate, there's nothing we can do to help him. He's probably just being arrested. We need to leave *now*, before they get us too. We need to get to Scotland."

"But—" She was shaking; she didn't know what to do.

"He's going to be fine. He's just going to jail. We can get him out. It's going to be fine."

This wasn't *happening*. Not again.

"*Kate*. Please," Tom said, looking back at her. "It's going to be all right."

She dissolved into tears.

"It's going to be all right," he repeated as he took the exit onto the motorway, like the reassurance was for himself as much as her.

She didn't know if she was crying for her Matt, *this* Matthew, or for every Matthew she'd known and lost. All throughout history they had been doing this, finding and loving each other and then being ripped apart before they even had a chance to live. Why did Matthew always leave her alone?

She wondered how anyone could survive such soul-wrenching pain and love. Matthew was hers, had apparently always been hers, and now he was gone. Why did it always end? Why did it always even *start*? Her thoughts kept flickering through thousands of memories; she couldn't focus or process any of the scenes flooding her mind. She couldn't place any of the moments, just had to let the snapshots of their lives together flow over her: images of Matthew smiling at her, snatches of conversation, kisses. They were on a boat, and then they were in a candlelit garden and now they were in a science lab, and she couldn't tell if that was an actual memory or one of her aunt's… No, they were all her own. All of those things had happened to them.

Matthew had been her servant – she could see him looking at her from the seat of a carriage – and he had taught her how to be a reporter, and in another century, she had flirted with him by email, and he had always, always loved her. Every time he met her. And every time, they lost each other.

She could remember him dying in her arms and her dying in his, time and time again. How many times had they done this dance, this horrific, beautiful dance through time? Why had they done it? What was so special about them that they were brought back – pulled together – by the universe?

Why did it always go wrong? Why couldn't it have worked, just this once? Kate closed her eyes, twisted her lip, and remembered how every Matthew throughout history had always looked at her as if she was the centre of his world.

Was she the centre of his? Or the centre of the world, full stop? That seemed arrogant and yet, the universe — or God, or some alien with nothing better to do — must have a reason for pulling them together like this again and again, pushing them through time itself even, just to keep them close before then ripping them apart just as easily. Why?

She needed to know the answers. She had to find whatever loose end they were leaving behind each time — the thread that the universe couldn't leave untied.

Kate dropped her head into her hands. She was exhausted.

They were nearly at the border now, nearly safe. But each mile was taking her further from Matt. How could they have left him behind?

"We'll go back," Tom said quietly, as if reading her mind. "Once we've sorted out the bacteria. We'll fix that, and then we'll go back for him."

"I'll always go back for him," she said. "I'm just worried that this time he won't be waiting."

Kate took a deep breath. What would Matt want her to do? The answer came quickly. Reveal the truth about CSL and the bacteria. Show everyone the vial.

Kate froze.

"Matt had the vial in his pocket," she heard herself say, voice blank. "We don't have the bacteria any more!"

Scottish student arrested on terrorism charges

45 Comments

Matt Galloway, 18, was arrested in Carlisle early this morning in a dramatic confrontation with police as he attempted to flee the country. He was under MI5 surveillance after being caught on CCTV, in the act of breaking into a government facility, apparently with the intention of stealing state secrets. He is accused of stealing equipment and classified documents, and of using a military vehicle to make his escape.

Due to the fast action taken by MI5, Galloway was caught before any acts of terrorism could be attempted.

Matt Galloway was, it seems, following in family footsteps. His uncle, named Matthew Galloway, was caught planning an act of treason against the government in the run up to the last war in 2019. He was apprehended, along with his wife, Katherine. Both later died of the injuries received while violently resisting arrest.

Matt Galloway is known to have two accomplices, Tom Galloway and Kate Finchley. They are currently on the run in Scotland, and there is an alert out for their arrest at all English borders. MI5 warn that they should be treated as highly dangerous as it is possible that they have a weapon in their possession.

If seen, please contact the police immediately. Use extreme caution, and do not approach them.

Crimea, Ukraine, 1854

Katy and Matthew ran for the tent where the generals were meeting. They barged past the guard and forced their way inside. The highest level officials of the British and French armies were all in there.

"We're under fire!" Katy burst out. "The Russians – they're firing at the encampment!"

For a moment, nobody moved. It was silent – there was no sound of gunfire or the whistle of an incoming rocket.

Lord Somerset stood up, face red. "Kit! Get out of here this *instant*," he exploded, as officers began shouting to each other in quick French. "I've had enough of your lies."

"I'm not lying," she said, desperate. "The tent's going to be hit by a rocket."

"You need to get somewhere safer, or everyone here is going to die," Matthew added, in a loud, determined voice.

"This is treason!" Lord Somerset raged as a French officer stood up. He looked between Lord Somerset and Matthew with equal suspicion, and then made his way carefully to the entrance of the tent. In a rush, the rest of the French generals followed him.

Lord Somerset shouted out orders for the rest of the men to stay put, but the exodus was underway. Katy stepped to the side to let them leave and returned Matthew's relieved glance. They'd done it. The officers weren't going to die. They'd saved them!

Lord Somerset, however, was outraged. "I'm arresting you both for treason," he said.

"Arrest us by all means," Matthew said. "But we need to get away from the tent."

"So you can escape? I don't think so." Lord Somerset sat down at the table and invited them to do the same. "I want to know what you're trying to achieve with this foolish interruption."

Matthew looked like he was going to resist, but then he sank down into a nearby chair.

"Fine. But let Kit go. He has nothing to do with this. He was just following my orders."

Lord Somerset nodded to the soldier who had grabbed hold of Katy. The man released her, and she took a quick step away.

"Kit, leave. Now," Matthew said.

"No!" she said, but the soldier began dragging her outside and she was powerless to resist.

"You do realize you have just ruined a meeting of great importance, don't you? Are you purposefully trying to help the Russians win this war?" Lord Somerset asked Matthew. He got no further, because just then there was a whistle, and a loud explosion, as a rocket hit the tent.

Carlisle, England, 1745

Matthew didn't get any better. Katherine nursed him unceasingly, but his condition deteriorated quickly. His skin was covered in ulcers; his now bald scalp was swollen. He threw up constantly, could rarely sit upright without fainting with dizziness, and he struggled to remember where he was. Katherine was beside herself with worry.

She had fetched a doctor, who hadn't recognized his disease and had wanted to let his blood. Katherine had stopped him, remembering Matthew's lesson about humours, and had sent him away with his fee. She was reduced to just keeping Matthew comfortable and hoping for the best.

"Katherine," he said to her as she was cleaning his sores, "I'm so sorry."

She looked at his swollen face and swallowed. "Don't be silly. You are going to get better. You – you have to survive this, Matthew. Please."

He brushed a hand against her cheek. "I'm not going to, Katherine. I'm so sorry. I'm dying. We both know it. I wasn't strong enough to make the transition, and it's killing me. I hope … I'm glad that I met you. I don't regret coming here, and keeping you for a few more days, even if it led to this – my death. I would return over and over if it gave me a little longer with you."

She tried not to cry, blinking away the tears rapidly. "I can't go on without you, Matthew. What do I do? What *can* I do?"

"Try to be happy."

"I can't," she said, and now she was weeping openly. "I can't lose you twice. How can this be fair?"

"It's more than fair, Katherine. You got to keep me after I died. How many times does that happen?"

He struggled to sit up, trying to wrap her in a hug, but

his strength was dwindling and he couldn't manage it. He settled for stroking her hair.

"Matthew, what if this happens to me as well? What if when you die I go back to the seventeenth century, where there is another version of you, and I don't survive the journey? What if it goes on for ever in an endless series? I'm scared."

"Me too. Oh God, Katy, I'm scared too. But I don't think that will happen. What would be the sense in that? Whoever has done this must have watched us our whole lives. They wouldn't send you back just to die. It serves no purpose. I think they made a mistake, sending me back like this. They were trying to help us, and they did it wrong. Maybe – maybe they'll find a way to send you back without getting ill. Or maybe it just won't happen at all. Maybe we fixed it, whatever it was that needed us both to be here. I hope we did."

He closed his eyes. The speech had taken him a long time, with frequent pauses for breath. He settled back in the bedding and went to sleep.

Katherine watched him, thinking over what he'd said until it was too dark to see, and she fell asleep curled up close to him.

When she woke up, he was dead.

> ALERT: Subject allocation "MATTHEW" in time-landscape 1745 timed out due to unconsidered high radiation levels of transfer

> Transfer between adjacent space threads not viable

> Operation terminated

> Reboot system

> Waiting for user input …

> … waiting …

>> Instruction acquired

>> Reboot of subjects initiated

> Calculating new path of execution

> Searching for time-landscape

> Transferring file

> File for subject allocation "MATTHEW" loading

> Subject allocation "MATTHEW" rebooting in 5 … 4 … 3 …
  2 … 1

> Subject transfer complete

> Awaiting completion of subject allocation "KATHERINE"
  in time-landscape 1745

> … waiting …

CHAPTER 32

Matthew Galloway tagged **Katherine Galloway** in the post:

MY WHOLE LIFE IS A CONSPIRACY! I don't understand anything any more. Thanks to … everyone I know … for their role in making my marriage happen. It's nice to know I can trust you all fully. Katherine, payback is coming. Don't think I'll be so easily influenced again.

Like • Comment • Share

Folios/v7/Time-landscape-2019/MS-165

Crimea, Ukraine, 1854

The rocket hit the tent with a screaming noise. There was a shock of heat and noise as the far end collapsed, with Lord Raglan and Matthew still inside.

Matthew.

Katy rushed in.

For a moment her heart stopped because she couldn't see Matthew at all. He wasn't here. He'd completely disappeared. *Where was he?* And then he crawled out from under the table, head tucked into his arm to protect it from the smoke. She sighed with relief because he was all right – he'd survived – and then the flames suddenly picked up in a roar of air and heat and everything seemed to collapse further inwards. The canvas pressed around her. A tent pole crashed against her shoulder. She couldn't see Matthew any more. He was hidden somewhere under layers of burning canvas, flames and smoke.

She coughed, trying to clear her throat of the thick burn. It was terrifying. The giant furnace blazing around them made her feel small and fragile and helpless.

She pulled her collar over her mouth and struggled forward to the table. She pulled and heaved until it was on its side. There was no sign of Matthew, and then she saw him, lying near by. He was pinned under a tent pole, the weight of it and the burning canvas pressing down on him. She crawled towards him.

"Get out! *Get away!*" Matthew shouted, but she ignored him and grabbed hold of the pole. She pulled and pulled, crying out in frustration when the pole wouldn't move at all. She was too weak, and the thick smoke was making her choke. Despair threatened to overwhelm her – she couldn't do it; she couldn't free Matthew.

```
> ALERT: Subject allocation "MATTHEW" in time-landscape 1854
  in critical danger

> Time out of subject imminent

> Intervention recommended

  >> Intervention denied
```

Then there were arms around her, pulling with her. It was Lord Somerset. At last, the pole jolted free and he guided it to the ground while Matthew scrambled to his knees, smacking his clothes to dash out the flames.

Disorientated, Katy looked around for the exit. Everything

was smoke. It stung her eyes and throat and nothing else mattered but getting out, into clean air and cool wind.

"This way!" she shouted to Somerset and Matthew, before covering her mouth with her sleeve. Matthew crawled behind her. She didn't look back, but forced herself to move, even though her limbs were heavy and stiff. And then they were outside in the light and fresh air.

She fell to the ground, taking a deep gasping breath of the cool air. Matthew collapsed beside her. He was black with ash and his eyes were running from the smoke – but he was alive. They'd made it. Katy closed her eyes, tears of relief sliding down her cheeks.

And then there was another crash, following by an agonized cry.

"Help!" Lord Somerset called. He was trapped inside the tent.

Katy didn't even hesitate. He had helped her to save Matthew. Ignoring Matthew's protests and the weak, panicked grasp of his hand on her arm, she ran back into the tent.

Lord Somerset was just inside the entrance, a tent pole across his chest. She pushed against it, straining to free him with everything she had. This was about more than just returning a favour. Lord Somerset couldn't die here. He was the Commander-in-Chief of the British Army. Who knew what would happen if he died? Who knew how that would impact the war? She had to save him.

The pole lifted up and then Lord Somerset was crawling free – but her grip slipped. She groaned as she pushed harder. Finally she managed to force it aside. But it must have dislodged the fragile tent, because another pole rose upwards. She tried to throw herself out of the way, but she wasn't quick enough. The pole swung towards her, pushing her backwards and sinking into her stomach.

```
> ALERT: Subject allocation "KATY" in critical condition

> Please advise on actions

> … waiting …
```

She gasped. For a moment she couldn't feel anything except for the sting of smoke in her lungs, and then the pain came. It filled every corner of her mind, until she couldn't remember how to breathe or think or do anything except close her eyes and push at the pain to try to stop it from overwhelming her.

Then Matthew was there, cupping her head.

"Katy!" he cried.

MatthewMatthewMatthew.

"Katy…" His voice was soft, agonized. How could she do this to him? They'd been so happy and they hadn't had enough time. Just like the last time.

"I love you," she tried to say, but the words wouldn't come and instead she just blinked up at him, with wonder and love. She knew exactly why he was brought back to her again and again. It was because he was *perfect.*

"I love you," he said over and over as she stared at him. He pressed kisses against her hair and ran his hands down her cheeks and lips. They came away blood red. "You'll be fine, you're fine, you're going to be fine."

"Matthew…" she mouthed. "It's all right."

"No! No – we can fix this."

> Situation cannot be fixed without adverse side effects

> Please advise on actions

> … waiting …

His tears dropped onto her face and mixed with her blood as he cradled her against his chest. She loved him so much. She had been so lucky to have him. Then she closed her eyes, flashes of Matthew smiling at her dancing across her vision, and she let herself stop breathing.

> ALERT: Subject allocation "KATY" timed out in time-landscape 1854

> Mission incomplete

> Permission requested to reboot system

>> Permission granted

Home > News > Terrorist Attack

Video provides "evidence" of government conspiracy

278 Comments

The accomplices of Matt Galloway, 18, who was arrested this morning in Carlisle, under terrorism charges, have released a press statement outlining their actions.

Tom Galloway, 22, the brother of the apprehended suspect, and Katherine Finchley, 18, an English national and fellow student at the University of Nottingham, allege that they have evidence that the English government has a biological Weapon of Mass Destruction, therefore breaking the International Treaty against WMDs of 2020.

This evidence consists of video footage, dating from 2019, which appears to show that their namesakes and relatives, Katherine and Matthew Galloway, were not only innocent of any acts of treason, but were, in fact, murdered during their efforts to uncover evidence of the WMD from their workplace, a closed wing of the Central Science Laboratories.

Tom Galloway and Katherine Finchley say that historical evidence, left by the Galloways, led them to uncover not only this video, but the biological weapon itself. They claim that the government still has a supply of this WMD, although they have failed to give any evidence to support this.

If true, however, this would have serious implications as the conflict between England and Europe continues to escalate, despite continual negotiations over trade and import disagreements.

Having evaded arrest and crossed the international border, Tom Galloway and Katherine Finchley are currently until the protection of the Scottish government. The refusal to extradite them has added to the current antagonism between the bordering countries.

There has been no comment from the British prime minister in response to these accusations.

Follow the livestream on this story as the news comes in at our website, and tell us your views at #BacteriaConspiracy.

Related news:

Were the Galloways murdered in 2019 to keep them quiet?

Scottish government vows to protect the civil rights of its citizens

Is Tom Galloway the notorious Spartacus?

Video: Tour the rooms of Kate Finchley and Matt Galloway at the University of Nottingham

King William "furious" as Scottish government confiscates Balmoral

Opinion: Should we close our borders?

ST ANDREWS, SCOTLAND, 2039

The video connection was fuzzy, but Nancy and Flo's worried expressions were still clearly visible. Kate and Tom were at Matt and Tom's parents' house. It had been three days since Matt's arrest.

"Kate, what on earth happened?" Flo exclaimed. "We let you into the loft and the next thing we know you're a fugitive from the law, hiding in Scotland, and your boyfriend has been arrested for terrorism offences!"

Kate scratched her head, embarrassed. "Yeah. It's been a hectic few days."

"Your parents are furious. They didn't even know you *had* a boyfriend."

Katherine sighed. "I know. I spoke to them." That hadn't been a fun conversation. "Sorry I took so long to call you. We've been tied up in continuous interviews since the press conference."

"Why are you risking this call? Couldn't MI5 trace it and find you?"

"Oh, they know exactly where we are. We're not even in hiding. We're staying with Matt's parents. They just can't do anything about it."

"Why?" Nancy asked, leaning forward and nudging Flo out of the way.

"England can't force Scotland to hand over criminals, especially not political ones."

"Kate, are you all right?" Nancy asked. "You don't have to joke about this, you know. This must be very scary for you."

"Nana, to be honest, if I stopped joking around I'm pretty sure I'd go to bed and never get up again. I'm only barely holding on to my sanity right now through a series of poorly thought-out puns."

"Well, you deal with this however you have to. But we're all here for you."

"Thanks, Nana." Kate wished her grandparents were here so that she could be held tightly and comforted. She swallowed, trying not to cry.

"So, you're staying with Matt's parents?" Flo said. "What are they like?"

"They're lovely. They've taken all of this completely in their stride, amazingly. I think they were expecting it to happen eventually – they knew about Tom's hacking. The fact that it was Matt who was arrested surprised them the most, actually."

"Have you heard from Matt?"

Kate sighed. She was calling from Matt's childhood bedroom. She looked around it now, pulling his pillow onto her lap. "No. Not yet. Matt's parents keep trying to get in touch with him, but he's still in questioning and he's not allowed phone calls."

"Hopefully when it's proven that you're telling the truth they'll let him out. They can't keep him in there when it's clear you aren't terrorists."

"*If* it ever gets proven. The English government are still refusing to discuss it. They say they 'don't acknowledge the claims of terrorists'. It's total crap."

"*What*? That's bullshit!" Nancy swore, outraged. Kate

missed her so much. "They can't do that – you have evidence!"

"I know. But apparently the video could easily be faked," Kate said with a frustrated sigh. "We need the bacteria, but Matt had it. Even if the police didn't find it in his pocket, the bacteria might be long dead by now, since it's not being stored in a freezer. It's lost."

"Can you not get another sample?"

Kate paused. "Maybe. I don't know how, though. It's not like they'll just let us wander back into CSL."

Kate scrubbed her hands over her face. She was so tired. She couldn't sleep for worrying. She'd thought that once people knew what was happening, someone else would take over and uncover the truth, but nothing had changed. And who knew what would happen if war with Europe was declared? The government might even decide to use the bacteria in warfare. The bacteria would spread across the globe, just because Kate and Matt couldn't prove their claims. If only they could get another sample, this would all be so easy to stop. She kept picturing what would happen – what the world would look like if the bacteria was released. Everything would almost certainly be destroyed and turned to dust.

The only thing that was reassuring was that Matthew and Katherine's video from 2019 was out there, for people to see. If the bacteria did get released, there was a chance someone would remember their claims and look it up. They might even be able to recreate the vaccine and stop the bacteria spreading – if it wasn't too late by then.

Her tablet beeped. Another call was coming in. *The*

Times hadn't stopped calling for an interview all day. Tom had been busy for hours fielding questions – in between making sure that the website they'd set up to host the videos didn't crash under the constant flood of views.

"I have to go, Nana, Gran. I'll call you in a few days, when everything's calmed down a bit, OK? I love you."

"All right, sweet pea. We're thinking of you. We're so proud of what you're doing. It's wonderful for us, Kate. I can't express just how much it means to us that you're trying to clear our daughter's name."

Kate ended the call and answered the one from the newspaper. They had a long list of questions, which she answered slowly as she tried to find the strength to carry on fighting without Matt.

Kate put down her cup of tea and ran to the bathroom, where she was sick again. She couldn't keep going on like this – the worry was making her ill. And the news this morning had just made everything much worse. She sat down on the edge of the bath as the conversation she'd had with Tom earlier came back to her. He'd been sitting at the kitchen table. When he saw her, he had pushed a newspaper towards her.

"Matt went on trial yesterday morning – a rush court order," he had said.

She'd scanned her eyes down past the headline to the picture of Matt, his head bowed, his hands cuffed. He'd looked small and defeated.

"They held the trial in secret for reasons of 'national

security'," Tom went on. "He was found guilty of terrorist acts. He got life imprisonment."

Kate closed her eyes now and took in a deep breath, but none of the air seemed to reach her lungs. After three months, the story had died down. No one had taken the time to prove their accusations, and the newspapers had forgotten about them, and now Matt had been charged and put in prison for life. She didn't know what to do.

She could break into prison and rescue Matt – assuming she could get into England without being captured herself. She could break back into the lab for another sample – assuming the vials hadn't been moved to a different location. Every plan she came up with seemed ludicrous. She couldn't do anything, not without Matt. She couldn't.

It looked like she was stuck in Scotland with Matt's family, waking up each day, waiting and hoping for news that the bacteria had been discovered and destroyed and dreading the news that it had been released and was spreading across Europe.

She swilled out her mouth and spat in the sink. Worry was sending her gut into a twist of nerves almost every morning. She'd even stopped having her period, with the strain of it all. She felt so ill. There must be something seriously wrong with her, or... She stared at her pale face in the mirror, and it suddenly clicked. How hadn't she realized before?

She was pregnant.

She tentatively pressed her hands against her stomach. She was *pregnant*?

Kate made a noise: a cut-off animal sound of pain. She

thought she was going to cry, and then she found herself laughing hysterically.

She was having a baby. Matt's baby. *Finally.*

They'd gone through so many different incarnations – and this time she was pregnant; this time they were both *still alive*; this time they had survived everything, even if they weren't together. This had to be the time they were happy, at peace. This had to be the time that they escaped alive.

Suddenly Kate knew what she was going to do. She couldn't just sit around and wait for someone else to fix this – not now. *She* had to make sure the world was safe from the bacteria, for her baby, and she had to get Matt out of prison.

Kate began planning. As her belly grew bigger, her rescue plan came together.

She did some research into their other lives, trying to work out where each memory fitted in their long series of lifetimes. She found Matthew's newspaper articles about the Crimean War: dense, narrow articles in the back issues of *The Times*. She spent an afternoon crying over his words and the proud byline "Our Own Correspondent".

Obscure wars of long ago that she hadn't thought about in this life suddenly became the most important moments in history. Together with Matt, she had stopped the world from collapsing six times before, and only now did she realize just what a difference they had made. They had helped end the Jacobite rebellion and made sure Scotland wasn't ravaged by famine. A century later they had saved the generals in the Crimea to make sure England and France didn't lose the war. And now they had to make sure the entire world wasn't completely destroyed by the bacteria.

After all the effort they'd put into protecting the world, she couldn't give up, because apparently humanity couldn't survive without them. Why else did they keep being brought back?

She wrote letters to the baby, just in case she failed in her rescue attempt and never came back. She wanted their child to know that it was loved, that neither of its parents had abandoned it easily. She was going to come back. She just had to find its father and finish saving the world first.

CHAPTER 33

Katherine,

We need to talk about something, something I've been thinking about for a while now. I'm taking you out for dinner tonight. Wear the black dress. You know the one. I love you (far more than is good for my mental health).

Matthew x

Folios/v7/Time-landscape-2019/MS-166

ST ANDREWS, SCOTLAND, 2039

Kate felt like she was about to explode. She was fighting her own body, pushing against the tightness of her skin, desperate to just get this finished, finally, after hours of pain and pulsing tightness and straining focus.

She was exhausted, but she couldn't stop pushing. She squeezed tight onto the rails of the bed, wishing it was Matt's hand that gripped hers, trying to convey the endless pressure that was pulling her in all directions. Finally the relentless, unyielding power she was pushing against stopped, and in a slither of release, she gave birth.

She dropped her head back and closed her eyes. "I am *never doing that again*," she stated, for the record. "I don't care if Matt comes back and demands ten more children. It's not happening." Everybody ignored her, just like they had for the last nine hours every time she'd screamed for somebody to bring her some more of those drugs, *right now I swear to God*.

She stared at the pink light filtering through her eyelids, trying not to think about the messy wetness she could feel covering the lower half of her body. No one had told her that childbirth was so disgusting.

She was drifting in a sea of adrenalin, when a small weight was pressed into her arms. She opened her eyes and looked down at the tiny bundle. Her breath caught in her throat. She was *exquisite*. Kate had hoped she would be able to look at her and see Matt, but for now she was just a round, chubby-cheeked baby. She smiled down wonderingly, touched her tiny fingers and stroked the long length of her eyelashes.

Kate wondered why she'd never done this before. She could have felt this joy so many times, in every life, but somehow it had never happened for them. How had they never managed to make a baby together before, in all those lives? How strange it would have been, if she had given birth in Carlisle, at the very beginning. Their baby would have been grown up when they were reborn in their next lives. She could have met her. She would have been younger than her own daughter. She could have followed her own descendants through history. But they'd missed out on children until now. They'd never managed to conceive before their time ran out.

The baby's eyes flickered open, blinking against the

bright light of the outside world, and everything clicked into place for Kate. The answer unfurled undramatically like it had been there all along, just waiting for her to pay attention. *She* – this baby – was why it had happened. They kept coming back, endlessly, trying and failing to create this person, this little girl. And now she was here.

Kate settled back on fresh pillows, and felt success tingle on her tongue and in her fingertips. It was *done*. Kate and Matt had made the baby they had always needed to make, finally, after all this time. Now their baby could go ahead and live her life – do whatever it was that was so important that they kept being brought back to make her.

Finally, they could stop living again and again. She smiled down at her sleeping daughter, knowing that this was it. She didn't have any more idea of who had manipulated time than she'd had in the eighteenth century, but at least now she knew why. She wouldn't be back for another life. It was time to let her baby girl take over. Hopefully she and Matt would be around to see some of her story, if everything went according to plan. Hopefully.

The only thing left was to choose a name. She liked the sound of Clove.

Three days later, she gave her baby to Tom and her ecstatic new grandparents. She was leaving their daughter in safe, loving hands. Kate was ready to finish their story.

> Objective achieved

> Mission complete

> Assignment "CLOVE" in operation

EPILOGUE

Home > News > Terrorist Attack

Terrorist prison break

113 Comments

Matt Galloway, the European terrorist sentenced to life imprisonment six months ago, disappeared from his prison cell at Wakefield Prison early yesterday morning, in a breakout assisted by his accomplice Kate Finchley. The couple, both 19, were sighted at the prison during the breakout but evaded capture before vanishing completely.

The police have issued warrants for their arrest, but have released no information about how the breakout occurred or whether they have any leads in uncovering their whereabouts.

Folios/v8/Time-landscape-2040/MS-3

Home > News > Politics

British government dissolved

2487 Comments

An emergency NATO meeting was called only hours after the escape of Scottish terrorist Matt Galloway. According to a statement from the international organization, "An anonymous source provided incontrovertible evidence of the possession of unethical biological weapons by the English government. A breach of international law so serious that control of the English military has been seized by NATO while the claims are investigated.

There is strong reason to suspect that this anonymous source is Matt Galloway.

The British shadow cabinet has declared emergency rule, after all officials connected to the conspiracy fled the country, and there have been reassurances that any biological weapons will be handed over to NATO for safe disposal if discovered. Hopes are high that peace talks will begin later today.

Folios/v8/Time-landscape-2040/MS-4

Matthew and Katherine Galloway

From the Free Encyclopedia

Katherine Galloway (née Finchley) and **Matthew Galloway** were the parents of the infamous <u>Clove Sutcliffe</u>. They are well known in their own right for their <u>Repeated Lives</u>, a system of <u>History Control</u> in which they played a vital role in the aversion of multiple possible historical catastrophes.

Their <u>Repeated Lives</u> spread from the 18th century to 21st century AD, and are discussed in great detail in the <u>Personal Lives</u> section. Most famous of their actions is the crucial role they played in both the creation and discovery of the <u>Bacteria Conspiracy</u>, but other notable achievements include preventing such events as the <u>Jacobite Independence Treaty of 1745</u>, <u>the Scottish famine of 1765</u>, and the <u>Russian invasion of London</u>. They were also instrumental in bringing about British success at the <u>Battle of Sebastopol</u> and in arresting <u>The Bletchley Park Murderer</u>, resulting in the subsequent WWII victory due to the cracking of the <u>Enigma code</u>.

Their lives caused the great wave of <u>History Revisions</u>, which began in 2056. These are discussed further in <u>Legacy and Historical Impact</u> and as such their importance cannot be understated.

Contents

References

Communications Through History: an Annotated Anthology of the Lives of Matthew and Katherine Galloway

The Last Beginning

Great Programmers of the 21st Century, Chapter 2: Clove "Anise" Sutcliffe: Time & Quantum, p. 19

ST ANDREWS, SCOTLAND, 2043

"Clove, come and get your dinner!"

The little girl made an indeterminate noise of refusal, and clung more tightly to her dad's tablet computer, anticipating the struggle that would come when Tom found her hiding place inside her duvet cover. She suspected that she might be visible from the outside, even though she was hunched over as small as possible, with white clouds of material drooping over her head.

She had things to do. She couldn't waste any time eating dinner, even if her stomach was grumbling insistently and Granny had made apple crumble for pudding.

She carried on typing on the tablet, letting out heavy sighs and grumbles just like Daddy did when he was working.

"Clove, where are you?" Tom called, coming upstairs.

She eyed his feet as he padded into the bedroom, and after a moment of exploration, she found the edge of the duvet and stuck her head out of the hole.

"Daddy, I'm *busy*. I can't eat dinner yet. I'm programming, look!"

Tom squatted down next to her bed, peering inside the duvet at her nest. "Hello there," he said, grinning at her.

"Daddy, *look*!" She thrust the tablet at him.

He wiped her sticky fingerprints off the screen, examining her efforts. "Very good, Clove. You're going to be a programmer like me, are you?"

She nodded proudly, puffing out her chest. "I'm gonna

be the best programmer in the entire world," she declared confidently.

"Well, you're nearly there," he agreed. "You're better than me already. But even programmers need to eat their tea. It's egg and chips."

"Are there mushy peas?" she asked, considering her choices.

"Of course there are, little 'un." He held out his arms, and she crawled into them, wrapping her own around his neck.

"All right then," she decided, still clutching the tablet. She took a moment to admire her work as Tom carried her downstairs. She was getting very good at programming.

```
> daddy fjsjs kkkkkki

> cloveclove clove

> ddd d kkkssssss

> clove sutcliffeonfddis;

> 12345678910

> a

> b

> cd

> dsdddddkk tifd tide tile time

> time time time12345

> time1745
```

> time1805 1854 191819411963 2039

> dddddaddddd mum mum mum clove

> vvvcclove sutcliffe

> clove sutcliffe

> clove sutcliffe

> clove

BIBLIOGRAPHY

Carlisle in 1745: Authentic Account of the Occupation of Carlisle in 1745 by Prince Charles Edward Stuart by John Waugh and George Gill Mounsey

In the Steps of Bonnie Prince Charlie by Winifred Duke

The Jacobite Wars – The Sieges of Carlisle 1745 by Rupert Matthews

Despatches from the Crimea by William Russell

Mrs Duberly's War: Journal and Letters from the Crimea, 1854–6 by Frances Isabella Duberly and Christine Kelly

The Crimean War by Denis Judd

AFTERWORD

The many historical errors are all in the name of dramatic licence, and should be taken as such.

After the siege of Carlisle, in 1745, the Jacobites marched further into England before they began to panic and retreated back into Scotland. By this time the British Army had mustered enough troops to defend the country. Carlisle fell under siege once again, this time by the English, who won. The Jacobites in residence there were hung after they surrendered. The uprising eventually ended at the Battle of Culloden with the defeat of the Jacobites. The Jacobite pretenders returned to France in a sulk, and the current "King of Scotland" lives in Nymphenburg Palace, Munich.

I couldn't have written this without the diaries of William Russell, the real *Times* correspondent, who is probably tuning in his grave at my romantic rewriting of his life. This man affected history so much it's kind of unbelievable and I fangirl him so hard. Thanks, dude – you rock!

The possible effects of travel through time are, of course, guesswork, but I have assumed that it would not be possible to survive the radiation poisoning. The symptoms Matthew displays are all medically accurate.

ACKNOWLEDGEMENTS

The Next Together is dedicated to Aisha Ahmad, who was this book's biggest fan from the very start, but never got to see the end. Aisha, you supported everything I did, and made me into a better person. I learnt so much from you, and I was so lucky to have you in my life, even for so short a time. Rest in peace.

I couldn't have written even half the novel I have without my agent, Claire Wilson, and my editor, Annalie Grainger, who both pulled the best book possible out of me. I promise the next one will have fewer *That's what she said* jokes. Maybe.

A huge thank you to everyone else at Walker Books and Rogers, Coleridge & White who worked on this book – especially Lexie Hamblin, Hannah Cooper, Sean Moss, Sorrel Packham and Jack Noel for the incredible page design and Jack for the cover.

Thank you to the Ogden Trust, whose support throughout my further education meant I could spend my summer holidays messing around writing instead of working. I'm very grateful for the opportunities the trust has given me.

Thank you to Claire's Coven, for being the best at Christmas parties and Twitter nonsense, especially Alice Oseman, Catherine Doyle, Alexia Casale, Sara Barnard, Melinda Salisbury, Gary Meehan and Ross Montgomery. Knowing you all makes me feel cool.

For the brilliant welcome to the scary world of

publishing and never-ending support, thank you to Louise O'Neill, Zoë Marriott, Katy Moran, Non Pratt, Sarah Sky, Kendra Leighton, Libby Drew, Lucy Powrie, Jim Dean and Charlotte Morris.

A huge, huge thank you to all my Real Life friends, who put up with my constant book talk with admirable patience, especially to Sarah Barnard, Madison Woodward, Maggie Kelso, Stephanie Whybrow, Cherra Mathis, Abbii Packer, Clare Samson, Bethany Longden and Cal Donnelly.

Thank you to my nana, Shirley Barnes, for always being willing to draw stuff for my stories, from illustrations for my "talking dogs" novel at age twelve to maps for *The Next Together* at eighteen. Thanks to Charlotte, Troy and Travis Smitten for their constant support.

For mentoring me over the years and always believing in me, thank you to Ghzala Ahmad, Alison Tumber and Sir Martyn Poliakoff.

Finally, the biggest, brightest thanks go to Mum and Dad and my brother Christopher Banks James, for supporting me on a daily (hourly) basis, being interested in even the dullest aspects of my life and book – and for always wanting to talk to me when I'm writing. I've got the best family in the world, and I love you so much.

LAUREN JAMES graduated in 2014 with a Masters degree in Natural Sciences from the University of Nottingham, where she studied chemistry and physics. She now lives in the village of Berkswell, West Midlands.

You can find her on Twitter at @Lauren_E_James, fancasting actors as her characters and panicking about all of her overly ambitious plans for the future, or her website, at lauren-e-james.tumblr.com, where she mainly posts pictures of her dogs.

Don't miss the sequel to *The Next Together*

THE
LAST
BEGINNING

Enjoyed this book? Tweet us your thoughts.
#TheNextTogether @WalkerBooksUK @Lauren_E_James